THE

FLYING

WOMAN

A NOVEL

DANIEL SHERRIER

The Flying Woman is a work of fiction. Any similarities to actual persons or events are entirely coincidental.

First print edition, October 2018.
Printed in the United States of America.
ISBN: 9781728616742

Edited by Matthew Limpede
Additional editing by Todd Barselow
Cover design by Justin Burks

For Rose, Jackie, and Josh

THE FLYING WOMAN

1

Miranda Thomas liked pretending to be someone else. Her true self receded behind a persona she had spent innumerable hours crafting, rehearsing, and perfecting to the greatest possible extent. And her hard work paid off as she made her regional theatre debut in *The Reluctant Guest*.

They enjoyed her. Several dozen strangers laughed at all the right moments. Everyone returned to their seats after intermission. They cheered when the lights went down at the play's conclusion. And audiences never lied. Miranda loved that about them.

She had graduated from Olympus University a mere three months earlier, and she was already doing her favorite thing in the world—as a professional. Her castmates were fun, the reviews were strong, and the nonprofit company owned a charming venue. This was not a poor start by any means.

Today's matinee wasn't quite finished. Miranda had one last moment on the stage, the only one as herself.

Warm light enveloping her, she crossed the polished floorboards of the Aeschylus Theater for her curtain call. The stage was smaller than most, and its house seated a mere eighty-eight on three sides. An intimate performance space, perfect for a four-person contemporary comedy. It minimized the barrier between actors and audience, filtering none of their reaction. Right now, it was Miranda's stage.

Difficult to see the audience's faces through the glare of the lights, but everyone saw her—a petite young woman with tremendous presence. Her eyes, large and vibrant, attracted all others. The applause sounded genuine, not merely polite. She knew the difference. Enthusiasm fortified each clap, and it all coalesced into an intoxicating fanfare. Some of those silhouettes rose from their seats. They didn't have to. Miranda earned that.

One tiny concern lay at the back of her mind, however. She wasn't positive they were truly seeing Miranda Thomas, the actress, rather than the humorously absentminded host she had played for the previous two hours. They needed to recognize *her* and recognize that they wanted to keep seeing her in various roles in so many other plays, television shows, and movies. This production couldn't be her pinnacle. If this was the pinnacle, then she failed, and odds were, she was going to fail at the only thing she ever wanted to do. But she couldn't think about that now, certainly not while people were applauding her. Besides, she'd no doubt receive plenty of reminders about her long odds during dinner immediately afterward.

Miranda bowed, and a burst of cheers cleaved through the overall applause, cheers all coming from the same narrow source. She didn't earn those. Her family gave them freely. Rest assured, they saw only Miranda—now and throughout the entire production. All that work, effort, and craftsmanship, and they perceived none of it. Until the curtain call, to avoid any distraction, she pretended they weren't even there.

Not that she didn't appreciate their attendance, of course. A cross-country trip from the East Coast to Olympus City wasn't a simple jaunt, and the timing just about worked out. Parents Naomi and Vern had just wrapped up a major project for the small architectural firm they founded, owned, and operated. Older sister Bianca was starting her next semester of medical school in a few days, and little sister Peyton had a week before she embarked on her first day of high school. They all found the time to support Miranda's first post-college production—and evaluate the overall status of her life.

They hadn't done the latter yet. As soon as she finished changing, Miranda met them in the lobby, received copious hugs and congratulatory sentiments, and led them across the busy street to Ambrosia, the touristy yet tasty restaurant they had made reservations at.

As they filed into a curved booth situated beneath a mural of Ancient Greek paintings, her family continued raving about the play, and Miranda considered it in her best interests to keep them focused on this topic.

"I was surprised at how talented the whole cast was," Naomi said while scanning the menu, which was written in a fancy calligraphy surrounded by ample white space to emphasize the fanciness. "We of course knew you'd be wonderful, but everyone was so funny."

It was a professional production. Why was that a surprise? But Miranda decided to ignore the backhanded compliment. Just let her keep talking. And Naomi did.

"I can't remember the last time I laughed so hard."

Miranda almost chuckled. "That would be a great review quote. You should write that up, and we'll plaster it across all the posters." She swept an arm across an imaginary billboard.

Naomi squinted at an item on the menu, then looked over her glasses as her daughter's words finally registered. In part, at least. "Is there some website where audiences can leave feedback? I'd do it if you think it would help."

"No, Mom. I'm kidding. But thank you."

Miranda smirked and expected Bianca to be smirking also at their mother's naivety, and they would share a silent laugh across the table as they had done countless times in their youth. But Bianca's phone distracted her. Probably a text from her boyfriend. Whatever was on her phone elicited a fond smile.

Flashing a grin, Bianca patted Naomi's shoulder as she put her phone away. "Don't worry, Mom. We always pick with love." The eldest Thomas girl looked like a barely older Miranda stretched out to accommodate an extra six inches of height—a bigger Miranda, like a funhouse mirror version.

A young waiter arrived to take their orders. Miranda could've sworn she had met him somewhere. Another actor? She might have seen him at the auditions for *The Reluctant Guest*. Poor guy.

Miranda didn't even want to contemplate what she might be doing that very moment if she hadn't gotten cast. She could have been serving the next table over, channeling the full force of her talents into convincing customers she wanted to be there and delighted in tending to their every Ambrosia-related need. Five days a week, maybe more, she would be coming to this same place, walking past those same replicas of Ancient Greek artifacts and artwork, internally mocking the establishment for trying to be a weird restaurant/museum hybrid, at least when she wasn't struggling to tune out the obligatory screaming child. A tantrum was already in progress across the room, easily making itself heard despite the considerable competition from the neighboring table of brash loud-talkers. The sole bright spot would be that the European cuisines smelled delicious, but they would no doubt transition from tantalizing to revolting after piling into her nose day after day. She'd give it two weeks before no longer being able to eat moussaka or coq au vin without shuddering in disgust.

Miranda wrapped her arms tight around herself in response to a perceived temperature drop. Vern asked if she was cold and offered his sports coat. Fitted for his protruding belly, it could easily blanket Miranda several times over. She declined. She already felt small enough after noticing little Peyton had surpassed her in height since their last visit.

All meals decided upon, her family resumed complimenting various aspects of the production, as if that would lend validity to their obviously biased praise of Miranda's performance. But she was happy to discuss the show for as long as they wanted. It was a safe topic that, once exhausted, would give way to a barrage of highly invasive questions. Those questions currently waited within a time bomb, one tactfully concealed so Miranda couldn't see its timer. She could, however, keep twisting the exposed dial back to delay the inevitable explosion.

"Oh, hey, fun fact—the guy who wrote this play also writes for that TV show you all love, the one about the doctors."

That led to a nice tangent that filled the remainder of their wait for the food. But Bianca grew quiet. She observed Miranda, something bugging her. Peyton was even less chatty, had been all night, and kept twirling her long hair around her fingers.

The waiter eventually returned with everyone's meals,

which for Peyton necessitated an inspection to gauge the edibility of its contents. She poked the pasta with her fork to make sure no unwanted elements lurked underneath. She moved lethargically, her eyes squinted. This distracted Miranda from her detailed explanation of the costume design process. What was up with the Little One?

Bianca, between bites, exploited the brief lull. "Has Brad seen the show yet? What did he think?"

Boom.

Brad was Miranda's boyfriend until a few weeks ago. She hadn't gotten around to informing her family about the break-up. In hindsight, it probably would have been better to share the news during a phone conversation, which she could have ended with the slightest vague excuse. She considered telling a little white lie to avoid prolonged discourse on the topic, but they were so nice to come all this way. And besides, Bianca's tone suggested she had an educated guess about her sister's relationship status. Bianca and her own boyfriend had been dating since their freshman year of college and would be getting engaged any second now, and somehow that elevated her to an expert on Miranda's relationships.

"I don't know," Miranda said.

"Has that boy not seen it?" Her father bristled at the very idea. "At a minimum, he should have been there opening night."

Time to get it over with. "Don't make a big deal about

this, but we broke up. It's fine, though!"

"Are you okay?" Naomi asked.

"It's fine." Miranda's hands shot up into a defensive posture, which she didn't realize until after the fact.

Vern wiped a speck of salad dressing off his goatee to ensure he asked his question with the requisite dignity and gravity. His eyes narrowed. "*Are* you okay?"

Because if Naomi's emphasis on the word "okay" failed to uncover any problems, then surely the emphasis on "are" would succeed. Maybe next, Bianca could emphasize the "you," just for kicks.

"I am still fine." Miranda put on a ridiculously huge smile and pointed to it. "See?"

Naomi persisted. "I'd still like to know what happened. You two seemed to be getting along just fine at the graduation ceremony."

"We were, and we're still on friendly terms. There's nothing to worry about."

"I know what happened," Bianca said, tapping the table and drawing attention back to herself. "You did what you always do. You latched onto a guy you figured would be fun for the short term, but who you knew wasn't a keeper. The guy came with an expiration date, and you reached it."

Miranda planned on taking a breath, focusing on her succulent lamb, and simply allowing everyone to keep talking until they purged the topic from their systems.

Instead, she found herself speaking extra quickly.

"I do not do that. Sometimes things just don't work out. You're luckier than most."

"It's not luck."

"Okay, so you're better than most."

"That's not what I meant."

"Do I look unhappy?" Miranda's speech continued its acceleration, and her hands tried to assist, gesturing this way and that without a discernible game plan. "Do I look like I'm pining away for some great lost love? No, I'm fine. I'm focused on the show, and focused on making sure another show follows."

She miscalculated. She opened the door for a new, potentially worse line of questioning—her most-likely-to-fail career.

His meal wasn't half finished, but Vern set his utensils down and folded his hands as he leaned forward. "What are your plans if there's not another show immediately after this?"

Naomi served the follow-up: "Is this show paying you enough to meet all your expenses? Rent is not cheap in this city. You could get the same square footage for three-quarters of the price back home. Maybe less. And oh, you could room with Alyssa. How fun would that be?"

Having not heard from her supposed best-friend-forever in nearly a month, Miranda wasn't entirely sure. Yet another topic she preferred not to explore in this live group discussion.

Miranda wondered if she could stage a last-minute segue to steer everyone back toward discussing the show, but a ship this size could not easily turn.

Naomi went on about the city's high tax rates. Vern offered multiple suggestions for part-time employment to "stop the bleeding," as he put it. Naomi suggested that if Miranda married a well-to-do young man, he could support her and allow her to act without any urgency for a paycheck and "just for the fun of it," and certainly Brad didn't seem poised for a lucrative career, so perhaps there was a silver lining to Miranda's heartbreak. Miranda reiterated that she was fine.

The conversation continued, but with Miranda firmly in the role of spectator. Bianca accused Naomi of suggesting her daughter become a "kept woman," which Naomi refuted. Peyton studied a portrait of Athena—the kid was utterly transfixed, her expression blank.

Miranda zoned out briefly and missed the transition into worries about her physical safety in the big city—the big city she had already survived through four years of college.

"I should look up the crime statistics when we get back to the hotel," Vern said. "Not every part of this city will be as safe as that campus was."

This, at least, was an easy one.

Miranda stated the obvious. "Dad. This city has never

been safer. Never."

. . .

The high sun surprised Miranda as they exited the restaurant. She could've sworn it was later, though she wasn't sure whether to blame the matinee or the dinner conversation for that confusion. But she knew what she needed to do.

She linked an arm around Peyton's, and they quickened their pace down the sidewalk.

"I'm showing her the huge bookstore right down the block," Miranda shouted back. "You'll see it."

Lest the kids forget, their parents issued the usual reminders to have fun and be careful. Of course Peyton would have fun in a bookstore. She was always reading around the house, always in the middle of a few novels of assorted genres, always on the hunt for the next great one.

Peyton whispered, "Where are we really going?"

"To a huge bookstore. I'm not getting into any more trouble here."

Miranda truly had expected the prospect of a bookstore to excite her, but Peyton's fog didn't lift. So Miranda employed a second tact—having fun with her growth spurt. Peyton had always seemed more on track to achieve Bianca's height rather than succumb to the same short genes that left Miranda barely scraping past the five-foot mark. While not shocking, Miranda was never going to be prepared for it.

"So I see you've grown. That really wasn't necessary. High schools don't actually have any of those 'You must be this tall to enter' signs. You're thinking roller coasters."

Peyton laughed. She still sounded young and girly, and she remained awkwardly scrawny, unsure how to carry those narrow shoulders. All as it should be. Only so much growing up permitted.

The giggling petered out sooner than usual, though, and Peyton withdrew into her own head.

"This is a used bookstore, so everything's super-cheap," Miranda said. "And I know this is a short trip, but you're still so many miles from home, so it counts as a vacation and Mom and Dad will get you a special vacation prize. Don't forget to claim it."

All she got in response was a mumbled "Yeah, okay."

Miranda guided her through a gap in the oncoming pedestrian traffic and into Olympus's premier seller of secondhand literature. Stacks upon stacks of potentially amazing discoveries awaited Peyton—and she still couldn't care less.

Something was bothering her, and it wasn't hard to guess what. "You'll do great in high school. Now middle school, that was the hard part. If you can get through that, consider yourself unstoppable."

"It's just ..." Peyton's mouth hung open long enough for the words to perish. "It's nothing."

Clearly not. The sidewalk had a few benches, so Miranda escorted Peyton back outside.

"I want to hear all about this 'nothing,'" Miranda said.

Peyton sat and then nodded. "So in high school, I'll basically be preparing for college, right?"

"There is a lot of college prep, yes."

"Then college is all about preparing for a career."

"It does help with that."

"And when you're working, you're preparing for retirement and your kids' educations."

Oh, yes—Miranda was supposed to be saving her oodles of excess income for retirement. She had intentionally forgotten, largely because those oodles were, in fact, nonexistent.

"What's wrong?"

Hardly even blinking, Peyton gazed straight ahead at the vehicles crawling down the street, futilely honking their horns. She scrunched her face, carefully considering her response before she spoke it.

"This summer is the end of my childhood, and then everything is about preparing for something else. What if I'm so busy always preparing that it all stops being fun?"

Their parents would have handled this much better, Miranda realized. They, or even Bianca, would have dispensed suitable wisdom to alleviate Peyton's anxieties about growing up. All Miranda managed to do was mutter the basic no, no, that would never happen, you'll be fine, you'll have a blast—did she actually just say "you'll have a blast"?

It sounded pathetic and unconvincing, and guilt over her poor showing blocked her brain from producing anything better. But any advice would have involved mere guesswork, if not outright lies. What did Miranda know? She didn't know what she'd be doing in four weeks when her play closed. Even her friendship with Alyssa— which was supposed to be her one enduring relationship from high school—no longer seemed a given.

She kept trying. She couldn't look at Peyton's melancholy face and not keep trying. So she started talking about how much fun she had in high school, then slowed down upon realizing she didn't want Peyton to partake in all the same types of fun. All the worst examples kept pushing to the front of Miranda's mind— that day she played hooky, her first party with alcohol, losing her virginity on the auditorium's well-concealed catwalk. Where were the PG examples? They existed, they happened, but the memories chose that moment to go into hibernation.

"Everything will be fine," Miranda said, knowing damn well how often she used "fine" to mean nothing of the sort. It reeked of insincerity—a sin for an actor.

Peyton rested her head on Miranda's shoulder, so Miranda put an arm around her. They watched the traffic, occasionally glimpsing the pedestrians on the far side.

But Miranda wasn't content. She felt she was failing her little sister with every second she proved unable to offer the perfect advice, the perfect wisdom, the perfect reassurance, anything perfect. Peyton deserved no less than perfect.

Her concentration collapsed altogether when a large, haggard man snatched a lady's purse across the street and dashed away, shoving people aside with his meaty arms.

He made it half a block before the equivalent of a giant camera flash blinded him, and the light congealed into a man.

Miranda tugged at Peyton, urging her to her feet. "Peyton! You'll want to see this."

Pedestrians on both sides of the street did, too, and the motorists ceased their honking, suddenly in no hurry. Many cell phones vacated pockets and purses. Everyone, whatever their background or current plans, stopped and watched the confrontation between the stupidly brazen purse-snatcher and the world's first and only superhero—Fantastic Man.

As of a month ago, an actual superhero existed. Not some martial arts enthusiast with a costume and death wish, but rather a uniquely talented man who could manipulate light by thinking about it—a man who was able to convert his entire body into a bunch of photons, transforming himself into living light, and return to human form unscathed. No one knew who he was or how he came to be, but everyone knew he protected Olympus City.

Miranda and Peyton angled for the best view of that radiant blue-and-amber uniform, whose radiance wasn't figurative. They couldn't hear a thing over all the commotion, but for a moment they had an unobstructed line of sight to the most sparkling smile ever seen outside a toothpaste commercial, beneath a mask shaped like a hazy setting sun. Even with some distance, Miranda could read him—his posture impeccable, his yellow cape fluttering behind him, he projected the image of a man who would never allow anything to go wrong, not on his watch.

And that purse-snatcher knew it. Rubbing his stunned eyeballs, he hustled away, not even attempting a fight.

Fantastic Man dematerialized into light and reappeared once again in front of the purse-snatcher. The superhero was tall and muscular in his own right, but still smaller than this hulking thief, a fact neither seemed aware of. Fantastic Man thrust an arm forward and unleashed another flash to disorient his opponent, and he followed by sweeping his leg through the purse-snatcher's, toppling him onto the pavement.

Two police officers cut through the crowd and handcuffed the criminal. Fantastic Man stuck around to shake their hands, his smile unrelenting. He returned the purse to its owner, who responded as if she had won the lottery, and the Beacon of Brightness waved at the cheering throngs surrounding him, then looked to the sky and disappeared in a brilliant flare.

Peyton was entranced. Her mouth hung open, and the grin looked permanent.

"That was the coolest thing ever," she said.

Her previous worries were now the last thing on her mind. Where Miranda had failed, Fantastic Man saved the day.

2

Greek gods lined the way to Mount Olympus—though these gods appeared in the form of meticulously maintained topiaries, and this Mount Olympus was a fat tower occupying a public park in the center of the city, standing taller than all else within a seven-mile radius.

Miranda hiked between looming bushes, down the long brick path that led straight to the elevator centered beneath the tower. As always, she found the nice old policeman, Officer Hoskins, patrolling the park with a friendly smile beneath his white mustache.

The overhead lights shaded and deepened his wrinkles as he nodded at her. "Welcome back, young lady. Enjoy yourself up there—but not too much, you hear?"

He said that every single time, and he chuckled at himself every time. But Miranda had to admire the old man's relentlessly positive attitude. He may not have gone far in his career, but he seemed happy where he was. An enviable quality.

"Yes, sir. I'll be sure to keep my ruckus to a minimum," Miranda said, mirroring the smile.

And she entered the elevator, as usual, alone.

Her family had retired to their hotel, but she continued to brim with restless energy from another successful performance. Going to bed would have resulted in a long night of staring at the ceiling. Better to gaze at the stars from the city's best vantage point, which was seldom busy this late, making it the perfect spot for quiet reflection and unwinding.

Sleeping would have been sensible. Monday was a day off from the play, but not from her side gig—acting in the background of a movie. She was going to be an extra. Extraneous. Expendable. But even that meager paycheck wasn't expendable, not to her. In any case, Miranda had plenty of experience in the background and therefore could background-act on a minimum of sleep.

The elevator car lifted off, embarking on its two-thousand-foot climb.

Her ears popped, and white noise was Miranda's only soundtrack as the car slid up the rails. Only external soundtrack, rather.

Involuntarily, she dwelled on Bianca's analysis of her love life. Miranda attempted to disprove the conclusion that she was somehow a saboteur of her own relationships, deliberately choosing the wrong guys. In the case of Brad, he had wanted to move in together. She didn't. So they were clearly incompatible at this stage in their lives. Miranda didn't *consciously* mean to attract a guy who would prematurely want to live together. The very notion was preposterous. But could she have, *unconsciously*?

The elevator settled and doors opened, granting passage to a steady, cool wind. The observation deck was, as expected, empty. Several times the square footage of her apartment, a sizable perimeter of railing—all hers for now. But she picked the same spot as always, which offered her a view over numerous skyscrapers, down the bridge connecting this island city to the rest of California, and to the distant Santa Monica skyline. Miranda intended much of her career to take place not far beyond. That was the direction of her future—she hoped.

She leaned on the bar, gazing down at the city through the protective grate. At this distance, the cars looked like fireflies that forgot how to fly, forcing them to conform to the city's preplanned grid.

Plenty of lights still on across Olympus, even at this hour. She noticed one unusually bright spot in the far north corner, in the otherwise dim suburbs. The glare spilled up from a street but stayed confined to a tight radius, its intensity never fluctuating. Miranda suspected it was the handiwork of a film crew. Probably the movie she'd be working on tomorrow. She wanted to be working there now. She had auditioned for one of the bit parts. Didn't get it. So many others didn't either.

She knew her dream was not unique. Every day, she encountered other young women pursuing the same career. Only a small percentage could achieve somewhat steady work, and only an infinitesimal percentage of *that* group could catapult to Miranda's ultimate goal—the A-list, the most talented, most bankable, most adored. Miranda was one of a gazillion—yet another over-ambitious and under-employed actress. But then she remembered the applause she received that afternoon, its delicious enthusiasm enveloping her ...

Miranda redirected her eyes to the starlight, and she thought of Peyton's excitement at seeing Fantastic Man. The kid could focus on nothing else the rest of the evening. At the first opportunity, Peyton took to her phone and scoured the internet for any and all tidbits. While lacking in depth, the tidbits were plentiful. Fantastic Man, though less than forthcoming on personal details, was not camera-shy. News and amateur websites alike provided ample coverage of the man who should have been impossible. Peyton had found an escape from her worries. But Miranda couldn't escape the dread of her inevitable failure to become a star, no matter what altitude she reached. Reality refused to untether her.

She had set the bar so high for herself she'd never be able to reach it, but she refused to lower it an inch. She tightened her grip on the railing. Her chest constricted, she couldn't breathe, goosebumps sprouted across her shivering arms as the wind picked up ...

"Miranda? Are you okay?"

The voice was familiar. A distinctive baritone. Once she ensured her eyes were dry, she summoned a huge smile and spun around—and she saw Ken Shield, an old friend from high school.

"I'm wonderful. Hey!" She rushed over to give him a quick hug. "Oh my God, how long has it been? A year? Two?"

"Three."

"Three! Well, that's just wrong."

Sure, they went to rival colleges on opposite sides of this island city, but they shared that hometown bond. Not that Miranda considered herself bonded with most of the people she went to school with back in Meadowville. She couldn't care less if she never saw ninety-five percent of them again. But Ken qualified for the other five percent that was worth seeing once a year or so—certainly sooner than three whole years.

Miranda swept her wind-blown hair from her face. "I see we're both terrible at sleeping."

Giving a small shoulder shrug and a soft, lopsided smile, Ken said, "Hasn't been my strong suit lately."

"But in our defense, we're insomniacs with exquisite taste in late-night hangout spots."

"We're not without our talents." Ken's humble face exuded warmth and sincerity. "So how's life as an actress?"

Miranda could've discussed her show, but she didn't trust herself to stop there, not when Ken had always been such a patient listener. She worried she'd sound ungrateful or like she was too good for regional theatre. She was acting professionally and yet wasn't satisfied—the nerve of her.

So she swatted the question away. "Oh, I don't want to bore you with all that."

"You wouldn't—"

"It's really not all that glamorous."

"Never thought it would be."

She lightly touched his thin arm—a small gesture to tug him away from his line of questioning and toward her own. "So you're teaching now, right? How is that? Everything you always dreamed? Or I guess the school year hasn't started. But you student-taught. Taught." She winced. "Student-*taught*. It's very late."

Ken wandered to the railing. He leaned on the sturdy bar, his posture slacking. Miranda followed, and standing beside him, she tracked his gaze to the city streets beyond the tower's dark moat of grass and sparse trees.

"Actually," he said, not blinking, not looking at her, not smiling, "I dropped out of my school's licensure program."

Miranda studied his profile. So sullen. But he was always so sure about this path, as sure as she was about her own. How did he descend from certainty to quitting? Miranda could never picture herself quitting.

She blurted out her question. "Wasn't that all you ever wanted to do?"

His head drifted down until he had fixed his gaze on the railing's rust. "I wasn't feeling like the right fit for it, and for a job that important, you better be the right fit." Ken brushed his thumb against a paint chip in the process of flaking off. "I have no idea what I'm doing."

Miranda needed to offer reassuring words, but they proved as elusive as they had with Peyton. She had gotten lucky with that conversation. If Fantastic Man hadn't shown up, what would she have said?

Ken continued, "I want to make sure I do something useful—but not something I'd screw up."

Then she realized—she didn't need Fantastic Man's presence to use him.

"Here's how I look at it," she said, making it up as she went. "If a man can turn himself into a beam of light, then surely we can turn ourselves into successful human beings."

The sullenness melted away as Ken absorbed her statement, and he let out a quick grunt, his standard mode of laughter. Miranda wanted to pat herself on the back for a job well done.

"That is very crazy," he said.

"I know, right? Tell you what—I'll promise to do amazing things if you promise to do amazing things. No excuses when anything's possible." Miranda extended a hand. "Deal?"

He nodded, and they shook on it. "Deal. I'll see you on the big screen, and you'll see me doing ... something of value."

"But you will figure it out," she said.

"I will figure it out."

His smile was fully restored—Miranda did that, and doing so bolstered her own, locking them in a smiling loop.

But Ken broke her out of it. "Hey, how's Alyssa doing? What's she up to?"

Miranda swiftly recovered from the unwelcome reminder, and she had no trouble supplying the basic, surface-level summary: Yes, Alyssa was still pursuing certification to become a dental hygienist. No, Miranda wasn't sure what the appeal of such a career was, but hey, job security was a thing for some people. And yes, Alyssa still lived near the old hometown. Ken told her to pass along a "hello" from him. Miranda didn't tell him that she expected to forget by the time Alyssa finally got around to returning a call or text.

From there, they drifted into conversation about their college days and life in Olympus. And when Miranda learned that he, too, was planning on sticking around the city for the foreseeable future, she developed an idea.

"You know, we should get together for coffee one day," Miranda said. "Sometime sooner than three years. We've got a lot of time to make up for."

Caught off guard, Ken's eyes widened and he tensed, like he wasn't sure what was going on exactly.

Miranda feared she had miscalculated, but Ken was

a genuinely nice guy—not one of those "nice guys" who expected some magnificent reward for the extraordinary feat of not being a blatant jerk. No, he was a good-hearted, honest soul. And, present uncertainties aside, he was responsible. Miranda had no doubt he'd figure out a rewarding, worthwhile career. His looks, though not of leading-man caliber, weren't bad by any means. He was tall and lean, had a nice solid chin devoid of any cleft, and his dark hair hadn't thinned any.

And Miranda had asked him out. No real build-up. No historical basis from their mutually friendly past. She blindsided the poor guy. Blindsided herself. Was this what she actually wanted?

She had no answer. But the thought of him declining, with any excuse, froze her, and the encroaching ice squeezed her every internal organ.

After a couple seconds' consideration, though, Ken relaxed and agreed, pulling off a casual air of *Sure, why not?* "Yeah, that'd be nice," he said.

Miranda masked her tension, dissipating it through light laughter as they fumbled with their phones and exchanged numbers. He promised to call sometime in the next couple of days.

Like a proper gentleman, he offered to walk her to the subway, but she declined, insisting that he not cut his Mount Olympus time short on her account.

"Are you sure?" he said. "It would be no trouble."

"I'm pretty sure I can get to the subway without a bodyguard." Miranda tossed a parting smirk at him. "But I'll be seeing you, Ken."

And she intended to do so—sometime after he started missing her.

3

As she descended in the elevator, Miranda considered what she just did. She had never felt any physical attraction toward Ken Shield. But, on an intellectual level, she acknowledged that he possessed many fine qualities. He wasn't right for a brief, passionate fling. A guy like him qualified as long-term boyfriend material. And Bianca was wrong that Miranda avoided long-term boyfriends—never mind that the longest of her numerous relationships lasted five months, back in high school ...

But yeah, Ken seemed like a decent option. What was the harm in a couple of dates?

The elevator carriage settled, and Miranda expected to find Officer Hoskins somewhere along the well-lit path, ever vigilant as he stood guard over the park. But once the door opened, she saw only a long, vacant stretch of brick surrounded by topiaries and impenetrable darkness. The park did span several acres around the tower. Perhaps something demanded Hoskins's attention.

Miranda kept her phone in hand as she began her brisk walk, reminding herself that this was one of the safer parts of town. Still, her parents had issued many warnings about the dangers a city held after dark, and her mind replayed the greatest hits. Miranda felt her ears expanding to catch even the faintest rustling of leaves.

She heard something else. Not leaves or wind or any scurrying critter. Nothing from nature. Nothing natural.

A moan. It was coming from somewhere behind those bushes. Miranda's senses all dialed up to maximum.

She decided to ignore it and stay on the path, stay under the lights. Keep her eyes on her phone and check the hell out of those text messages. Or pretend to while secretly poised to dial 9-1-1 if the need arose—a need like someone leaping out and strangling her.

Whatever it was, Officer Hoskins was probably already on it. That explained his absence. But what if he was the one moaning?

"I'm hurt," the moaning person called out from the darkness, her voice hoarse.

It was definitely a woman's voice, not the policeman's. And he wasn't around to respond to the cry for help.

This could have been a trap—some creepy man lurking, sheathed in the dark, ready to throw the first unsuspecting good citizen into a black van. And if not, well, really, what could Miranda do to help? Aside from the simple task of dialing 9-1-1.

It would be the right thing to do, in case someone *was* suffering. Miranda could make the call and run away.

"Help. Please."

Miranda wanted to keep walking until she exited the

park, but her feet refused to budge and she cringed. She remained physically capable of forward momentum, just not mentally.

Her stomach folded in on itself, threatening to incite debilitating queasiness unless she did the right thing. If she walked away, she'd spend days or weeks dwelling on whatever she walked away from, constantly checking the news for any hints about what the hell this was. All food would lose its appeal, and she would look back on the concept of sleep with nostalgic fondness.

She considered running back up to Ken, but he was nearly half a mile above the ground. And someone right here might be hurt.

Miranda dialed the digits 9-1-1 and positioned her thumb over the "call" icon. Without hitting it just yet, she advanced toward the source of the moaning and commanded herself not to dissolve into a shivering mess of nerves. She did not heed herself. Her shaking thumb almost jabbed "call" by accident.

Didn't happen, though. A flash of light cut through the park for just a second, and she stopped. Where did it come from? Not the park's lighting system. Was it … Fantastic Man? Was she about to meet Fantastic Man? This seemed more like something he should handle, not her.

"That was me," the woman said, each word scraping against Miranda's ears. So scratchy and parched. She wasn't far, maybe only a few feet into the darkness. "Want to make sure I ... have your attention."

Without stepping off the path, Miranda dared to look between the bushes. A new source of light flickered low to the ground, revealing a much older woman lying on the grass. The light came from the strange electricity that was cascading over her unusual outfit, which looked like a superhero costume—emerald tights with a scarlet cape. A deep red symbol occupied the center of the chest, the silhouette of a bird's wing melding into a fierce, sharp beak. The costume lacked a mask, though. But this woman had to be at least fifty, maybe sixty, and Miranda had never seen her before. Surely if an older female superhero had emerged, she would have dominated the news as much as Fantastic Man did, probably more so on account of her unexpected demographic affiliation.

Or was she a supervillain? Was this a trap? Was Miranda stupidly falling into a trap?

The woman was clutching her side, pressing her hand against a dark liquid ...

Blood. The super electric woman was wounded to the point where she was bleeding all over the grass. Miranda did not care to stick around to learn who did the wounding, nor did she relish the idea of running away and unwittingly intercepting such a person.

The woman reached toward Miranda with her free hand, which glowed as bright as a standard light bulb, no more intense than that. The electricity never sparked beyond her elbow, so the hand appeared safe.

"Come here," the woman said. "Help me up. The pain ... is too great."

If she was actually in pain. Miranda started to wonder. The injury seemed real, but the woman almost looked like she was smirking. Miranda's eyes were still adjusting to the aura of electrical light, though, and she wanted any excuse to get the hell away with a clear conscience.

Paranoia was not an excuse to let someone suffer, so Miranda started to reach for that bright, quivering hand. And paranoia froze her anyway, after only an inch of movement.

"Should I call an ambulance or the police?" Miranda asked, continuing rapidly without pause, "And who are you and where is that electricity coming from? Am I in danger just by standing here? Are you going to kill me? Please don't kill me."

The woman chuckled through gritted teeth, as if Miranda had told a joke. "Just grab my hand, dear."

So many dangers a city held at night ... "Where—" Miranda cleared her throat to stop from squeaking. "Where did you come from?"

"Very far. It's quite a story." The woman coughed, and her scratchiness worsened. "Come here and I'll tell you all about—"

Another loud moan. She writhed, and the electricity

sparked brighter, flashing like lightning. In that split-second of illumination, something glinted across the field, and the glint looked person-shaped. Miranda tensed, and hoped her imagination was embellishing a garbage can, which was indeed a possibility. But still ...

Time for 9-1-1. Miranda tapped her phone, but the screen had shut off from disuse. She was about to wake it up, but the woman managed to speak again.

"Not much time. *Come here.*"

She sounded so forceful, almost rude, but why wouldn't she be? She was clearly in agony, probably dying, and the only person close enough to help her was struggling to lift a finger. Another lightning flash would have been helpful—Miranda could have confirmed if the glinting had reflected off some mundane, harmless object.

But if there *was* a dangerous individual nearby, what safer place to be than beside a super-person, even a wounded one?

"Okay," Miranda said, stepping further onto the grass. "Let's, um, get you out of here."

Miranda reached forward. The strange glow warmed her, and it brightened and grew hot as the woman reached up. Miranda wasn't sure if this was the best course of action, but she'd still be able to live with herself afterward. If she was still living, that is.

The electrical woman's fingertips brushed against

Miranda's, casting an unexpected chill.

And the woman quickly withdrew. She gazed at her own shivering hand, horrified by it.

"You were willing to help me," she said. "And I almost—but why do I feel this way? I've never—"

The woman descended into nonsense, most of it inaudible, something about a strange sensation in her head, an unnatural migraine she was struggling to identify. Her rambling further devolved into incoherent utterances about good and evil, during which Miranda was utterly baffled about what the hell she should do.

Before Miranda could make any decision, the woman landed on a clear question: "What have I done with my life?"

The woman hacked out the nastiest cough yet, and her whole body convulsed. She required serious medical attention that Miranda had no idea how to render. Where the hell was Officer Hoskins? She tapped her phone's screen, but it wouldn't turn on. The battery died. It had been halfway charged minutes earlier, but now the phone was useless.

And the woman was still convulsing, ever more violently, her electric energy intensifying ...

A brighter glare washed over Miranda, and she raised her hands to shield her eyes from the light. Her arms itched, and the sensation swept across her skin, passing an instant later, only to be replaced by nausea. She could feel nothing beneath her feet, as if she somehow lost track of the ground. But that, too, passed, and the light dimmed.

She lowered her arms, and the woman was gone. In her place, charred grass formed a silhouette, like a crime scene outline.

Did Miranda just watch a woman die?

She did. The woman died, some kind of supernatural death that didn't even leave a body behind, and if Miranda reported it ... who would believe her? Maybe more people these days, but still ... what concrete information could she even supply?

Queasiness overcame her after all, forcing Miranda to her knees as she dry-heaved. Lightheadedness arrived next, followed by crawling skin and a vague sense of movement as the night faded away.

4

"**A**re you awake?" Peyton asked.

Miranda was now, though she couldn't recall when she fell asleep—or why she collapsed on her couch as opposed to pulling out her bed inside it, or when her family let themselves in. For that matter, Miranda wasn't sure when she returned home the previous night. That poor super-person died, and then ...?

She needed several moments alone to process and unpack last night's events. But her visitors denied her even one.

Five people tested her studio apartment's capacity. Naomi and Vern inspected her food supply in the kitchen nook while Bianca, seated comfortably on a stool, rummaged through several weeks' worth of junk mail like it was her own. At least she organized the pile into a neat stack, which was an improvement over Miranda's system of tossing the envelopes and fliers onto the counter and forgetting they existed.

"Why are you still in the same clothes as yesterday?" Peyton asked, leaning on the fraying armrest.

Naomi closed a cabinet and noticed Miranda had woken up. "Did you forget you were supposed to meet us at the hotel? We left messages on your phone."

Defying her pre-caffeine grogginess, Miranda pulled herself into a sitting position and rose quickly. A sudden familial invasion of privacy substituted for coffee just fine, it seemed.

"I'm so sorry. I just ... I guess I overslept." But how? She pinched the bridge of her nose and closed her eyes, replaying what she could of last night, trying to visualize a memory of leaving the park ...

"Well, you weren't getting out of seeing us one more time," Naomi said.

"I wasn't trying to." How could she not remember leaving the park? She tried to picture the subway. She must have ridden the subway.

An image began to form ...

The refrigerator door opened, and Naomi sighed. "And when was the last time you went to the store? This fridge is empty."

Miranda lost the image. "It's not empty. It's almost empty. That's a noteworthy distinction."

"These coupons expired three weeks ago." Bianca held up a piece of junk mail, which apparently wasn't always junk.

Something under the sink fascinated Vern. "Your wood is rotting. Might be a leak. You should notify your landlord."

Miranda muttered a noncommittal acknowledgment,

then turned to Peyton. "Do you have any comments about my home?"

"Nope."

"You're my favorite little sister."

Naomi swooped in for closer examination. Her hand descended on Miranda's forehead. "You look pale. Are you feeling well? You're warm."

"I'm fine."

"So what were you doing last night that you couldn't be bothered to set an alarm?"

Pleasant moods raised fewer questions, so Miranda pretended to be in one. Instinct produced a smile, though she kept it subdued—didn't want to overdo it this early in the day. "I ran into an old friend. You might remember him. Ken Shield. From high school."

Just as Miranda intended, a look of fond recognition swept across Naomi's face. "Oh, yes. Barb and Keith's little boy. How's he doing?"

"Fine. He's doing fine."

"Always such a nice young man."

A memory resurfaced. Miranda saw herself riding home on the subway, everything around her hazy. But before that ...?

Bianca set the final piece of junk mail on the stack and evened the edges as much as possible. "He's not your type," she said without turning around.

"What? Did I say he was?"

Naomi pointed at Vern, drawing his attention. "We haven't seen the Shields in ages. We should really give them a call, especially if our kids are seeing each other."

"We happened to be at the same place. That's all." Parental notification of anything further was premature. Miranda's statement omitted much, but she didn't consider it a lie.

She realized she was repeatedly bouncing her leg on the ball of her foot, so she stopped. And she remembered hearing sirens sometime before she got on the subway. Did she ever find out where Officer Hoskins disappeared to?

Naomi and Vern discussed what nice people the Shields were, and Miranda lost all ability to pay attention. The thing with Ken seemed so trivial now.

She needed a shower. She excused herself, and Naomi reminded her to not to get lost in there—they were already running behind schedule and couldn't miss their flight.

Miranda's phone sat dormant on the corner of the side table. Behind that dark screen lurked the internet and, perhaps, a few answers. She discreetly grabbed it as she made her way into the bathroom, locking the door behind her.

Somehow, the phone had regained a charge. Did she charge it? No time to waste figuring that out. She opened the browser and searched for any news about Mount

Olympus. And she found something.

An article posted early in the morning detailed how veteran police officer Earl Hoskins was found unconscious on the Mount Olympus grounds. No evidence of a struggle, no visible wounds, but he was admitted to the hospital in critical condition. As of press time, his condition had stabilized, and though they couldn't go into details, the hospital staff expected him to make a full recovery. The park's security footage proved useless—nonexistent, actually. Whether due to a technical malfunction or foul play, the entire day's recordings had been wiped out.

So, Officer Hoskins was alive. The super-powered woman wasn't, but the nice old man was. That lifted some weight off Miranda's mind but not all. The article mentioned nothing about whoever found Officer Hoskins, nor anything about a woman in a superhero costume. Miranda feared she'd never learn who the woman was or why she was there or even what that brilliant flash of light was. All of it a perpetual mystery to haunt her.

She showered, taking long enough to make her parents anxious.

The family shared a quick breakfast at a café. Miranda contributed to the conversation just enough, but most of it fled her mind immediately afterward. Something about the diverse architectural styles across various parts of the city.

She rode with them to the airport, distracting herself with Peyton's souvenir—a commemorative extra edition of the local newspaper, *The Olympian Herald*, compiling its coverage of Fantastic Man. Miranda stared at the words, registering few. Neat photo of Fantastic Man in mid-transformation, though. It would have qualified as surrealist art, were the photo not taken from reality.

She waited as her family checked their luggage, and as she accompanied them to the security line, Bianca pulled her back several steps behind the others.

"Something's bothering you," she said, quiet enough that no one would overhear.

Miranda didn't think, just responded. "Nothing's bothering me."

Bianca leaned in closer. "You have to let someone in, Miri." She invoked the childhood nickname, a reminder of when they were much closer. "Doesn't have to be me, but someone, okay? This isn't good for your mental health."

"Are you switching tracks to psychiatry?"

Bianca pointed at her face. "See? Someone reaches out, and you deflect."

They reached security, mercifully freeing Miranda from any need to respond. Her parents launched into their goodbyes, and Miranda gave Peyton a good long squeeze.

Bianca still got the last word in, barely above a whisper. "Just think about it."

Her family merged into the line, and Miranda watched them retreat from her city.

Soon, she was alone again. Just her and her mental picture of a dying woman.

She looked forward to a long day of crummy work.

5

Miranda hated being an extra, but she excelled at it. She always knew how to get in front of the camera without calling undue attention to herself. There were benefits, though, namely the networking opportunities.

Today's job was a romantic comedy, one content to coast on the name recognition of its leads. Titled *Huge*, it featured Courtney Byrd and Tuck Lewis, both true movie stars capable of elevating a mediocre script. They deserved tremendous professional respect, in Miranda's estimation. She was a bit embarrassed that movie posters bearing Tuck's image had adorned her bedroom wall in far less mature days.

All Miranda had to do today, however, was run behind him and not trip. Her background role was a jogger hustling down a sidewalk that was pretending to be part of New York City. She'd jog from Point A to Point B while Tuck and Courtney said their lines, and they'd all reset as many times as necessary—which would doubtless be a lot. The scene was long, talky, and would have bombed with anything less than these gifted actors, and it would require numerous takes over several hours, equating to lots of exercise for Miranda on this fine hot day.

Miranda was getting paid to spend the afternoon trapped in a manmade time loop.

But the more she jogged, the more energetic she felt. It escalated quickly. After the fourth take, Miranda wanted to run a mile, hell, a whole marathon. She never craved running—she considered any form of exercise a chore, especially in this summer heat. But now her muscles demanded to go, go, go. A full hour into her intermittent jogging, and she hadn't even begun to tire. Rather, she kept having to remind herself to slow down and not run so fast that no one could get a good look at her.

In the middle of the afternoon, filming paused so the camera crew could make some adjustments. For the background actors, this meant a break.

Miranda grabbed a complimentary water bottle, mostly out of habit. She took a sip and realized she wasn't all that thirsty. Nevertheless, she forced more down and scoped out the set for a fellow extra to strike up conversation with.

"... but look at her nose."

The assistant director, a perpetually scowling British man, was speaking to a scrawny guy who looked like a freakishly elongated child but was actually a production assistant. They were standing in the middle of the closed-off street and staring right at Miranda like she was something less than a person.

"What about it?" the PA asked.

"It's just like hers."

"Well, sure, it's small ..."

"Just like hers!"

Miranda hoped the assistant director simply recognized her from her current play. She clamped down on her jittery foot, which she noticed was tapping dead-center on a small spider-web crack in the sidewalk. Of all the places to step, her foot just had to land on a crack. Not the greatest omen.

"Once I saw it, I couldn't stop seeing it," the assistant director continued. "She's going to confuse people."

Miranda put everything else on hold—even breathing—until she heard the rest.

"You in the shorts—jogger girl, come here."

She did as told, and the two men managed the feat of simultaneously examining and ignoring her.

"Yeah, spitting image of Sadie," the PA said, referring to the most prominent supporting character.

"People are going to see her jogging across the screen and wonder why she's giving the cold shoulder to her best friend."

Aside from both being tiny brunettes, Miranda and the actress playing Sadie looked nothing alike. Maybe the noses were similar, *maybe*, but the other woman had a longer face, shorter hair, and at least a decade more in age.

"Sorry, darling," the assistant director said without

pity. "You're wrapped. Go see B.J. for your timesheet."

The men carried on with their business, and Miranda began her walk of shame off the set and toward the production's trailer office. The route soon brought her past Tuck Lewis as the director was giving him notes. And, *of course*, he stood facing her, witnessing her embarrassment.

"Excuse me," Tuck told his director, and he approached Miranda.

She reminded herself she was a professional about to meet a much more experienced professional and she was not about to meet her first celebrity crush.

That handsomely chiseled face projected confidence without arrogance, and his posture relaxed just enough that he almost seemed like a normal person, one who happened to keep in excellent shape. His lean arms were exceptionally well toned. Not a trace of flab that Miranda could see. He looked even better in his thirties than he had in his twenties.

"Hey, I saw what happened there," he said, his lazy smile offering sympathy. "Don't feel bad about it. A lot of what goes on in this business boils down to dumb luck—right place, right time, all that kind of stuff. It's nothing you did."

Miranda would have preferred this to be her fault—then she could learn and correct herself next time. But random bad luck offered no lesson of any value. In this case, it brought only Tuck Lewis's pity. So many times she imagined meeting him ...

"Thank you," she said, feeling she should add something but failing to do so.

The tall leading man hooked his thumbs into his jeans' front pockets, and his deep blue eyes locked on to hers with a penetrating gaze that was both exciting and uncomfortable.

"You shouldn't worry at all," he said. "No one will remember this. At your age, tomorrow's always a fresh start."

"Thank you." She wanted to replace that with something she hadn't already said, but too late. The moment passed, and Tuck turned to walk away.

Yeah, that matched none of her adolescent fantasies about the guy.

Almost immediately, though, Tuck stopped and glanced back. "They're wrong, by the way," he said quietly, a hand over his mouth, like he was telling a secret. "You don't look like her. You're actually prettier."

Miranda was beaming. *That* was more like what she had imagined.

But Tuck had said no one would remember this. Did he include himself in that? How many young women did he flirt with on any given day? According to the tabloids, a fair number.

Those two seconds of feeling special were nice, and

Miranda was right back to the reality of being fired.

So if tomorrow was a fresh start, what was the rest of today? Her dismissal granted her an extra six hours of free time, six hours without anything to distract her.

She'd start with a walk. Still lots of excess energy to burn off. She'd just keep moving.

Three miles of walking, and Miranda had yet to tire. She set out with no destination in mind, and her wandering brought her back to Mount Olympus.

The place was far busier in the middle of the afternoon. Families gathered and kids played on the grass. Couples enjoyed picnics together. Joggers jogged for real, not to color the background for more important people.

And none of them had the first clue that a woman died there several hours earlier under mysterious circumstances. As far as they knew, the worst thing that happened last night was that a veteran police officer's age caught up with him.

Miranda approached *the* spot, near the Hermes topiary. She felt disrespectful visiting in workout clothes. No evidence of last night's events, though. Like the woman was never there. To all these people milling around, the woman never existed in the first place.

She felt her throat closing and gasped for air. Nobody rushed to check on her. Would anyone notice if she passed out? She didn't, though. All that surplus energy boiled inside without anywhere to go, her tightening chest bottling it up. If she could just breathe …

Miranda sucked in a lungful, and the ground disappeared and her hair whipped into her face. All sense of weight abandoned her, as if gravity decided to untether just this one person.

Everything was spinning—no, *she* was spinning. Spinning where? By what means? She felt nothing except her own clothes and the relentless wind that kept changing its mind about which way it wanted to blow. A commotion rang out among the park-goers, their volume swiftly diminishing to nothing. Miranda reached out to grab whatever she could, but empty air offered no support.

She found herself outside the Mount Olympus observation deck, looking straight in. She almost expected to see herself in there. Instead, several stunned faces turned toward her, only just beginning to register the sight of a flying woman. And Miranda realized that *she*, somehow, was a flying woman.

But she had no idea how to fly, so she swirled, tumbling head over feet along an ever-changing axis. Whether the ground was above, below, or to a side, it remained far away, easily hundreds of feet removed from her. The scenery shifted with her every revolution. Blurs of people became blurs of cars, which morphed into blurs of skyscraper windows. And the windows zoomed toward her.

Miranda shouted and covered her face, and the wind shifted, sweeping her away as the world spun.

She had flown several blocks from the park, to a street full of sleek, towering office buildings with full-length windows. Her aerial somersaults interrupted many workers' daily routines, and a few close brushes spiked some heart rates. But no one got a good look at her. She was a human rocket with a broken guidance system, swerving toward and away from buildings, in search of a destination.

At the street's terminus, an especially wide office building offered itself up as a target. It seemed to charge toward her. She thought, wished, and prayed to move in a different direction. Any would do.

Right as she flinched, no collision happened. Instead, she saw a street packed with cars and people, and it all retreated from her as she rose straight up. A series of windows flashed beside her until the supply ran out, but rooftops came into view, as did more streets. The streets grew longer and narrower as the rooftops shrank and the wind bore down harder on her back.

Mount Olympus reentered her field of vision, the whole thing. The highest point in Olympus City, and she was looking down on it. Felt like she was looking up, though. The whole world was upside-down.

She wasn't slowing. Some weird force yanked her ever higher. But what force?

The air thinned. So thin and cold now. And her view resembled a topographical map. People and vehicles were imperceptible, and soon even Mount Olympus would share their fate.

No plane, no parachute, no safety net of any kind, and yet she needed to return to that receding ground.

Finally, her ascent slowed, and a familiar knot tightened in her stomach, like she was reaching the top of a roller coaster, about to ride that steep first drop. But she had no tracks to guide her.

She came to a full stop and hung above the clouds, a howling wind drying her skin. Staring down miles of empty air, she clutched her shivering arms and had barely a second to reflect on the fact that however this ended, her life would forever be different.

And she fell. Frigid air smacked her in the face, attempting to suffocate her, and she tumbled, losing all sense of direction. At least the screaming helped clear her lungs.

The fall kept going. She expected it to be over already, but the ground—wherever it was right this second—taunted her. At any time, it could crush her, and she'd die as no one and nothing. But it kept her waiting. Occasionally, she'd catch a glimpse of a distant landscape, always a little closer but never arriving.

Wasn't there a certain pose she was supposed to strike? She recalled skydivers holding their arms and legs up above their flat torsos, so she did that and the tumbling soon stopped. It didn't solve her lack of a parachute, but now she had a better view of her approaching demise.

The ground continued its steady march toward her, but she didn't feel like she was falling anymore. She blinked rapidly against the constant wind rushing up against her, and she otherwise lost all sense of motion.

Details emerged on the landscape—clusters of trees with a road cutting through. The vehicles grew, and she panicked.

This would be it, with no profound final thought, just *How the hell is any of this happening?*

But the fall remained generous with its time, allowing her another thought: What if *she* was somehow responsible? What if she lifted herself several thousand miles into the upper atmosphere, and what if she decided to drop?

What if she could she redirect her fall?

She pictured herself moving to the right, and the very thought propelled her that way. She hurtled across the sky at more miles per hour than she expected—at least as fast as her recent freefall. Now she was falling sideways.

She took a breath. Leveled her body. Pointed her fists straight ahead. And she thought *forward*.

No more falling. Now, she was flying, sailing above the world under her own power. She laughed. She howled with unbridled glee.

Flying. The impossible happened, and of all people, it happened to her.

7

Miranda lost track of time. She was too busy relishing the *fact* that she was flying.

But how long would this last? What if it wore off while she was thousands of feet in the air? What if she landed and was never able to take off again?

She flew faster, unconsciously at first, and the clouds melded into endless, wispy lines streaking past her on all sides. As her speed increased, so did the wind's intensity, like they were in competition. But she hardly blinked, her eyes suddenly impervious to dryness, and she breathed at a healthy, normal rate. Wondering how far she could push this, she willed herself to keep accelerating. The wind responded by howling louder. And louder ...

And silence. Still windy, the windiest yet, but a mute wind. Miranda worried she went deaf, then realized the more likely explanation:

She broke the sound barrier. All by herself. No supersonic jet or other technology required. It was one hell of an accomplishment, unprecedented in human history, and strangely relaxing. Nothing at all to bother her. No noises competing for her attention. It was just her, the sky, and the greatest view ever. She was sailing through a giant work of art, currently over the Grand Canyon, which she could now observe from a tremendous altitude using only the naked eye. This definitely beat seeing the world through a foggy old airplane window.

Too soon to come down.

She pirouetted, spinning under her own control this time, and when she again leveled herself, she noticed something in the distance, appearing as a speck at first glance. By the second glance, though, it had already swollen into a jumbo passenger airplane, and they were on a collision course.

All she had to do was swerve to the side, think about redirecting left or right, didn't matter which. She just needed to choose. Right now.

Miranda steered her fists to the right, but she was soaring so much faster than before. For some reason, traveling faster meant a slower course correction. She cursed the inconvenient physics.

Her teeny amount of flesh and bone versus a massive hunk of flying metal? Yeah, she wasn't particularly concerned about the plane's welfare. An inexplicable thud might startle some passengers for half a minute, but they'd forget about it by the time Miranda's pulped remains splattered across the desert.

Miranda refused to die like a bird. She steered harder, pulling her fists almost entirely rightward, which made the plane appear to lurch to the left. Had she done this earlier, it might have worked.

The plane consumed her vision, and she tossed her hands over her face and averted her tightly closed eyes. And she barreled through what felt like aluminum foil.

Turned out, it was a wing. Miranda, without receiving a scratch or bruise anywhere, ripped off an airplane's wing by flying through it.

She watched the severed wing plummet toward a barren desert.

Her aversion to littering kicked in, compelling Miranda to swoop down and snatch the falling debris. Huge piece, totally dwarfed her, but it weighed ounces, was merely awkward to handle. Good for her, because if that wing crashed into the desert …

"Oh, no, no, no."

The plane was spiraling out of control, no doubt sending its innumerable passengers and crew into a panic. To anyone on board, the peaceful sky had become violent for no discernible reason. Miranda, however, knew exactly whose fault this was.

She dropped the wing and pursued, having no idea what, if anything, she could do to steady a plane of that size, but she had to try.

She tried too hard. Miranda swiftly overtook the falling plane, zooming far ahead of it. Realizing her error, she stopped—much more suddenly than she expected.

The gap between the two aerial opponents didn't last

long. The plane hurtled toward the tiny flying woman, who instinctively thrust her hands forward as a shield, and the result was something of a draw.

"Oof!"

Her palms punctured the airplane's nose, but the nose walloped her in the face at hundreds of miles per hour. Somehow, this did not kill her. Didn't knock her unconscious either. Contact with the hull didn't even chill her. It definitely stung, though.

The vessel carried Miranda along, her arms stuck near the bottom of the nose. It remained in the air for now, but at a rapidly decreasing altitude.

Miranda extracted her arms, flipped over, and pushed back, gradually increasing her momentum, assuming it would be sufficient to counteract the plane's. She never felt more arrogant, but the ground was well on its way. She could just fly away, but not the people on board.

How scared they must have been. She hadn't even considered them beyond the abstract. They probably assumed they were all dead. How many people? Dozens? Hundreds? Someone could have been suffering a heart attack in there that very second.

The plane's hull bent under her mounting pressure. She blinked, and a street appeared, growing closer. Plenty of desert on both sides, but the current trajectory would send them crashing on or beside the highway. This didn't look like a well-traveled route, but of course two cars and a trailer truck were driving in the danger zone this very moment, potentially increasing the casualty count that Miranda absolutely would be responsible for.

"Move, you stupid cars!" she shouted. "Move faster!"

Despite her culpability, she was everyone's only chance for a safe landing, the only force other than the unforgiving ground that might be able to bring the plane to a complete stop.

She pushed against the plane, slowing it ... slowing it a bit more ... needing to slow it a hell of lot more in the next half a second ...

"Rrrrgh ...!"

And it stopped. Miranda and the jumbo vessel rested about a hundred feet above the ground.

Or they *did*, until physics again decided to point and laugh at her for deigning to think she could hold an airplane by its nose.

The plane's tail came swinging back down, so Miranda slipped beneath the center of the cabin, spread her arms and legs, and let it crash onto her whole front.

"Ugh!" A painful jolt shot through her every limb, but she carried the weight.

The plane wobbled, so she adjusted to keep it more or less steady. Compensating for the broken wing wasn't easy, but she managed. Finding a landing spot, however, would be much more challenging with her face pressed against the hull. She regretted not catching the plane on her back, but too late. She didn't want to risk losing her balance to fix her latest stupid mistake.

So, Miranda clung to the hull like some kind of airplane barnacle, and she tilted her head for a better view of her surroundings.

She passed over the highway to a vast expanse of undeveloped land. This would do.

Positioning herself and the plane above a wide patch of desert, she gradually descended, wondering how she was going to set the plane down without it burying her.

Weeds scratched her back, and she brushed against dirt. She inched to the left, allowing the plane's right side to connect with the ground. A bumpy landing ensued for everyone on board, but it would be a landing they could walk away from.

Sticking close to the hull, out of the windows' sight-lines, Miranda debated whether to go inside and check on them. She couldn't bear to find anyone hurt. She was wracked with guilt for causing the crash landing in the first place.

She heard faint sirens, which weren't faint for long. A few ambulances and a firetruck sped down the highway.

She watched them. They just needed to turn onto the dirt, and she could fly away feeling slightly less terrible. She did an internal double take at the notion of flying away.

If they would just turn …

"C'mon ... c'mon ..."

They turned. They navigated the bumpy landscape on their way to the plane, and Miranda fled, taking off in any direction for now. She could figure out the correct way to Olympus later, when she was out of sight.

Olympus City awaited a mile off the coast, and Miranda came in high and fast, determined to neither crash into a building nor show up in any pictures.

The city's main retail district was situated shortly beyond the Poseidon Bridge. The area had plenty of tall buildings with flat roofs, but none of the more imposing skyscrapers. Miranda designated a random rooftop as her landing pad and aimed herself at it, flinching the whole way down, assaulted by visions of crashing through floor after floor like a cartoon character. But she avoided that embarrassing fate by stopping slightly too early. Hovering a few feet above the roof, she reached down with one foot until she connected with the solid surface. Then she planted her other foot, thus completing a safe return trip that imperiled no one else. She congratulated herself with zero enthusiasm.

A breeze tickled a small patch of exposed skin—a tear in her shirt. Miranda shuddered.

Standing in the middle of that rooftop, unsure how to move forward, she stared deeper into the city, where a cluster of the tallest skyscrapers loomed over everything, high enough to eclipse the low evening sun. They dwarfed her utterly. Clever people had built them up over the course of decades, creating this thoroughly modern metropolis that surrounded Miranda. She was a single speck within, incapable of building a skyscraper, starting a business, or creating anything else of lasting value.

But she could wreck it all. The world had become fragile. If she wasn't careful, it could break apart in her hands. She could do so many terrible things if she were a worse person.

Flying had been the greatest thing. Better than sex. Better than applause. Then it became the worst thing. How could she ever fly again? Yet, how could she not?

A glare peeked between two backlit skyscrapers. The scarlet sky, so peaceful now, seemed to invite her up.

Lowering her gaze, Miranda happened to look straight ahead at an aging apartment building a couple of streets over, right as a person tumbled out a top-story window.

Miranda leapt and projected herself toward the apartments, her eyes locked on the falling person. Wind rushed against her, and soft flesh landed in her outstretched arms. A middle-aged woman, plump but seemingly weightless, screamed and flailed in Miranda's grasp, almost squirming herself back into a freefall.

"I've got you! Hold still!" Miranda said, constantly readjusting her grip, careful not to grab too hard. *No squeezing* became her mantra.

The woman's face was bruised. The eyes were puffy.

Miranda focused all her attention forward, on their destination—the adjacent alleyway.

Without touching down herself, she gently released the woman onto the ground in front of a tall solid fence. Resisting the urge to take off right away, Miranda hovered as the disoriented woman struggled to catch her breath, clasping a hand tight to her chest.

Miranda wondered if she should take her to a hospital. This would have been difficult to explain, but if the woman needed it ...

The situation had drawn many curious onlookers, several of whom rushed into the alley, inquiring about the woman's wellbeing. They'd take care of this poor lady. Miranda kept her back to them as she began rising.

"Wait!" the woman shouted through labored breaths.

Miranda winced. But without turning around, she stopped and hovered.

"He—he pushed me out!" The woman sounded like she was crying. Tears mixed with anger. "He's horrible."

Her hands clenching into fists, Miranda started, "The police can—"

"*You* can stop him. Whatever you are, you can do it."

Miranda had no idea how large the audience had grown, but she felt numerous eyes on her, perhaps marveling at her wondrous abilities, perhaps fearing her unknown power ...

That horrible jerk would fear her.

She shot up to the top floor and found the open window. Perching on the ledge, she ducked her head into the untidy apartment. The scent of beer lingered, and without any lights turned on, the waning daylight provided scant illumination.

A tall, potbellied man was rushing toward the door, unaware of his visitor. He was just trying to get the hell away from the scene of his crime.

Trespassing into a stranger's home felt wrong, repulsive even. Miranda thought of that poor woman's bruises and got over it. Before the man took another step, she raced across the apartment and blocked the door.

He kept coming. Without thinking, Miranda shoved him.

The large man cried out as he landed halfway across the apartment, barely missing the coffee table, and he immediately scrambled to his feet. Phrasing his questions as ninety percent expletives, he asked who she was, what she was, and why she was there.

Miranda needed to figure out those answers, too. What was her endgame here? Arrest him? Scare him? Hurt him?

He couldn't hurt *her*.

"You—" Her voice squeaked out, so she tried again, louder but still shaky. "You pushed a person out a window."

"*That* was an accident!" He wagged a finger a bit too

vigorously, as if trying to convince himself as much as her.

Miranda floated to exceed his height, and she grabbed him by his sweat-stained tee-shirt, hoisting him off the floor. This required no effort. He was an insubstantial man.

Her voice stopped quavering. "That is *not* an excuse."

The man stared at his own dangling feet, and he shook his head with several short, quick jerks. "This can't—you're just a little girl!"

"No," she said. "I'm not."

Miranda tossed him near the door. A tiny motion of her hand sent the full-grown bastard flying. His back slammed against the wall, and he slumped hard onto the floor, grunting and cursing.

She continued to float in place, and the whimpering man didn't even try to pull himself back up. She *was* going to land, but staying airborne seemed to terrify him more.

"The bruises," she said, deepening her voice. "On her face. Tell me those were accidents, too."

"That's none of your business, freak!" The anger flashed, then dissipated. A ray of concern slipped through. "Did she ... Is she okay?" Took him long enough to ask.

"Let's see how okay *you* are after falling out a window."

Relishing the man's escalating terror, Miranda glided toward him, slowly. But she still had no idea what to do with him. She could take him out for a high-speed flight, maybe drop and catch him a few times, except she didn't yet trust her abilities enough to risk a person's life with them. But if she accidentally dropped a piece of garbage like *him* ...

The thought attempted its seduction, and at first, she humored it. It was one damn attractive thought, after all. She wanted it to win her over. This man deserved worse. But there was something about it she couldn't quite get past.

Nevertheless, *he* didn't know that.

So, she closed in on him, slowing her pace even further, stretching out the experience. She effected a sadistic smile, telling herself this was just an act, a means of persuading him to improve his behavior, to ensure no one else ever suffered at his slimy hands.

An intense glare encroached on her peripheral vision and cast her shadow large over her quarry. From behind, a confident baritone asserted itself.

"Young lady, I'd stop right there."

Miranda dropped to the floor and turned around. Indeed, it was him—Fantastic Man had arrived. He stood in front of the window, arms crossed, his entire form glowing.

"This isn't how we do things." His voice sounded like that of a 1950s TV dad. He projected no anger, just self-assured patience tinged with disappointment.

This did look pretty bad, Miranda realized. If Fantastic Man started battling her over a misunderstanding, *she* would be the villain in everyone's eyes.

Her jumbled words flooded out. "I wasn't going to— he's a bad man, but I wouldn't—I was just—"

Fantastic Man lifted a steady, calming hand, and she shut herself up.

"Yes, I'm aware of the situation, and the authorities are on their way," he said. "Meet me on the roof. I'll be up in a jiffy, after I've resolved this fracas *properly*." Wearing a slight sneer, Fantastic Man cast a blinding spotlight on the horrible jerk, who didn't dare move an inch. "Don't worry—this vermin isn't getting away."

As he strode forth, Fantastic Man glanced at Miranda.

"The roof, young lady," he whispered forcefully. "Don't let anyone else see you."

Miranda started for the door, then redirected herself, remembering the window was a valid option.

She hopped out, landed on the roof, and loitered there, wondering what exactly Fantastic Man wanted with her. She felt like she had been sent to the principal's office for disciplinary action. Did he know about the plane? And if he did, what did he intend to do about it? What *could* he do to her?

Miranda stared at her own arms, at countless cells imbued with extraordinary power. Flight, strength, and speed were all hers now. But what was the price? Would there be side effects? Would these powers corrupt her?

Had they already? Would they fade away tomorrow?

She considered fleeing, just running home and locking herself in her apartment so she could figure everything out. But Fantastic Man could follow her anywhere. She doubted she was faster than a living beam of light. While he seemed physically normal in human form, he could become untouchable anytime he wanted. Her strength was useless against photons. He could hound her tirelessly.

So she was stuck waiting to defend herself, as time seemed to slow at an exponential rate. She thought about how to convince him she wasn't a threat—convince herself, too. She stared ahead, her mind blanking.

The roof provided a clear view of the water separating Olympus from the rest of the state. The waves reflected the departing sun, and the Santa Monica skyline began to light up for the evening. Her future seemed farther away now, her goals out of reach ...

A flare assaulted her eyes. She embarrassed herself with a startled shout.

Fantastic Man materialized in front of her, blocking her view of the water. He swiftly dimmed down until he appeared as a regular masked man in tights, which diminished his authority only a little.

"The police have taken the suspect into custody," he said. "Now let's talk about *you* ..."

Miranda's throat clamped up, and he continued, his

tone maddeningly matter-of-fact:

"I heard about the plane crash."

She felt every internal organ caving in, the pressure mounting ...

He opened his mouth to continue. Miranda needed to defend herself *now*.

"It was an accident! I'm not a bad person! I was just flying, and, and, and—plane! I had no idea how strong I was, how strong I am." The words kept coming. Too much momentum to stop. "When I woke up this morning, never in a billion years would I have guessed my day would include flying, let alone the rest of it. I was just supposed to be working today, working a dumb easy job, and now I'm on a rooftop with *you* of all people and you probably think I'm some incredible mess of a person." The mask somehow made him easier to ramble at, like she was speaking through a confessional veil. "You're right—I have no clue what I'm doing. It seemed wonderful for about two seconds, and then ..." She let out a quick, frustrated roar. "I don't understand how any of this is even possible. It *wasn't*, not until you came along, you with your shiny—your shiny light tricks!"

"Young lady—"

"The world made sense. I had a plan. And now here I am, a klutzy Godzilla compressed into a peanut—I got lucky catching that woman, just stupid luck I didn't crush her as I grabbed her ... or fly us into the side of a building!

What do I do? What am I? What the hell am I now?"

Fantastic Man slowly set a hand on her shoulder and gave her a gentle squeeze. "You're a hero."

Miranda stared at that sun-shaped mask. It looked so ridiculous up close without his usual special effects. "What? No, I'm—"

"My apologies. I misspoke. You're a *super*hero."

"Huh?"

9

"You saved everyone on that plane," Fantastic Man said, smiling at her. A warm, paternal smile, almost proud.

Miranda knew one of them was seriously misunderstanding something, but she wasn't entirely certain who. "But I—"

His tone grew more insistent. "You saved them."

He explained how he followed up after he heard the news of a slowly crashing airplane in Arizona. He confirmed that not one person on board sustained a serious injury—nothing more than a few bumps and scrapes here and there.

He repeated, emphasizing each word, "You saved them."

They're okay. The words rattled around in Miranda's head. She hesitated to believe it, but even the possibility removed several thousand pounds off her soul.

Fantastic Man commended her quick thinking and action, totally glossing over the reason the plane lost a wing in the first place.

Did he even know? What did he think happened? Even as Miranda fretted those details, she took a deep, soothing breath she hadn't realized she needed.

Arms akimbo, Fantastic Man spoke through a cheesy grin, his confident tone never wavering. "From the start, I suspected I wouldn't be the only one of our kind. I feel it's in humanity's best interests that we join forces, build up a team of like-minded do-gooders dedicated to thwarting evil at every nefarious turn. Young lady, the world needs *your* astonishing abilities!"

He was crazy. The sun-shaped mask indicated bona fide insanity. Miranda wasn't a hero, super or otherwise. She was just an actress ...

This crazy guy—Peyton loved this crazy guy. Just a glimpse of him in action, and she was spellbound, instant fangirl. She loved Miranda, too, of course, but nepotism helped out. Fantastic Man earned the kid's adoration without the aid of any shared genetics.

A team of superheroes? This would be a first. Miranda could be part of something historic. Was he recruiting anyone else? *Was* there anyone else? She could be the first female super—

The dead woman at Mount Olympus. Should she mention her?

Another woman *wasn't* dead because of Miranda.

But she still crashed that plane ...

She could stop terrible people. Or she could try and screw up, making everything so much worse ...

People loved Fantastic Man—they would love *her*.

She wasn't a hero, but she could play the role. It

would be the right thing to do. She had to try.

What would she call herself? How would this character act in public? What costume would she wear? She did not want to match Fantastic Man's.

Flying was amazing, until—it was amazing. With practice, it could always be amazing.

At some point, she had started smiling.

"I'm in. Absolutely in." She extended a hand to shake on it. "I'm M—"

"No real names!"

Fantastic Man recoiled, and a weariness emerged from beneath his sunny façade. In that split-second, Miranda noticed how much older he was. Mid-thirties at a minimum, maybe early forties. What was he before this? What was he when he *wasn't* this?

Whatever he was, it all receded behind that cheesy grin, which he doubled down on. "We must become something more than we were. We can't inspire the good citizens if we keep reminding each other of our ... less super selves."

"Oh. Okay." The rule struck her as odd, but what did she know? He was the expert on these matters.

"You can't tell anyone else about your secret either," he continued, "no matter how tempting it may feel to do so."

Miranda blanched at that. "What? Why?"

"Being a superhero is a burden you must shoulder

on your own. It wouldn't be very heroic to place such a weight on anyone else," he said in a gentle, counseling tone.

"But if I just told my—"

Fantastic Man's patience slipped a bit, supplanted by slowly escalating urgency. "Then you wouldn't be a superhero, not in their eyes. The effect needs to be airtight. Whenever you don your uniform and answer to your superhero name, you will bury all your personal foibles and daily concerns. You must brush your ego aside and become this new persona."

Miranda had heard similar advice from a few bad directors.

"We have to be perfect," he said. "Nothing can interfere with that. Promise me you won't share this secret with anyone."

The hell with that, Miranda thought. He didn't want to know her name? Fine. Fair enough. He had no right to dictate anything beyond that.

But if he expected her to lie to her family and friends, then how was lying to him any worse?

"Sure. I promise," she said.

He gave her hand a firm shake. "Excellent!"

Instructions followed: She was to meet him on a tiny undeveloped island a few miles north of Olympus at 7 p.m. tomorrow, and that was her deadline to construct a uniform and decide on her superhero name. No public displays before then. He was firm on that point. Her new identity deserved a proper debut, but only after the requisite work went into it.

His glow returned. He bid her a swell evening and disintegrated into photons. After a flash, he left Miranda alone on the rooftop under the darkening sky.

The whole day flooded through her mind out of order, the events popping up like whack-a-moles. Before she could squash one, another surfaced, then another and another ...

What were people saying about her? A flying woman must have made the news. It must have been *the* news story of the day. Were people excited? Fearful? Jealous that they couldn't fly? She could find out by going home and turning on the TV or computer.

She needed to talk to someone. A real person not hiding behind a mask, someone she could talk *with*, not *at*.

And the conversation could be face to face—she could visit anyone anywhere. The sky was open to her. The sky was also getting darker, and only more so further east. Flying in clear daylight had hardly gone smooth. The very idea of diving into that gloom constricted her breathing.

Who to visit? Fantastic Man's directions popped up at the front of her mind, reframing the question for her: Who to burden?

Her closest college friends had already moved elsewhere to start their new lives. It didn't seem right to dump this on any of them. Some of the younger ones were due back to Olympus University soon, but the semester hadn't started and she wasn't exactly sure where to find any of them. Her castmates seemed like lovely people, but they were mostly just coworkers to her at this point. She wouldn't see them for a couple more days anyway.

Ken was an option, but ... no. Miranda worried her abilities might threaten a male ego, even a nice male's ego. Better to start with a woman and take it from there.

Bianca, maybe? She was the logical choice. Actually, her parents were the most logical. They were guaranteed to think no less of her for any mistake she made, and they'd give the best advice by far. They'd also worry the most. Telling them seemed cruel, at least until after she proved herself successful. And Bianca might feel obligated to inform their parents, regardless of Miranda's wishes on the matter.

She wanted to tell Peyton. The kid would be so impressed. But she was too young. Maybe later. For now, Miranda needed a mature sounding board. She needed her oldest friend.

But Alyssa might not want to see her. Miranda felt ridiculous even thinking that. Alyssa had probably just been busy, and that was why communication had become so infrequent.

If Miranda flew across one dark sky for the length of a country, she could resuscitate a friendship, inject the excitement of a shared secret into it. Even after Miranda told others, Alyssa would forever be the first to know—she'd appreciate that.

One country ... all the distance separating them. As long as Miranda didn't crash into anything on the way.

She took off into the night sky.

10

This flight proved far more enjoyable. Miranda paced herself at just above the speed of sound and didn't try to push herself further. The light pollution from cities and towns streaked below her, providing a neat show, only a minimal distraction. She kept her eyes focused straight ahead, vigilant for any oncoming airplanes. And she maintained a lower elevation than last time, trusting that would place her below cruising altitude.

Visiting home was going to be so much easier now. No more layovers in random cities. Just a direct flight at supersonic speed. And if she decided to be more relaxed about the secret identity, or dispose of it altogether, her parents wouldn't have to waste all that money on airfare. Actually, she realized, without a secret identity, she'd be *the* hometown success story—local girl turned big-shot superhero.

Not a superhero yet, though. She still needed a name, but she tabled the brainstorming for now. The flight required her full concentration. Alyssa would help her pick a good one, might have thoughts on the costume design, too.

Miranda couldn't wait to surprise her with this spontaneous visit. She remained a tiny bit nervous about how it would go, but they had many years ago proclaimed themselves *best friends forever*. That meant unconditional acceptance, right? Alyssa wasn't drifting—she was busy. Nothing more than that.

It was almost ten o'clock on the East Coast. Alyssa could have been at work. The clothing store was in an outlet mall located a thirty-minute drive from Meadowville, so Miranda wasn't likely to run into her family there this late. Seemed like a good first stop.

Miranda landed in the darkness behind the shops and walked around to the front. It took her that long to accept the fact that she was back east, having bypassed all conventional modes of transportation to arrive here. Paranoia gripped her for a second—if her powers faded …

She caught herself, noting she felt as strong and vigorous as ever, even after flying across the whole continental United States. She wasn't even winded.

Alyssa worked part-time at the Titanic T-Shirt Factory, as she had since the end of high school. Several times she had mentioned wanting to try something else, but her managers kept giving her periodic raises and always respected her academic schedules. And, in her never-ending battle to become a responsible adult, Alyssa wasn't done with academics yet. A dental hygiene program claimed the next year or two of her life, and that meant another year or two of putting up with this store.

It *was* the responsible thing to do, Miranda reluctantly had to admit, much more responsible than subsisting off stipends from nonprofit theatre.

Miranda had been here before, and she could have sworn the store was bigger last time. The "Titanic" part of the name seemed quite the overcompensation. Pretty much the entire sales floor was visible from the entrance. A clothes-filled cage for its employees. Thinking of poor Alyssa stuck between these walls for hours on end, Miranda wanted to jump back into the sky and stretch— but not until she brandished her thrilling news to cleave through the tedium and free her friend.

Her eyes swept across the store. Several shoppers examined the racks while a few employees fixed the disarray left in their wake, no doubt wanting to be rid of these nuisances so they could close up and go home.

A teenage girl forced a smile as she greeted Miranda and asked if she needed help finding anything.

Miranda, super-polite, smiled back. "I'm actually just looking for my friend. Is Alyssa Henson working today?"

As she finished asking the question, she spotted her. Alyssa emerged from the back room carrying a stack of folded tee-shirts, going through a routine she had performed countless times, looking like she'd rather be sleeping.

Though Alyssa was always thin, she had gotten even skinnier since Miranda last saw her, which was ... winter break? Miranda tried not to do the math, but involuntary mathematics occurred anyway. Over seven months. In that time, Alyssa had literally lost some of herself, and this new boniness only accentuated her air of malaise.

Alyssa instantly woke up when she noticed her visitor. A quick laugh overtook her previously blank expression, and she smirked.

"The hell are you doing here?" Alyssa called across the sales floor, only to be immediately chastised by a supervisor. "Oh! Sorry!"

"Surprise," Miranda said sheepishly, meeting her halfway for a hug.

Alyssa's hairstyle had changed. Same natural auburn color, but it was cut shoulder length. It had always been so long, and the shorter hair produced an unnerving effect—Alyssa looked like an actual adult now. Naturally, Miranda complimented her on the new style straightaway, and Alyssa simply said it was time for the change, as though it were inevitable.

"I am so sorry I've like vanished off the face of the planet lately," Alyssa said. "Really, I've mostly been here. Got to get the hours in before classes start. Again, so sorry."

Miranda declared the apology totally unnecessary, and her stomach settled. She wanted to launch into everything at once with maximum youthful enthusiasm: *Alyssa! I have powers now! I flew across the country! I saved a person! I'm going to be a superhero!*

Unfortunately, the store was small, so she had to wait.

"Walk with me while I work," Alyssa said, ushering her to a table of shirts in desperate need of folding. "How long you in town for?"

"Not long. This is very much a quick, impromptu visit."

"Damn straight it's impromptu, not that I'm complaining." Alyssa pointed at the small tear in Miranda's shirt. "What happened there?"

"Oh, just a long day of traveling." Not entirely a lie, but Miranda wanted all these inconvenient people to wander somewhere far away so she could get on with the truth.

Alyssa wheeled a small mobile countertop around the corner and parked it alongside the solid-color tees. Collectively, the tees had become an almost tie-dyed swirl at the hands of careless shoppers. She grabbed a folding board from the mobile counter and went about repairing the damage, one crumpled shirt at a time.

"I want to hear all about this play of yours," she said. "Congratulations, by the way."

Miranda thanked her as she watched Alyssa fold a shirt around the board so very slowly. Her soul shriveled. Miranda could have knocked out these chores in seconds, or straightened the whole store within minutes. Instead, she stood there uselessly while her friend toiled in this manmade purgatory.

Alyssa sounded genuinely interested in the play— what it was about, Miranda's role, audience reactions, and so on. And Miranda enjoyed answering all questions.

As Miranda expounded on how wonderfully the show was going, a voice in the back of her mind raised an important question: How would being a superhero interfere with her performance schedule and future commitments? Surely people wouldn't expect her to be on duty every minute of the day, would they?

The wisdom behind Fantastic Man's team idea became apparent. If she was busy with a professional obligation, he—and maybe others someday—could provide adequate coverage, and she could do the same whenever he needed to tend to his life. In any case, society got along just fine without superheroes until recently, and nobody ever asked a volunteer to give up absolutely everything else for the sake of community service.

"I'm so glad that's working out for you," Alyssa said.

"It's really just a start."

"Yeah, already a better start than most get in that business. Keep doing us all proud. I'll take any and all vicarious thrills."

Alyssa was still smiling, but it was such a weary smile.

"Is everything okay?" Miranda asked.

The folding stopped, and Alyssa seemed to age as she scowled. "I know what you're getting at, but we are not talking about *my future* again."

"I just want you to be happy."

"You sound like your mother."

"Can you seriously tell me you're looking forward to cleaning teeth for the rest of your life?"

Alyssa resumed folding. "Are you looking forward to a life of constantly wondering where your next paycheck is coming from and if it'll cover the bills?"

Miranda backed up a step and raised her hands in surrender. "Okay, okay, we don't have to get into that." She winced as she spoke. "Just—"

"Just you're going to keep getting into it."

Miranda's heart was hammering. A whole cross-country flight? Steady beat. This? Manic drumming.

If these other people would get out of earshot, if she could say what she came all this way to say, if she could make Alyssa realize how exciting life was becoming …

"So have you seen the news coming out of Olympus?" It struck Miranda as the best approach. Drop the argument and start hinting at her developments. "What do you think of all that?"

Alyssa placed a freshly folded tee-shirt in the middle of the same-colored stack, ensuring everything was arranged in the proper size order.

"I don't get it," she said.

One of them must have misheard something. "Don't get … what?"

"An actual superhero." Alyssa adjusted the stack's edges for maximum neatness. "It's weird. Everyone everywhere is talking about this guy like he's Mr. Perfect.

No way that's true."

"Fantastic Man?"

"I refuse to call a grown man 'Fantastic Man'—especially when he dresses like *that*."

Such disdain in her voice. But the man was a hero! Wasn't he?

"Well," Miranda said, as if she were playing devil's advocate, "he has helped a bunch of people."

Alyssa's eyes narrowed and her face scrunched for two full seconds. Then she released.

"I hear he has some power that allows him to change his entire body into light, like, you know, sunlight or something?" Alyssa threw her arms up to punctuate her confusion. "Do you get that? He becomes *light*. That means half the time, the guy isn't even a guy. He can't be a guy because he's a ball of light and therefore has no balls of his own, unless he has little photon balls. Think about it, Miranda. This supposedly selfless hero doesn't even have a shape sometimes. And so what really is he when he's light? There's no body, no head, nothing." She shook her head and calmed down somewhat. "I don't know. I just find it creepy."

"Um ..." Miranda grasped for whatever rhetorical ammunition she could find. "Peyton thinks he's great."

"Well, yeah, of course. I love Peyton, but she's a kid. Give it a few years. Give everyone a few years for the novelty to wear off."

No way, Miranda thought. This was all so incredibly world-altering, how could people tire of it in her lifetime?

Alyssa got herself revved up again and continued her diatribe against the "man-child in his pajamas," but Miranda was hearing only every few words.

Maybe if it wasn't just one strange guy in tights ... "I hear there's also a flying woman now," Miranda said, tentatively.

"Oh, God!" Alyssa's elbows crashed onto her mobile counter as she leaned forward, cringing. "I've been stuck here all day. Tell me you're kidding."

Miranda shook her head, and Alyssa groaned.

"Does she at least have a jetpack or something? Any means of propulsion? Or is it just like magic?"

Was *thinking* about flying an acceptable means of propulsion? "It's ... I don't know, but no jetpack. Just her."

Alyssa buried her face in her palms. "Someone is giving a giant middle finger to science."

The supervisor walked by. "Alyssa, we don't want to be here all night."

"Right! Sorry!" She resumed folding at an accelerated rate. "That is one crazy city you decided to move to."

"It wasn't like this in college."

"Yeah, what the hell happened?"

A customer approached Alyssa and asked if they had a particular shirt in a particular size. She effortlessly slipped back into professional mode and went to the back to hunt down the desired merchandise.

And Miranda stared at that folding board, picturing the countless shirts Alyssa had folded and refolded over the years, always more to fold. So many things Alyssa could have done with her life, so many chances she could have taken, but she settled for such a boring path. Miranda didn't get it. And why didn't Alyssa get the appeal of an *actual* superhero?

Her heart was beating even faster, alarmingly fast, so fast that anyone else would have dropped dead by now. Several beats per second. Hundreds per minute. Inhuman.

Alyssa returned with a few options for the customer, one of which sufficed. Then it was right back to folding.

"So what did you want to tell me?" Alyssa asked, knocking out another shirt in the span of that question.

"Tell you?"

"You're dying to tell me something. Can't fool me."

Miranda laughed to stall. Maybe if Alyssa knew her own friend was the flying woman, then she might be more amenable to the concept. Maybe …

Another shirt folded around the board.

The best-friends-forever didn't understand each other anymore.

"I met Tuck Lewis," Miranda said, instantly chipper. "I was working as an extra for a movie he's in. It was totally awkward, but he was so nice."

Alyssa grinned, amused. "Your inner fourteen-year-old must be pleased."

"Seriously! And he's only improved with age. I will spare no detail, but it looks like you're all ready to close up any second now. I should get out of your way."

Closing time was indeed too imminent for Alyssa to protest, but she had a counteroffer. "Oh, hey—I'm getting together with college friends after work. Just hanging out in a bar downtown. You're more than welcome to join us. I think you've met at least a couple of them."

Miranda almost agreed but realized she didn't want to spend an evening lying to Alyssa, even by omission.

"I would love that, but you know how my family is. They've got me booked solid all morning, and then it's right back to Olympus. And it's been such a long day already. I'd be terrible company."

"Completely understand. But I'm glad you stopped in." Alyssa leaned in and added, quietly, "Highlight of my day." She squeezed her tight for a parting hug. "I'll try not to be so awful about staying in touch. I promise."

Miranda thought about her last promise to Fantastic Man and what a blatant lie it was. Although, it had inadvertently become truthful.

"Have fun tonight," Miranda said, maintaining her smile long enough to exit the store.

She was careful not to walk too quickly as she made her way around the back for a discreet takeoff. But she didn't depart yet. She felt too heavy, had lost that sense of weightlessness. She could still fly; she tested herself by rising a few inches above the pavement. It would be such a long, dark trip, though. She dropped back onto her feet, slumped against a wall, and slid down to the pavement.

Alyssa would never understand the rush of soaring across a sunny sky under nothing but her own power. Neither would her sisters, nor anyone in her life. Even Fantastic Man's experience was different. Miranda was unique to the point of freakishness, and people detested freakishness. Alyssa was right—the novelty factor had an expiration date.

From her low vantage point, Miranda fixed her gaze on a random star. So many more were visible here compared to in California. She could get closer to them than anyone who wasn't an astronaut, but still nowhere near a single one.

She was under no obligation to become a superhero. Most people wouldn't even consider anything like that. It wasn't too late to back out. The only person who got a good look at her face was Fantastic Man. All she had to do was not show up to his meeting tomorrow night, and the mysterious flying woman would simply disappear. No one could judge her, roll their eyes, or mock any silly costume if she disappeared.

Fantastic Man's costume *was* absurd. Alyssa was correct on that count, too. What the hell was with his sun-shaped mask? It was like something out of an elementary school pageant.

And he was such a cartoon, like he had escaped a piece of celluloid, but he was *someone* underneath all that sparkling. Miranda wondered who. Others would, too—already were wondering, no doubt. He was hiding something. What was he hiding? Why? Nobody liked a phony. No one would like Miranda if she followed his phony path. Not for long.

People outgrew cartoons.

But they loved heroes.

11

The media was trying to pin the name "Ultra Girl" on her. It was exactly the sort of direction Miranda had decided to steer away from. She'd come up with her own name, thank you very much.

At least the coverage was mostly positive so far. Even the most cynical journalists had difficulty criticizing someone who saved a woman from plunging to her death.

In the privacy of her apartment, Miranda flipped through the news channels and kept finding *she* was the story. It was surreal every single time a different set of talking heads "analyzed" her. They didn't know much beyond what shadowy cell phone footage had captured, but from so little, they generated an astonishing amount of chatter.

Miranda was only half-listening at this point. She had a costume to figure out.

Floating upside-down near the ceiling, she stared at a bunch of colorful clothes she had spread across her apartment. Some came from school plays, others from old Halloween costumes, and few ever left her closet. All were candidates to dress Miranda as ... whoever this superhero was going to be.

She decided on a few parameters right away: no cape, no tights, nothing a normal person would refuse to wear in a public setting. But the look still needed to be distinctive, iconic even.

If only she had paid more attention during her costume design course in college, then she might have had some idea how to extract "iconic" from a weird assortment of thrift purchases. The candy striper outfit was a hard pass. She could also eliminate the blue wig as a contender.

The neon-green leather jacket kept catching her eye, though, and the ski goggles were the obvious choice for a mask. They had a green tint that wasn't the same shade as the jacket, but close enough. She spent way too much of her parents' money on those goggles for a one-act play in high school. Not reusing them now that an opportunity had presented itself would've been a waste.

Her phone rang, and she welcomed the opportunity to procrastinate.

She muted the TV, landed on her floor, and answered a call from Ken. They exchanged hellos.

Ken sounded in much better spirits this time. Miranda figured she was obviously a good influence on the boy.

"So I was thinking," he said, "you had this really great idea about us meeting up for coffee or something."

"I am wise like that."

"Let's do it. What's your schedule like later this week?"

Such confidence. Miranda had no idea where it was coming from, but a coffee date truly did seem like a great idea now. They made plans for Thursday afternoon.

"You're in an awfully good mood today," Miranda said.

"Just some things starting to fall into place. I'll tell you all about it on Thursday."

A breaking news alert flashed on the television. A young anchor addressed the camera, her demeanor grave. A graphic displayed the words "Hostage Crisis."

"I look forward to it," Miranda said. "Oh, I've got a call coming in from my director. Really got to take this. See you soon!"

The second she hung up, she restored the TV's volume.

A gang of ten armed criminals, all wearing Kabuki masks, was demanding ten million dollars from the city government, in exchange for the lives of everyone in a local grocery store. If Fantastic Man interfered, the hostages' lives were forfeit.

Police had the building surrounded, and a negotiator was in communication with the gang's leader. So far, they were at a stalemate, and Fantastic Man was nowhere to be found.

Miranda narrowed her gaze onto her costuming options, and a design solidified.

Red jeans, matching shirt, and matching sneakers,

plus a long wig that was nearly the same shade. She'd break up the red with the retro leather jacket, and the goggles would help conceal her identity.

And she had settled on a name for herself: "Astraea." A person, not some "Ultra Girl." The name could have been her real one for all anyone knew, and she wouldn't be the first public figure to opt for the mononymous route.

She threw on the costume and took off.

12

This could go horribly. Miranda's heart became an unwitting homing beacon—the closer she flew toward the C&P Market, the faster the beat.

And there it was, in a transitional area between businesses to the south and suburbs to the north. A long, flat building, all doors reportedly locked.

The police had taken over the sizable parking lot in the front of the building, as well as the thin alleys to the sides and rear. Dozens of sworn officers stood ready, all poised to swoop in as soon as the order was given. But no order could be given, not without any visual on the shoppers and employees trapped inside at gunpoint.

With the entire perimeter already spoken for, Miranda chose the roof. She zoomed in as an unidentifiable blur, hopefully perceived as a passing figment of the imagination. She miscalculated when to stop short, though, and landed slightly too hard. A patch of roof cracked under her knee, but it didn't break. She silently cursed at herself, praying the commotion below drowned out the thud, and she flattened herself onto her stomach.

She couldn't see the parking lot, so no one in the parking lot could see her. That would have been a terrible start if the police mistook her for part of the gang. She needed to be more careful.

Crawling toward a vent, she realized it wasn't too late to back out. How arrogant of her to think she could save everyone. So many ways she could screw this up! Better to fly away unseen and let the professionals handle this, right? But the professionals couldn't do things like fly or run around at superhuman speed, and their usual tactics had so far proven unsuccessful.

She checked her wig. The spirit gum was doing its job. No going back after this, she realized.

Miranda yanked the grate off and slipped head-first into the vent, never more thankful for her under-sized frame. Feeling her way down the shaft, against the current, she aimed for the faint glow of light intruding into this darkness. At the source, she pushed out another grate, accidentally letting it clank hard on the floor, and she squeezed through into the musty stockroom.

Two men in Kabuki masks came rushing toward the disturbance—one mask depicted a grinning face while a weeping expression was painted on the other. Handguns drawn, they rounded the corner and hustled down rows of crates and boxes. Their quarry scurried behind a tub of merchandise waiting to be stocked.

"Hey! Stop!"

The man in the grinning mask pulled Miranda from her hiding spot, seizing her by the wrist.

"How'd you get back here?" he growled, his eyes a mystery behind the reflective lenses affixed to the mask. Not a traditional Kabuki feature.

"Don't hurt me!" she sobbed convincingly. "Please! I got scared, I hid—I'm sorry! Just please, please, please, I don't want to die!"

She didn't have to act much, not with those handguns pointed at her. She had no idea if she was bulletproof. Probably. Maybe. Kind of a tricky thing to test.

She could toss these guys to the police waiting out the back door. It would be so easy, would take two seconds. So tempting. But that could prompt retaliation from the rest of the gang.

"What's with the shades?" The grinning-masked man patted her down while the other kept his aim on her. "Little warm for a jacket, isn't it? You wearing a wire?"

"No! I promise! This is just cosplay!"

Of course, the man found nothing on her, not even a phone or wallet. But that only further aroused his suspicions.

"Can't remember the last time I saw a youth without a phone," he said.

"My ... my parents took it away. As punishment. Really!"

That rigid, false face simply stared at her, and Miranda had no idea how much skepticism the Kabuki mask hid.

The men argued with each other over how they could

let someone sneak this far past them, while the "grinning" man took charge and dragged Miranda to the front, squeezing her arm with his meaty hand. A couple of days earlier, it probably would have hurt.

"Ow! You're hurting me!"

"Shut up or I'll do worse."

He dragged her into the dimly lit store. The gang had herded all customers and employees into the back aisle, where they lay in clusters face-down on the hard floor, several shivering near the open-air refrigerators.

Masked men and women strode around the hostages, inspecting their compliance. Tips of guns sailed over innocent heads.

Teens. Seniors. Children. Parents. Couples. Singles. So many different people, none guilty of anything worse than choosing the wrong day to replenish their groceries.

And yet Miranda entered this scene willingly, a status only the criminals shared. What the hell was she doing? One misstep could launch a bullet. Someone could die, and those poor children would witness real death right in front of their little faces. This was a bad idea, the worst, most terrible, stupidest damn idea she ever had!

"I found this one trying to hide in the back," the grinning-masked man said, shoving Miranda to the floor.

Right next to her, a woman clutched her small child to her side. The girl couldn't have been more than six. Quiet sobs bubbled out despite the mother's constant, gentle consoling.

No backing out. Miranda had committed. She was seeing this through. She was saving these people—if she didn't screw it up. And, oh God, she could so screw this up ...

Gang members loomed over her. The grinning-masked man mentioned her lack of phone and ID.

"That's weird, right?" he said. "What do we think about her? She just a lone crazy person, or she with the police?"

"If she's with the police, that means they're not taking us seriously." A tall man in a black leather jacket approached at a leisurely pace, his words oozing out just as confidently. "It's time to show them how serious we are."

The man, no doubt the leader, pulled Miranda to her feet. In his other hand was a pistol, clean enough that even this soft light glinted off its body. A fiery demon's head concealed his face.

The pistol chilled Miranda's temple, and a cell phone rose to the leader's ear. "Still with me, buddy? We got ourselves a little riddle in here. Since you're my new pal and everything, maybe you can clear this up. We found this young lady in the back. Nothing on her but clothes. Odd clothes, too. But she's a cute girl, kind of scrawny but just pretty enough. So I'm thinking it would be a waste to blow her brains out, such a damn waste."

A loaded bullet was so close to her. That much

concentrated force, at this range ...

Would it kill her? Hurt her? Penetrate just enough to give her permanent brain damage?

Someone gently touched her shoulder, but she saw no one there.

"You wouldn't be stupid enough to send in an undercover cop, would you?" the leader said, as he kept waving that pistol in Miranda's face.

Time to get into character. She inhaled a deep breath through her nose, inhabited her costume, felt the newfound power of her muscles, and remembered who she was supposed to be. This was just another type of performance—one with potentially life-or-death consequences, but a performance nevertheless. And at that, she was the professional here.

In her mind, the houselights had dimmed, and the stage lights were coming up. A little stage manager in her head whispered, *Go! Now! What are you waiting for, idiot? You're on!*

But then the pistol left her face, and she fumbled to recapture her character work.

"Not sure I believe you," the leader said into his phone. "And if she is one of yours, then I'm thinking shooting *her* might not teach the most effective lesson."

The leader moved his aim from hostage to hostage, as if trying to decide whom to punish for Miranda's interference.

All my fault. Can't be my fault.

"Hey!" Miranda summoned a confident smirk, hoping it would conceal her terror. "You honestly believe you have the upper hand here, don't you?"

"Hold on a second." The leader lowered the phone. "Girl, I do not like this mouth on you."

"I don't like this criminal behavior on you." The more she spoke, the more she deluded herself into embracing her role, even if she couldn't tame her jittery leg. "Shame on you all. Shame!"

Everyone was focused on her, criminals and innocents alike. And only one gun steadied its aim on a target—the leader's, on Miranda. Perfect.

The leader drew out a long sigh. "You are one crazy bi—"

"Watch the mouth!" she interrupted, wagging her finger at him. "There are children present. Think of the example you're setting."

The leader tightened his grip on his pistol, his finger tensing over the trigger but not pulling it yet. But the gun wouldn't hurt her, she told herself, possibly lying.

"You think you're cute or something?" he said.

She flashed a huge smile. "No, just disarming."

"Okay, you're done."

His finger began to squeeze.

She couldn't help but think, *I'm going to die.*

No, remember: I'm a superhero. Time to be super.

Miranda snatched the pistol before any shot was launched. She became a whirlwind, swiping all firearms from the rest of the gang, then coming to a rest.

Everyone looked up.

Miranda hovered over everyone's heads. Plastic shopping bags hung from her arm, each loaded with the gang's firearms. She pulled a pistol from one, grabbing it by the barrel.

"Like I said." She bent the barrel, trapping all bullets in the chamber. "Disarming."

The hostages' faces filled with awe at the impossible spectacle. Most of the criminals stared at her, stupefied into inaction.

The leader, however, muttered through clenched teeth, "This goddamn city."

He pulled a second pistol from his jacket and pointed it at the nearest hostage, a teenage boy. He was poised to shoot at any second ...

Everything froze, and Miranda forgot how to move. She needed to swoop down there, but what about all these guns she was carrying? Where to stash them for a second? Anywhere for a second! Move!

As she started to, a flare erupted.

Fantastic Man materialized beside the leader, immediately grabbing his arm and pulling up.

A shot fired.

The hostages ducked tight to the floor. Children cried.

Miranda averted her eyes, but then remembered she didn't get to do that anymore. Dreading what she'd see, she forced herself to look down.

No one was hurt. Not the boy, not any other hostage. The bullet had sliced through a tub of butter.

Fantastic Man launched an uppercut at the gang leader and swiped his gun, then impatiently glanced at Miranda. "The masks!"

Miranda hung the plastic bags on ceiling fixtures and dove in to yank the masks off the criminals. She handled these with far less care than the guns, flinging the masks any which way so long as they'd land out of immediate reach.

"Thanks, Ultra Girl!" Fantastic Man said.

"That's not—"

She recoiled as he exploded with blinding light, but he limited the effect to head level, leaving only the criminals caught in the intolerable glare.

"Citizens, remain calm!" he announced. "This ordeal will be over momentarily!"

Fantastic Man handed Miranda the swiped pistol. She bent the barrel in half, flew to the ceiling, and pitched it in one of the bags.

In that quick moment, fisticuffs broke out—ten dazed criminals versus one luminescent Fantastic Man.

A clumsy fist swung at him, only to pass harmlessly through photons. Fantastic Man instantly solidified and decked his attacker, then turned to the next oncoming criminal.

Miranda started with the ones who, in their half-blind states, were tripping over hostages. She plucked the criminals up one at a time and slid them down an aisle feet-first, careful not to use her full strength. They slammed against a checkout counter and each other as their comrades followed. Gum, breath mints, and energy shots rained on them.

She defeated seven that way. Fantastic Man was still exchanging blows with two more, including the leader.

She grabbed the subordinate first and added him to her pile.

Lastly, the leader. Miranda snatched him up, yanking his face to hers. He blinked rapidly, still reeling from Fantastic Man's assault. His eyes were no longer hidden, and his fear was on full display.

"I—I was just bluffing!" he said, his legs flailing over empty air. "I wasn't really going to hurt anyone."

"Sure." Miranda smirked. "You're done." And she slid him down the aisle at the rest of his gang.

Fantastic Man nodded approvingly at her handiwork, the result a tangle of disoriented villainy. "Let's bring the police in before these hooligans can cause more mischief!"

Miranda counted nine gang members, but weren't there ten?

A masked woman appeared from around a corner

and raised a pistol at Fantastic Man. She fired.

Miranda lunged in front of him. A bullet punched her sternum.

Mild pain registered at the point of impact, eliciting a quick shout from Miranda, mostly due to shock and the anticipation of impending agony. But there was no damage, just a tiny hole in her shirt, and even that flicker of pain was nothing worse than a tiny fist jabbing her.

She perceived the ricochet in a surreal slow motion, and she caught it, stared at the dented bullet in her palm, squinted at it. An actual bullet, yes, it was.

The bulletproof young woman nabbed the last gang member.

Day saved.

13

The police swarmed into the store and arrested the gang. Fantastic Man zapped himself outside to talk with the officer in command. The former hostages reunited with their loved ones in the parking lot. And Miranda stood by the refrigerators and realized she was squeezing the bullet within her fist. She opened her hand and found a flattened piece of metal.

People were safe because of her. All those happy reunions outside—she made them happen. She didn't screw it up.

"Ma'am?" a young officer said. "You're free now. You can come outside if you'd like."

Miranda flung the ruined bullet into a wastebasket and flashed a grin at the officer.

"Thank you. I think I'll do just that."

She enjoyed his confused double take as she flew over him.

Once she exited the store and stepped into the light of day, nearly every head turned to her. The volume of chatter plummeted, but she kept hearing "Ultra Girl" among the whispers. Her smile smothered a groan. She'd correct everyone soon enough, and "Astraea" would be on all tongues.

The reporters launched themselves at her, but beyond them she spotted the young children who were among the hostages. They were understandably shaken, had more than a few tears among them, but they all studied her with total fascination. And Miranda understood— only one force could prevent this horrible situation from being purely traumatic. Well, perhaps two, but Fantastic Man was still busy with the police.

Miranda hopped over the press and slowly descended near the families. She focused all eye contact at kid level and boosted her enthusiasm.

"Hey, kids! I wanted to thank you all for being *so* brave in there. I was so impressed."

Two boys and two girls, all elementary age, detached from their respective parental units and rushed at her. No hesitation, no fear. The tears dried up, and they let her know exactly what they thought of her.

"That was so cool how you bent that gun!"

"You are like the fastest person ever!" The boy flung his hands every which way in his best imitation of super-speed. "You were all zoom, zoom, zoom!"

"You're really short," another observed.

Miranda laughed. "You see, what happened is when I was your age, I ate my fruits but not my vegetables. So I grew up strong, but not big. If only I had eaten those vegetables, too!" She shook her fist in a show of lamentation.

The kids giggled.

"You're awesome, Ultra Girl!"

"How'd you become Ultra Girl?"

"Ultra Girl, how do you fly?"

"I like your hair, Ultra Girl."

The barrage persisted, and the kids were absolutely certain that her name was Ultra Girl. They liked it, even. Why did they have to like it?

The reporters had formed a semicircle around them. Cameras recorded everything.

If Miranda was going to correct the record on her superhero name, this would be her best opportunity, her only opportunity. The cement was drying.

"Hold on a second, kids," she said patiently.

The kids fell silent, leaning forward to catch her next words. The reporters were doing the same.

"We've got to get something straight here," she continued. "I'm not Ultra *Girl*. I'm Ultra *Woman*."

14

So she was Ultra Woman. Done.

Miranda's anonymous performance wasn't over yet, though. On to the next act.

The reporters lost their patience and began pelting Miranda with questions: Where did she come from? How did she acquire her powers? What exactly were her powers? What was her relationship to Fantastic Man? Who was she wearing?

Miranda smiled at the children, told them to run along back to their parents, and turned around to face a much larger audience. She recognized the media logos as a mix of local and national outlets, and she wondered how many people were watching her live. Thousands? Millions?

"What's your real name?" a reporter asked.

Miranda was tempted to answer that one. Surely she deserved to take credit for saving a bunch of people. Miranda Thomas—saver of lives!

Just do it, she told herself. *Take the goggles off. Instant fame.*

She watched the camera flashes continually burst around her, until one flash solidified into Fantastic Man, standing right beside her. The abrupt entrance stunned the reporters, wedging an opening for him to speak.

"Ladies and gentlemen of the press, good day to you!" he said, cheesy grin in full force. "I'd like to commend Ultra Woman's heroic actions today, and I heartily endorse her aid in the ongoing fight for justice!"

Miranda noticed the flaw in her costume. The goggles obscured her eyes. Effective for identity concealment, terrible for performance. She couldn't properly display the bemused expression she wanted. So she settled on a shrug.

"Well. I've never gotten an endorsement before, let alone a hearty one. I feel special now. Thanks, Fantastic Man." Instinctively, she used the International Phonetic Alphabet to expunge any hint of a regional accent, and she disguised her voice by going an octave above normal.

Fantastic Man's grin didn't lapse, but it struggled. The reporters chuckled, fueling Miranda's theatrical instincts. She struck a lighthearted tone, like she was sharing a laugh with him.

"You make me sound like I'm on some gravely important mission or something." She comically deepened her voice. "Fighting for justice, apple pie, and the safety of puppies everywhere!"

She waited as the laughter climbed to its peak, and the second it began to fade, she continued in her rehearsed voice.

"Look, I'm just here to help. I've got some unusual talents, so I figure, hey, why not pitch in and lend a hand where I can? Plus, flying is really awesome—oh my God, I wish you could all experience it. So really, any excuse to go zipping around, I am totally in."

The parking lot wasn't exactly the Aeschylus Theater, but Miranda achieved a similar performer-audience intimacy. The daylight and closeness of the crowd helped, but she again regretted the goggles. She worried they made her off-putting, hindered eye contact.

Her concerns proved unfounded. Enchanted people surrounded her. But how much better would she have fared with visible eyes?

As she indulged in a glance at the crowd, Miranda spotted the teenager who almost got shot due to her carelessness. She tensed, suddenly glad she didn't reveal her name. She hadn't earned full credit yet.

One smiling reporter asked, "So what's next for you, Ultra Woman?"

Arms akimbo, Fantastic Man proclaimed, "You can expect to see plenty more of this exceptional young lady— whenever danger strikes!"

Miranda smirked. "So, apparently, my powers came with a free spokesman." She turned to him, lifting her hands into a casual *stop* signal. "Lighten up, Fantastic Man. I got this."

That drew another burst of laughter. But Miranda

didn't receive the same charge as before.

Was she being rude to Fantastic Man? She feared she was. She was trying to distance herself from his style, but perhaps she overshot. He wasn't innocent either, though. He overstepped. Who the hell was he, trying to speak for her?

She decided it best to stop while she was ahead. Behind the press, the police were about to depart with the defeated gang members stewing in the backs of their cars.

"Anyway, that's enough about little ol' me for now." She gestured at the criminals. "I wouldn't want to steal focus from the main attraction. Their day sure didn't go as planned. Take lots of pictures before they're gone. Really zoom in on their disappointment."

The reporters seemed to agree, and for a brief moment, most attention centered on the police cars.

Leaning toward her, Fantastic Man whispered, "You need to work on your professionalism. Let's talk."

Miranda wanted to brush him off, tell him their appointment was later. But that *would* be too rude. She didn't have to become his subordinate, but they should at least remain cordial allies. People would expect that of them.

"Pick a roof," she whispered back, and he nodded.

Miranda bid the crowd a nice day as she rose into the air. They gasped at the sight of a flying woman—in person, right in front of them! And they cheered.

She expected Fantastic Man would be a tougher audience to please.

15

Miranda followed a zig-zagging ball of light to Olympus's office district, where the buildings all looked like clones of each other. Nevertheless, these homogenous structures had high, wide roofs that could facilitate a private meeting between superheroes.

The ball of light cut through the clear sky and swerved down to a rooftop, where Fantastic Man appeared, arms crossed, his cape fluttering behind him. No cheesy grin this time.

Miranda mustered up her most polite tone as she landed, and she lifted the goggles from her eyes to aid the effort. She had to raise her voice over the wind, though. "Hey, thanks for helping out against that gang. I could not have done it without you."

His posture stiffened. "I had expressly told you to abstain from any further public displays until after we met this evening, but I suppose one can never plan for a hostage crisis. Given the circumstances, your makeshift uniform is understandable, but I look forward to seeing the final version."

It took some effort to avoid rolling her eyes, but Miranda dialed it down to a simple flap of the arms. "This is pretty much it."

"That's not a superhero uniform."

She wagged a finger, as if she were a clever professor responding to a student's fallacious thinking. "Ahh, but you see, in the real world, there's not a whole lot of precedent for anything we're doing. So what really *is* a superhero costume?"

Fantastic Man resembled a statue for a few more seconds. Then his shoulders slacked and he rubbed the bridge of his nose.

"You're starting off on the wrong foot," he said, sighing.

Miranda opened her mouth, but Fantastic Man preempted her before the first syllable emerged.

"When I look at you," he continued, "I don't see a superhero. I see a young woman playing at being a superhero. I see someone who's more concerned with getting a laugh than getting the job done."

Cocking an eyebrow, Miranda responded, "So when you 'endorsed' me, were you basically lying?"

"It's better the people trust you rather than fear you, but I expect you'll earn the endorsement in time."

"Okay, you were lying. And that's kind of the issue here. When I see you, I see someone trying to hide."

Glancing off to the side, Fantastic Man clenched his mouth, swallowing whatever retort he wanted to unleash.

Miranda softened her tone, aiming to sound reasonable rather than combative. "I get that you feel we should act like we stepped out of an old comic book, but that feels insincere to me. So I'm trying a different approach."

Fantastic Man frowned. "Your approach almost got a boy killed."

Miranda floundered as she tried to form an appropriate response, because yes, she should feel bad about that, but *he* shouldn't make her feel bad about it. "I made a mistake."

"Superheroes don't make mistakes."

"People do, and like it or not, we're—"

"*I* am a superhero. If you'd like to get serious about this line of work, our appointment this evening still stands. We'll train and determine how our skills best complement each other. Otherwise, I'll do my best to prevent your mistakes from turning into tragedies."

His cape swished as he turned away, but he remembered one more item.

"If you *are* serious," he said, not bothering to reestablish eye contact, "I've left a communication device for you at Hephaestus Enterprises. See the co-owner, one Dr. Luna."

He flashed and disappeared.

Miranda reminded herself that no tragedy occurred that afternoon. She rescued those people. Indeed, she completed the vast majority of the rescuing, and if Fantastic Man hadn't shown up, she would've reacted in time to save that boy. She kept replaying the moment in her mind, trying to convince herself that she had enough time to dive down and intercept the bullet. It would have been an inexcusably close call, but she was the swiftest person ever. And she totally proved she was willing to throw herself into the line of fire.

Just as she was starting to relax, she recalled seeing the boy's relieved parents embracing him in the parking lot after the crisis had passed. Her brain took it upon itself to edit the moment, rewriting events to show her how devastated those parents would have been if they had lost their son. She knew her own parents would never recover if ...

That hostage situation probably made national news.

Miranda dashed back to her apartment.

16

Four texts and two voice messages awaited Miranda as she rushed back into her apartment. All were from her mother, seeking confirmation that her daughter was not anywhere near that terrible hostage situation. Naomi asked her to call her back immediately—she asked all six times.

Miranda berated herself as she hit the call button. She should've sent a quick text on her way out, could've spared her family so much worry. How thoughtless of her.

Naomi picked up on the first ring. "Are you okay? Where were you? I must have left ten messages."

"I'm fine. I'm sorry. I was nowhere near there. I was practicing for an audition and just tuning out the world, and apparently my timing was awful. I'm so sorry."

Lying came far too easily, but the sincere apology alleviated some of her guilt.

"Do you feel safe there?" Naomi asked.

"That store is on the other side of the city." She quickly debated bringing up Ultra Woman. "And you might have heard, there's another superhero here now."

"I saw that, but crime is still crime—and no one can be everywhere at once."

Miranda spent a few more minutes convincing Naomi she was indeed safe and not scared for her life.

As she calmed down, Naomi transitioned to questions about the audition, thereby requiring Miranda to fabricate a production on the spot. Details about a hypothetical student film flowed out, and Miranda scribbled down a few notes on a scrap of paper, in case this ever came up again.

But wouldn't it be simpler, and kinder, to tell Naomi she had a bulletproof daughter?

No rash decisions, Miranda decided. Besides, her parents were constitutionally incapable of *not* worrying about her for one reason or another.

She heard Peyton's voice in the background, and the kid was on the phone seconds later.

"You have two superheroes there now!" Peyton said in lieu of any conventional greeting.

"That does seem to be the case. I just caught a glimpse of her on the news—an Ultra something?"

"*Ultra Woman!*"

Miranda smiled. It may not have been her top choice of name, but hearing her little sister speak it with such enthusiasm presented a strong case in its favor.

Barely pausing for a breath, Peyton volunteered her opinion of Ultra Woman, calling her "awesome," "amazing," "so cool," and other superlatives as she went on and on. Miranda was beaming several feet above the floor.

After all that rambling praise, Peyton added, "She just needs a better costume."

Miranda dropped back down. "What? I thought it looked good. What didn't you like about it?"

"It's just clothes. Anyone can wear clothes."

"And a neon jacket. Not just anyone can pull that off."

"She'd look so great flying in a cape. She also needs a real mask. And tights with maybe a symbol on them. But other than that, I really like her."

So, Peyton would like Ultra Woman better if she dressed more like Fantastic Man. Wonderful. Miranda understood her costume didn't fit the standard superhero template, but people would get used to it. She just needed to give it time. Besides, Peyton seemed otherwise thrilled about her.

Miranda wondered which superhero her sister liked better. She was about to ask, but there existed the possibility that the answer might not be Ultra Woman. She felt silly worrying about it, but she had already moved on and started wrapping up the conversation.

"I should get back to work, but you can tell Mom I'm just staying home and preparing audition stuff, okay?"

As they said their goodbyes, Miranda tried not to dwell on how she lied to her little sister, but the part about getting back to work was accurate. She had her Ultra Woman errand to run. Because she *was* serious about this. She'd pick up that communication device, maybe perform a few good deeds, go to that training session, and before long she'd unseat Fantastic Man as everyone's favorite superhero.

She put her goggles back on, sped up to the roof, and dove upward, into the clear sky.

17

Hephaestus Enterprises was a scientific research facility on the Olympus City coast; its main focus was exploring sources of clean, alternative energy. Miranda recalled her environmental science professor gushing about it when she was fulfilling that particular subject requirement. It was pretty much the only thing she remembered from the class.

However, Miranda wasn't clear on Fantastic Man's connection to the place. Was *he* this Dr. Luna he mentioned? Did he really expect he'd fool her just by taking the mask off? He'd have to be a hell of an actor. Miranda hoped Ultra Woman never met anyone she already knew.

She spotted the facility from above. From the outside, Hephaestus Enterprises was a large enclosed hangar situated along a plateau's edge, high above crashing waves and jagged boulders. Only a handful of cars occupied the spacious parking lot, but one well-worn sedan proved distinctive, in that its hood was on fire. And the fire was blue.

A lanky man in a lab coat leapt out the driver's door. With surprising fluidity, he rolled onto the pavement and leapt to his feet, but then became rigid as he watched the blaze, likely unclear as to how one might go about extinguishing a discolored car fire.

Miranda landed beside him. He flinched and raised his arms as if to ward off an imminent attack.

"You're the flying girl," he said, not yet lowering those arms.

"I'm Ultra Woman. Yes. Hi." She pointed at the blue flames. "Please tell me you know what's going on with this."

Beads of sweat crawled down his balding forehead. "There is no earthly reason for blue fire to be happening," he said.

The blaze flared up, rising several feet higher while emitting almost no smoke. But Miranda started feeling the heat, and it was growing hotter and larger still. So, without giving the matter much thought, she lifted the car above her head and tossed it over the plateau. The flaming vehicle sailed hundreds of feet through the air, crashed into the water, and sank. The mysterious fire was no match for the Pacific Ocean.

The scientist's face descended into his palm as he groaned. "Do you realize the ecological damage you've just caused? Did you even think about that?"

"I was just—there was a fire, and all that water right there ..." She looked at the water, then the scientist, then settled on the water. "Um, I'll go get the car."

Miranda tossed her jacket onto the pavement and flew into the ocean. The car wasn't hard to find. She lifted it from underneath, and water flooded through the open windows as it emerged. Sopping wet herself, she placed the vehicle in the same parking space she had originally found it. More water poured out as she opened a door.

"Ecological catastrophe averted. And you'll notice there's not a flame to be seen, blue or otherwise. That's the part I prefer to focus on."

The scientist groaned again.

Miranda picked up her jacket. "So you're really not sure what was up with the blue flame? What exactly were you doing with this car?"

"That's proprietary and confidential."

So a weird science project went awry. "Okay. Anyway, the main reason I came by was to see Dr. Luna."

She hoped this guy wasn't Dr. Luna. He definitely wasn't Fantastic Man, though. Similar height, but the head shape was all wrong. Too long, too narrow, too much forehead.

"Dr. Luna is busy with another experiment and can't be interrupted. I'm the other owner here. Dr. Warner Pinkney." He did not extend a hand to shake. "Is there something I can do for you?"

"I was told specifically to see Dr. Luna."

"By whom?"

Miranda had no idea if she was allowed to say.

"Maybe I should just try again later."

Pinkney scowled at her evasion, but the matter was entirely forgotten when, despite the clear sky, thunder boomed. It wasn't the car.

The boom repeated. Miranda and Pinkney appeared equally befuddled as they both looked around for a possible source.

Miranda instantly compiled a list of horrific possibilities: plane crash, arsonist, power company explosion, terrorist attack. What if there was lots of blood? What if she didn't know how to handle the situation? What if she wasn't able to help and looked stupid in front of everyone?

But maybe it was just a simple, freak lightning strike.

The dark smoke in the distance suggested not. A few thin columns rose between buildings deep inside the city.

Lightning shot up from that same area—a wide, jagged bolt sliced through the blue sky.

Miranda checked with the second set of eyes beside her. "Did that lightning come up *from* the street?"

Pinkney nodded vacantly as he, too, stared at the smoke, apparently overwhelmed by the grotesquely unscientific notion.

Another horrific possibility occurred to Miranda, one she definitely had no idea how to handle:

What if other people had acquired super-powers, too?

18

Lightning from the street. Miranda was flying *toward* lightning from the street.

Rushing into danger was never going to stop feeling weird, she suspected. And the thousand-foot view didn't help.

A tight cyclone of electricity swirled in the middle of the road, less than a block away from the city's largest hospital. Bright sparks danced around a male silhouette, obscuring his features.

Distant sirens wailed. Traffic had totally stopped in both directions. Three cars caught fire. No, four cars. People abandoned their vehicles and were fleeing.

Some couldn't flee—they were lying on the sidewalk, unmoving.

A small group, dressed in scrubs and wheeling stretchers, was running toward the injured victims, against the flow.

The electric cyclone spat a lightning bolt at another car, igniting a fifth fire.

Miranda paused, hovering high above the chaos. She wanted to curl up into the tiniest ball she could and pretend none of this was happening.

I don't know what to do. I can't do this. Someone is going to die.

Lightning zapped the brick building next to the victims, breaking off chunks of masonry, throwing the pieces into freefall toward helpless, unconscious innocents.

Miranda swooped down and caught the debris, then flung it all at the electrical man. She used a fraction of her strength, hoping to draw his attention, maybe disorient him. But no matter the size or shape of the projectile, the electric cyclone pulverized it all into dust. No reaction from the figure within.

The cyclone flashed. The victims and medics were totally exposed to any stray lightning that might strike in their direction.

Miranda could give them a shield, though.

She placed her hands on an abandoned sedan's roof and attempted to lift the vehicle. She succeeded only in tearing the roof open.

Inwardly cursing at herself, she lifted from the bottom. That worked.

She raised the vehicle with its underside facing the electrical man, covering the medics' rescue operation. She was almost too late.

Lightning pounded the car. The tires deflected the brunt, but part of the charge slipped through and jolted Miranda—not enough to knock her down, but enough to reveal an unpleasant truth.

I can be hurt, she realized. *Oh, God. I could die here.*

The medics gawked at the impossibly strong woman who somehow endured a powerful electric charge. Whether out of awe or fear, they froze.

"Help those people!" Miranda snapped, nodding her head at the unconscious victims. "I'll cover you. I promise I'll cover you."

The car received another hit. Miranda stifled a groan as her skin jumped.

Why the hell did she promise that? She couldn't guarantee anyone's safety! If any of those nurses or doctors got hurt, people would never trust her again.

Shielding them wasn't enough.

Miranda rammed the car at the electrical man. Harsher lightning flung it out of her grasp and bowled her over. The vehicle somersaulted and crashed onto another car halfway down the block.

An explosion rattled her ears. She climbed to her feet, and a small bolt stung her, throwing her right back down. Her head collided with a car's grill. The impact was more disorienting than painful, but she ached from the repeated electrocution. Pins and needles pricked every inch of her, and the fires impaired her breathing.

She was failing to save the day. What was the guy's problem? What motivated this rampage?

A few young adults were hiding in an alley on the

other side of the street. They were sticking their cell phones out, recording the carnage, capturing Miranda's embarrassing performance, increasing the number of people she needed to protect. The idiots.

What if Peyton saw Ultra Woman getting knocked around like an amateur? She *was* an amateur.

They were utter idiots for putting themselves in harm's way.

"Hey! You three!" she yelled and pointed. "Get out or I will fly you out! And no, you would not like it! I will make it very unpleasant!"

The electricity was flaring up again. Miranda stomped against the bumper of a parked SUV, sending it rolling in front of the alley just in time to block the lightning and save the idiots.

"Go!"

The idiots still weren't running the hell away. They preferred to gape, alternately, at Miranda and the foot imprint she left on the SUV.

"Yes." A hoarse voice emerged from the cyclone. The man lifted his head, as if coming out of a trance, and his voice gained strength. "Go away! Get out of here!"

He sounded genuinely desperate ... sounded familiar. An older voice.

The idiots finally got the message and scrammed. Miranda wished she could join them.

The medics. She left them unprotected. Amateur.

They were hoisting the victims onto stretchers as quickly as they dared. And the electric cyclone spewed more lightning, several bolts at once.

One bolt struck above their heads, blasting a hole in the wall behind them. They all ducked, scared but unharmed. Pure dumb luck saved their lives.

Miranda launched herself in front of them, arriving in time for the next bolt—barely. The margin was so slim, she had no choice but to take a direct hit to her chest.

Her nerve endings screamed. Everything burned.

But she did have a choice, she realized as she suppressed a scream. She could have fled like all the sensible people did—she could still flee.

No, she couldn't.

She needed to stop this jerk. Whatever his stupid problem was, she'd put an end to this.

As soon as she figured out how.

Their patients secure, the medics hurried back to the hospital. Good. No more bystanders in the danger zone.

The cyclone had gaps, thicker than Miranda initially believed. The glare cast the illusion of a mostly solid barrier, but it was mere illusion. Problem was, those gaps kept shifting at varying speeds.

Static crawled across Miranda's skin as she stepped forward, trying to find the best gap to exploit, trying not to flinch at the thought of another painful jolt.

She saw the man's face, his old, frightened face.

"Help me," he said pitifully. "I don't know what's happening."

Another gap passed over him and she recognized the man. It was Officer Hoskins—the police officer patrolling Mount Olympus on *that* night.

A glare erupted beside Miranda. She feared it was more lightning, but it was only Fantastic Man. Hands on hips, he gazed ahead, effecting his usual air of unflappable confidence.

"What's the ..." His voice trailed off. "... situation?"

The next lightning bolt created a pothole a few feet away. Fantastic Man's eyes widened.

Miranda pointed at the cyclone. "This is all an accident. This man can't control his powers. What the hell do we do?"

Fantastic Man's jaw hung open for a few long seconds until an idea clawed its way out, restoring a semblance of confidence. "Why, simple."

This better be worth the wait, Miranda thought as lightning assaulted the cars and buildings.

"Just fly in there and tackle him."

Wasn't worth the wait.

"I don't know if I'd survive!" she said. "The lightning hurts me. And he's innocent! What good is tackling him if he's just going to keep blowing up?"

Stress lines flanked Fantastic Man's mouth. Miranda hadn't noticed that before.

He snapped his fingers, and his tone was unusually harried. "I met a young man who might be able to help. Maybe I can find him. Contain the situation until I return!"

"Wait, how—"

He was gone, leaving Miranda alone with a dangerous innocent man.

Sirens were louder. Maybe backup would arrive soon.

But what if the police felt they had no choice but to shoot Hoskins? This wasn't his fault, and Miranda knew it could just as easily have been her in the middle of that electric cyclone. She was lucky. Although, she somehow wound up in charge of handling an unprecedented crisis, so perhaps not so lucky.

Lightning blew up a car's engine. Another sliced through the corner of a building. An even larger bolt fired straight up.

And Miranda was just standing there.

"I want to help you." She advanced cautiously. "It's Officer Hoskins, right?"

He nodded, his eyes full of shame.

Miranda continued, "Is there anything you can do to help me? Can you concentrate, dial it down even a little? If you can do that, I'll get you out of here."

To where? Fantastic Man had mentioned a vacant island. What if Hoskins blew up on her in transit?

"I promise I'll do everything I can to help you," she said.

Again with the promises! But Miranda had upheld her

promise to the medics.

"I don't know how!" Hoskins said. "I'm too dangerous. I need to be put down. It's the right thing to do."

"No. That is totally unnecessary." Was it, though? What if his power grew further out of control? "There's a solution. Look, I've met you before—you seem like a good man."

"I hurt people. I don't want to hurt people!"

Wind blew from above, accompanied by a steady whup-whup-whup. A police chopper. An officer was aiming a rifle out the door, and the gaps between the lightning widened, as if inviting the fire.

Either the sniper would shoot Hoskins, or Hoskins would shoot them and crash the helicopter.

The cyclone swelled.

"Do it now!" Hoskins shouted up. Miranda could barely hear him over the chopper, but he persisted anyway. "Take the shot while you can!"

Miranda *could* stop a bullet from killing him, but then she'd be responsible for whatever or whomever he hurt next.

For the love of God, she just wanted to act in plays and movies! When was she ever anything less than clear about that? Why was the universe entrusting her with life-and-death decisions?

Maybe because the universe knew she didn't consider death a valid option. Not for an innocent old man, not for innocent bystanders, and preferably not for herself either.

So how not to die? Checking the surrounding wreckage for options, she noticed a trailer truck and its thick, durable tires.

This was still going to hurt, though. No doubt about that.

Miranda punctured a tire with her finger and ripped it off, her whole body tightening in anticipation of the inevitable pain, all nerve endings flaring up to warn her. As if she needed the warning. She didn't deserve this pain.

But neither did Officer Hoskins.

The long strip of tire was ready to serve as her not-so-mighty shield. She held it in front of her, and her sense of self-preservation, more insistent than ever, begged her not to act. She almost surrendered to that impulse. Then she remembered the last time she hesitated, and the boy who almost got shot.

She flew into the electric cyclone, wrapped the material around Hoskins, and lifted him into the sky.

Sparks pinched Miranda constantly as she carried Hoskins out of Olympus. Charges ran up her arms. Spots dotted her vision, and they multiplied. The pain exceeded expectations, but she endured.

Was she flying in the right direction? She wasn't sure, and thinking proved challenging at the moment. She was relying on Fantastic Man's directions, which were only slightly more detailed than Peter Pan's directions to Neverland.

"Just drop me!" Hoskins shouted, writhing in her grip. "I'm not worth this!"

She tuned him out and focused.

There—a land mass, couldn't have been more than a square mile. Nothing but ample beach surrounding a forest.

Miranda swerved to land near the water, and she released Hoskins.

Once she let go and dropped the tire insulation, the electric cyclone sprang back to full power, throwing her across the beach like a rag doll.

"There's no one to hurt here," Miranda said, spitting out sand.

"Except you."

"Well ... I'm tough." She brushed herself off. "Apparently."

Hoskins turned to the sea and sighed. "I appreciate your effort. Thank you for getting me out of the city." As he glanced back at her, the cyclone's turbulence diminished, highlighting his somber eyes. "Now it's time for you to leave and forget all about me."

Miranda recalled her chaotic first flight. But she figured it out. He could, too. He just needed to achieve the right focus. What could get a seasoned police officer to focus?

"You could help me," she said. "I'm pretty sure we got our powers the same night. There was an older woman in a superhero costume. I watched her die. Did you see her?"

Miranda wondered if that was her ulterior motive for saving him. She hoped she was better than that.

Hoskins tilted his head back, and his brow crinkled. "I thought I dreamt that in the coma. But then I stepped out of the hospital, and I ... exploded. It all happened, didn't it?"

"What happened?"

Sparks continued flying around him, but the intensity had steadied and no further lightning struck.

"A lady fell out of thin air," he said.

19

Hoskins said nothing else for an indiscernible amount of time, though Miranda would have estimated it at somewhere between a few hours and a few eons. In actuality, he scratched the side of his face and angled his head toward the sand for about thirty seconds of infuriating silence.

After a calming breath, Miranda gently prodded him along. "And ...?"

"Sorry. I'm just wondering if the coma damaged my brain. That night makes less sense than any dream I could've had."

The woman's self-generated electricity was the first detail he mentioned, as he glanced at his own electrified hands. He went on to describe the woman's costume, and his recollection matched Miranda's. But he also noted that the woman was concerned about a missing mask, which irritated her to no end. She was a belligerent lady all around, and appalled that Hoskins didn't recognize her—no, he corrected himself, she was appalled *before* she noticed her mask was missing, and then his confusion made perfect sense to her. Not that she could let it stand.

To eradicate said confusion, she grabbed him by the neck, hoisted him off the ground, and identified herself as Dame Disaster, Predator of the Earth.

That woman was a supervillain? Miranda thought. *How am I not dead? How is she dead? Who can murder a supervillain?*

She didn't want to interrupt, though, so she kept quiet as Hoskins continued piecing together the evening.

He said Dame Disaster demanded to know where the Golden Gladiator was.

"You ever hear of a 'Golden Gladiator'?" he asked Miranda.

She shook her head. "There's only Fantastic Man. Oh, and I guess me now."

"Yeah, I told her about Fantastic Man, but she was as confused about him as I was about this gladiator fellow. She didn't believe me. So, next thing I know, she removes her hand from my throat, but I'm still choking and floating over nothing."

On account of the choking, Hoskins wasn't entirely clear what happened next. He heard Dame Disaster asking where her ship was—he was positive he had seen no vessel of any sort that evening—and she muttered something about a "voyage between realities."

Miranda wondered how reality could be plural. Maybe Hoskins misheard? He *was* being supernaturally choked.

Hoskins recalled seeing a shiny figure in the corner of his eye. It looked like a person.

"The Golden Gladiator?" Miranda asked.

"It was silver."

Whatever he, she, or it was, Dame Disaster recognized it, initially perceived no threat from it. She smiled for the first time since she popped out of nowhere, but any happiness or relief faded as soon as a recorded voice spoke.

Hoskins took a second to recall the words exactly. "The voice, a male voice, said, 'The Golden Gladiator arrived a few months ago. You two broke this world.' "

The shiny person fired a bright scarlet beam at Dame Disaster. Her electricity flared up as the beam hit her side. Hoskins found himself flung onto the grass.

"... and then I must have blacked out," he concluded.

Miranda had formulated a few theories about the old woman, but she never seriously considered she might have come from another world, let alone another reality. And that shiny person or shiny whatever—she had glimpsed it, too, hadn't she?

"Yeah, I can understand why you might have mistaken that for a dream," Miranda said. "You're right, though. I met her after you did." After she was murdered.

That supervillain was a murder victim. The idea kept echoing in her mind: It was possible to murder a super-person.

And what did the speaker mean by "broke this world"? In what way had it been broken? The whole world? Was that the scale of this situation? Had Miranda gotten herself involved in a global problem? She just wanted to help out here and there, do her bit of community service. World breakage—and any subsequent consequences of said breakage—was most certainly not part of the plan.

The electricity had almost entirely settled, producing little more than the occasional crackle and static.

This was a scope Miranda was more comfortable with—one person. She could concentrate on one person and take it from there.

"So how are we going to stop this killer?" she asked.

He didn't seem to comprehend. "Stop ...?"

"You're a police officer, right? And you're the only person who might be able to identify this guy."

The sparks grew brighter; the crackling, louder.

"I'm no detective. I'm a career beat cop, and for a reason." Surrounded by small lightning, his face fell. "And this sure as heck isn't the same world I started out in."

"Whatever you were, you're more now."

Lightning struck the sand.

"I'm serious," Miranda said. "When you were talking, your, um, electricity almost completely calmed down. And now I've said something that makes you a little uncomfortable, so it's ramping back up. You've been controlling it all along, just unconsciously. But we can make it conscious."

"If I *can* control it, that means I really am responsible for everyone I hurt."

Miranda positioned herself in front of him, trying to get him to look at her rather than his own guilt. "That's not what I'm saying. I'm saying ... hey, why did you want to become a cop in the first place?"

A long breath. "Always wanted to help people."

"And you can still do it. You can do it in a different way, and you can do it better than ever. Just focus. Focus on taming the electricity. Contain it."

He seemed skeptical, but Hoskins closed his eyes and slowly breathed in. He seemed to inhale the electricity. It still crackled around his arms, but no lightning escaped him.

"See?" Miranda said, stepping closer. "You're just learning a new muscle, that's all."

Cautiously, he extended a hand. As he squinted, the electricity faded.

"You must be that Ultra Woman I've heard about," he said.

She shook his hand and smiled. "Yes, that's me. And hey, not even the tiniest shock there. Well done."

"So we've got a suspect to track down, don't we?" Hoskins said.

She saved him. She didn't fail.

This was the way to go, she decided. Just focus on

helping individuals. Let others worry about the fate of the world, the big picture stuff.

"We need to involve my precinct." Gazing off to the side, Hoskins scratched his chin as he mapped out a plan. "That's the proper way to go about this. We need to get our observations on record. I should stay here for a little while until I'm sure I'm safe, but you can—"

A scarlet laser beam sliced through Hoskins, punching a hole in his chest.

He toppled onto the sand, his eyes wide open but not moving, not even blinking. He didn't move at all. No electricity sparked, not the slightest crackle.

He was dead. He had a hole as big as a watermelon where no such hole existed seconds before.

Dead.

Miranda almost threw up.

As she recoiled from the gruesome sight and the noxious odor of burnt flesh, her eyes landed on what had to be the killer.

It stood stiffly on the beach, its tall but gaunt body reflecting the sunlight. The size and shape of a man, almost. But it wasn't human.

A robot. A shiny, silver robot.

Its face lacked any features other than a pair of eye slits. It stared vacantly at its victim, then swiveled at the waist toward Miranda.

Its eyes blasted her.

A burst of light. Blistering heat. The force of a high-speed train. All at once.

Miranda was unconscious before she hit the ground.

She failed.

20

"**U**ltra Woman?"

A deep voice woke Miranda up, and something was crawling all over her—an army of rough, tiny nuisances.

Sand. Sand was everywhere, under her clothes, on her skin, in her wig. So unclean.

Whose voice was that?

A tall, slender man in a tweed three-piece suit stood over her. A matching mask covered his entire head, gray and blank, like the robot's.

The robot.

"You killed him," she muttered.

"I ... what?"

Miranda sprang up, grabbed the man's tie, and yanked him toward her.

"Your robot!" she shouted as she stared into an empty face. "Where's your robot?"

"What robot?"

She shoved him. He tumbled through the air backward, heels over head three times ... and then just stopped, without even touching the ground. He reoriented himself upright, and his sneakers slowly reconnected with the beach.

Miranda floated toward him, scowling. "Why did you kill him?"

"I didn't kill anyone. Just stop."

"Tell me why!"

Her arms were shaking.

The man raised his hands to chest level and pushed forward, against nothing.

Something invisible pushed against Miranda, forcing her backward. She tried to fly against this force, but it strengthened in retaliation, locking them in a stalemate.

"I'm a friend." His voice was strained, like he was struggling to lift too great a weight.

"I don't believe you!" she yelled.

Rooting herself on the ground, Miranda marched against the unseen force, one slow step at a time, the pressure aggravating her sunburns.

Not sunburns. Laser burns.

She pushed harder. Another step.

"Calm down," the masked man said. "Please."

Her fists clenched, Miranda took another step toward him. And another.

A clump of sand rose from the ground, seemingly with a mind of its own, and it covered Miranda's goggles. She jerked her head from side to side and swatted at it, but the clump spread around her.

"I'm sorry," he said.

The force attacked from behind this time, slamming

into the backs of Miranda's knees, toppling her.

The frontal assault resumed. Miranda felt herself being dragged across the sand, away from her opponent.

She flipped over and dug her hands into the ground, stopping herself. She lifted her head and looked straight ahead at someone else lying in the sand, dozens of feet away, so still. A dark bird had landed on the body and was picking away at the flesh.

The invisible force relented.

The masked man asked, in a kind tone, "Did you know him well?"

A putrid odor wafted across the beach, threatening to choke Miranda. Already, Officer Hoskins was decaying, his body baking in the heat as peaceful waves carried on around him.

An open hand reached toward Miranda and waited for her to accept.

"I couldn't save him." Her eyes moistened. She blinked rapidly to thwart any tears and was thankful for the goggles. "Didn't even see it coming. I was useless."

The masked man's response came a few seconds later. "I'm sure you did everything you could, probably more than anyone else could have."

His voice was odd, almost comically deep, like some- one trying too hard to effect a superhero voice.

Miranda stood up without his aid. She appeared a total mess. The laser had burned a hole in the shirt over her stomach, and the jacket was scorched along the zipper. Sand coated her jeans and infiltrated her hair beneath her wig. Only her goggles were in decent shape, just a few smudges to wipe away.

"So you are ...?" she asked.

Miranda tried to look at his eyes. She had to settle for estimating their location. That empty face stared dumbly back at her.

"What's your name?" she tried again.

"Name?" He looked away as he coughed, then recovered his deepened voice. "Yes, my name. I'm—"

A flash of light turned both heads, and Fantastic Man materialized beside them.

"Ultra Woman, there you are! I see you've met Mr. Amazing. He's the young man I spoke of, a veritable titan of telekinesis." He frowned at Mr. Amazing's attire. "That's not your uniform, is it?"

"I don't own spandex." Mr. Amazing started to turn toward the body. "But forget that for now—"

"I advise dispensing with the tie at once," Fantastic Man continued. "It seems precariously impractical."

"You wear a cape. Now—"

Fantastic Man patted Miranda's shoulder, kicking up a faint cloud of sand in the process. "Ultra Woman, I got concerned when you disappeared with the electrical man, but it seems I worried for naught! Tell me, how did you manage to neutralize that uncanny menace? Where is he now?"

Miranda stepped aside and pointed at Hoskins's body.

Fantastic Man went pale, his eyes unblinking. "Leaping luminosity!"

"Did you just ..."

Miranda wobbled as lightheadedness struck. Did the man just speak a catchphrase? Now? Jerk.

She steadied herself. "Where did you run off to?"

He spoke patiently. "I was looking for Mr. Amazing."

The blank face perked up. "You were? Where?"

"You didn't help!" Miranda shouted. "You could've helped. You could've saved that man, that innocent man. You could've warned us about the robot and he'd be alive now, but he's dead. He's just ..."

A second bird was pecking at Hoskins's body. One pecked, then the other, then the first again. They were taking turns. So polite as they desecrated a corpse.

"Shoo!"

Miranda fanned her arm at the birds—fanned at super-speed, which, combined with her strength, unleashed a startling, powerful gust that frightened the birds away.

The sand settled as the residual breeze died out. Fantastic Man, with a dignity that belied his costume, walked past Miranda, toward the body, not saying a word.

Fantastic Man knelt beside the body, removed his

cape, and carefully draped it over Hoskins's face. He smoothed out the fabric, stretching it to maximum length, and stood up slowly. He stayed there a moment, gazing down at the body as the calm ocean waves provided a soothing backdrop.

Wearing a solemn expression, he marched back to the others, and he kept walking past, gesturing for them to follow him down the beach.

They didn't immediately react, so he stopped and turned over his shoulder.

"Ultra Woman," he said, "tell us everything that happened, and we, all three of us, will do everything in our power to avenge that gentleman's death. I promise you, we will bring the killer to justice."

Miranda knew he couldn't guarantee that. But, despite herself, she believed he meant it.

21

Miranda told Fantastic Man and Mr. Amazing about everything except her own encounter with Dame Disaster. That part didn't seem relevant at the moment.

"The killer thinks this Dame Disaster somehow damaged the whole world when she arrived—or maybe when some 'Golden Gladiator' arrived ahead of her," Miranda said. "I don't know what 'broke this world' means. I'm not seeing any huge cataclysms or anything, but maybe one is about to happen?"

Fantastic Man paced on the beach, stroking his chin. Mr. Amazing stood still, just staring at Miranda, his reactions entirely concealed.

The silence compelled Miranda to keep talking. "I just, I don't know. How can anyone know? Or maybe the killer doesn't know what he's talking about and it's all meaningless anyway. Maybe he's just paranoid and losing his grip on reality. How much should we trust a killer?"

"I suspect," Fantastic Man said, "he was referring to the scientific laws governing our physical reality. Those have changed. You could say they're 'broken.' "

Mr. Amazing nodded. "Our abilities wouldn't be possible otherwise."

"Exactly," Fantastic Man said, pointing at him. Then his hand returned to his chin, and hesitation slowed his speech. "A ... reputable scientist has informed me that recent experiments have been behaving oddly of late, since shortly before I acquired my abilities."

Fantastic Man continued his conjectures. He suggested that Dame Disaster's mode of transit altered the fabric of reality, and he speculated about faster-than-light travel, wormholes, black holes, and other concepts that hardly seemed to matter when a nice man's body was rotting a quarter-mile down the beach.

As Fantastic Man droned on, the rolling waves competed for Miranda's attention. Though she still listened to him, her eyes drifted toward the clean water. The waves went about their business, rising and crashing, as they had done for eons, emitting that familiar saltwater odor.

Beyond the water, she saw the Olympus City skyline. She had seen it from the Santa Monica coast many times, but never from this angle or distance. With its tallest structures pointing up in the center and tapering toward sea level, Olympus looked like it belonged in a snow globe—and it looked exactly that fragile.

"We're at a crossroads in our planet's history," Fantastic Man said. "We are the first of our kind. Humanity will either embrace us and welcome our assistance, or it will reject us—which is why it's imperative we do everything *perfectly*."

He punched the word, and Miranda's stomach received the blow. Perfect was unattainable. It was phony. There existed no human frame of reference for perfection.

"If this alleged assassin has his way," Fantastic Man said, "he may well succeed in scaring other super-powered individuals into hiding, depriving the world of their terrific talents. Their potential, all the good they can do ... it will simply go to waste. By stopping this malcontent, whoever he may be, we'll save not only lives in the present, but also the lives *they* would help. The entire future is at stake."

So they were responsible for not just the city, not just the world ... but all future generations?

Beneath her goggles, Miranda's eyes popped wide open. Was this supposed to be motivational?

"My original idea seems all the more prudent," Fantastic Man said. "We must ally ourselves as a formal team, organize ourselves in a way that will reassure the populace rather than agitate them against us. Will you both join me in this endeavor?" He fixed his gaze on Miranda. "Are you willing to follow my instructions? The situation is bigger than any one of us. There is no room for mistakes."

Her stomach twisted.

She glanced at Olympus across the water. The killer was likely somewhere within, perhaps building another robot—or an army of robots. A faint burning sensation lingered where the laser hit.

"You want to be in charge of all this?" Miranda said. "Fine. To a point. But fine."

Mr. Amazing shrugged. "I certainly don't know what I'm doing. I'm here to learn, and I'm here to help. Just tell me how I can do that."

"I appreciate the open-mindedness, Mr. Amazing."

A breeze swept the cape off Hoskins's body. Miranda recoiled. She wondered if she should rush over there and reset it, but the body was so … dead.

"What are we doing about …" She didn't want to sound disrespectful. "There's a dead man—a murdered man—right over there. What are we doing?"

Fantastic Man looked at the body as if it were something far less traumatic than a corpse. "Ah. Yes."

"We should involve the police." Miranda began gesturing incoherently, playing conductor to her own rambling. "That was his suggestion, and he's—he was a police officer. We should respect—it was the final thing he was saying. We have to respect the final thing he said. And what do we know about investigating a crime? We have to—"

Fantastic Man raised a steady hand, and Miranda stopped.

"I agree," he said. "We *should* work with the authorities. I have a couple of contacts on the force. I'll shoot over there momentarily and notify them of what transpired here. We'll leave the body where it is so they can conduct a proper investigation."

"Leave him?" Miranda said. "Just fly away and leave him to rot?"

"He'll no doubt receive a respectful burial after the police collect their evidence. You're right—we shouldn't tamper with an active crime scene," Fantastic Man said.

Miranda watched the cape tumble across the sand, fleeing from its new role as a shroud.

Fantastic Man raised one more bit of business before they went their separate ways.

"Ultra Woman, did you get a chance to pick up the communication device from Dr. Luna?"

"Oh, that." It had nearly slipped out of her mind. "I got as far as the parking lot before ... this. I helped out some other scientist who was doing an experiment out there."

Fantastic Man cocked an eyebrow, curious. "An experiment ... in the parking lot?"

"Yeah. His car caught fire with these weird blue flames."

"Was his name Dr. Pinkney by any chance?"

"That's right. Pinkney."

"Huh. Interesting." Following a moment's contemplation, Fantastic Man pivoted back to his original point. "We still need those communication devices, including one for you as well, Mr. Amazing. Let's gather at Hephaestus Enterprises Thursday evening at eight for a follow-up meeting."

Miranda would be performing then. The play seemed

suddenly trivial, but she had an obligation to the production and everyone who had purchased a ticket for that night.

"I can't do that time." Discussing a scheduling conflict near the scene of a homicide. She felt like a jerk. "I have a—"

"Don't say what," Fantastic Man snapped.

"I was just going to say I have a prior commitment. Not something I can reschedule. You want me to maintain my real identity, right?"

"All right. What if we pushed it up to six o'clock Thursday?"

"Okay. Fine."

Mr. Amazing was staring at her again. Probably judging her for being a jerk, she decided.

"It's settled then," Fantastic Man said. "Remain vigilant in the meantime. Let's see if we can find some indication of where the deceased woman's spaceship may have crashed, if indeed it ever arrived at all. Remember—the future depends on us!"

He brightened and vanished.

Mr. Amazing stepped toward Miranda.

"Are you okay?" His voice remained muffled and unnaturally deep, but the tone softened. "Everything you went through today ... I'm sorry I wasn't there to help."

Aside from the mask, he appeared refreshingly human. Maybe he wasn't judging her after all.

Whatever face that mask hid, Miranda suspected it was a kind one. No, she wanted it to be a kind one.

Was she sure about this guy? For that matter, was she sure about Fantastic Man? What were their alibis for the night of the murder? Or for Officer Hoskins's murder just now?

"Thank you," Miranda said. "I'll be fine."

Mr. Amazing reached slightly toward her, as if about to speak. Soon, he did. "If you don't mind my asking ..." He paused briefly. "What's your—"

Another flash. Fantastic Man reappeared.

"I almost forgot," he said, still aglow. "I can help you both acquire more suitable uniforms." He gestured to Miranda's ruined shirt. "Ultra Woman, I see you've discovered the limitations of your selection. I can—"

"No," Miranda said, shaking her head. "You get no say in how I dress."

"I'm referring primarily to a more durable material—"

"No."

He turned to Mr. Amazing. "What about you?"

"I'll pass for now. But thank you."

"Very well."

Fantastic Man swallowed his evident displeasure and departed. The gentle waves filled the silence.

"Um, anyway," Miranda said, "it was nice meeting you, Mr. Amazing."

"Yes. Sorry it couldn't have been under better circumstances."

Miranda ascended a few inches. "Are you ... You can fly, right?"

"Not as fast as you, but I can get myself back. Go on. I don't want to hold you up."

"Okay. I guess I'll see you Thursday."

"Um, yeah. Thursday."

The water rippled as Miranda left the island, alone.

22

Miranda stepped onto the floorboards of the Aeschylus Theater and knew exactly what to do. Every word and movement were already predetermined, thoroughly rehearsed, and tested in front of live audiences. And this was merely a run-through to keep in shape for tomorrow night's performance. No pressure whatsoever.

All thoughts of day-saving, life-saving, and world-saving receded to the back of her mind, and old instincts kicked back in. She still had it, hadn't forgotten a beat, lost none of her comedic timing. After a few days of near-constant worry, this was the equivalent of a lazy morning watching movies in her pajamas. The stage was her bed, and the warm lights were a comfy blanket. Here, she could just be herself.

The curtain call concluded the run-through, and Miranda thought she did as well as ever, maybe even better.

The director wanted a word.

Heather Kinnear set her notepad on the adjacent armrest, and Miranda left a couple of chairs between them as she took a seat.

"You seemed distracted tonight," Heather said. The

frumpy older woman adjusted her shawl and relaxed into her chair. "It wasn't like you."

Miranda replayed bits of her performance, trying to pinpoint what Heather was referring to. What did she do wrong? She had no idea, and that made it worse.

"I'm so sorry," Miranda said. "Were there any specific moments that stood out?"

"You just generally seemed to be going through the motions. Everyone has an off day. I'm not worried about tomorrow. I just wanted to check in with you." Heather leaned forward and smiled softly. "A theater is not the place to bottle anything up. You're always welcome to come talk to me if something's on your mind. The Olympus theatre community, we're kind of like one big family."

Miranda wondered how a stepping stone could be a family.

She hated thinking of them in such terms. They were such lovely people, the ones she had met so far. Anyone would be lucky to consider them family. Some people no longer had family because they were dead.

Miranda squashed that thought at once and focused on listening to Heather.

"Anything you're going through, you can let us in. We're all here for each other."

Bianca had offered similar advice—let someone in, anyone.

"I appreciate that." Miranda truly did. "I've just been

feeling a little worn down the past couple of days." What a fine way to show her appreciation—a bald-faced lie. "I'll go home, rest up, and come back refreshed tomorrow. All will be well." Bianca had also mentioned something about a tendency to deflect, hadn't she?

"I'm sure it will," Heather said. "I trust you."

Miranda thanked her and flashed her most charming, most convincing smile.

As she exited the theater, she kept trying to diagnose what went wrong during the rehearsal. Normally, she would have been hyperaware of any stumbles, flubs, or low-energy scenes. But how did she let a man die right in front of her?

She wasn't thinking about that now. She was just walking toward the subway, pretending everything was normal as she kept checking every alley she passed. More than once, she flinched when excess street lighting glinted off any random piece of metal.

She realized her phone was in her hand, and she had started a new text message to Bianca.

Just let her in, she told herself. Let someone in, and why not her? Type a message, hit send, and done. No chickening out like with Alyssa. Alyssa could run away from Miranda's life, but family couldn't.

Miranda typed, *Call me next time you're alone. Something important for your ears only.*

Her finger hovered over the send button.

Ten minutes later, after having bypassed the subway by flying to her apartment, Miranda hit send.

23

The phone sat on the coffee table, dim and silent.

Miranda hadn't told Bianca anything yet. It wasn't too late to back out, invent some other reason for the cryptic text. Curled up on her couch, she watched the phone as her apartment gradually darkened. She could have turned on a light but didn't bother.

What if the text didn't actually send? Or there was a delay and it would arrive in Bianca's inbox a day later? Then Miranda would spend all that time dwelling, going over and over in her mind exactly how she would break the news that Bianca was related to Ultra Woman.

How much would she tell her? How much would Bianca want to know?

The phone rang. Miranda considered letting it go to voicemail.

She brought this on herself, was about to bring this on Bianca, giving her sister the irresistible combination of concern and curiosity.

Half a second before the call went to voicemail, Miranda answered.

"Hey," she said.

Silence, then: "That's all you've got for me?" Bianca

said. "I receive this ominous text, and just 'hey'?"

"You have to promise not to tell anyone. No one."

"I need to know what it is first."

"Then I'm not telling."

"Too late. You have to tell me now."

"Nope."

"In that case," Bianca said with calculated patience, "I'll keep bugging you until you tell me."

"Then I'll hang up."

"You try that."

"Okay."

Miranda hung up.

The phone rang. And rang.

Miranda picked up. "Just promise me you won't tell anyone! How hard is that?"

"Very. Secrets are corrosive. There are studies in which—"

"I'm trying to let you in on a secret. Isn't this exactly the advice you had for me?"

"Not exactly. I advised you to let someone into your life, not to construct an elaborate network of selective honesty."

As obnoxious as Bianca was being, Miranda found their bickering refreshingly normal, like time had shifted back ten years.

"It's not elaborate," Miranda said. "I'm just telling you."

"And I, in turn, need to remember not to slip up

around anyone ever, or else, God forbid, the wrong person might learn the wrong thing about your life."

"I could've told you my thing like twenty times over already. If you want my secret, I need your promise."

A pause. "I suppose that's a reasonable exchange. Fine. I'll let your secret fester within me until I receive your consent to tell another living soul."

"Thank you," Miranda said. "Now, you've seen the news about Ultra Woman, right?"

"Yes, you're all over the news."

"Wait, what?"

"Oops. Did I slip?" A soft laugh slipped through the phone. "Are you sure I'm the one you want to tell this to?"

"You knew? How did you know?"

Miranda had no trouble picturing the giant grin Bianca was undoubtedly wearing.

"We have basically the same nose," Bianca said. "So when I saw our nose on Ultra Woman's face, I knew she had to be one of us. And I was pretty sure she wasn't me. Oh, and I've known you for the length of my entire memory, so that also helped."

"Who else knows? Do Mom and Dad—"

"No, their denial will protect your secret. Peyton's blinded by hero worship. I'm guessing your friends are too self-centered. I'm really the only one you can't fool."

Miranda remembered why she had hesitated in telling her, not that it ultimately mattered, apparently.

"If you already knew, why were you being so difficult?"

"Because you've taken whole days to tell me. Like I wouldn't figure it out. Come on." Bianca took a breath. Her playfulness departed, and no judgment or mockery took its place, only genuine concern. "So what exactly is going on? How did this happen?"

Miranda told her everything, from the encounter at Mount Olympus through Hoskins's murder and the subsequent meeting with Fantastic Man and Mr. Amazing. The more she unburdened, the lighter she felt. Never before had she held in so much information, certainly never information this intense.

Bianca listened without interruption, and she remained quiet even as Miranda finished.

"So?" Miranda asked, wondering if the connection had failed. "What are you thinking?"

"I don't like this Fantastic Man. I'm getting a bad vibe about him."

"My options for allies are pretty limited."

"Not really. With these new abilities, you could join any police department in the country, or the FBI, CIA."

Those suggestions nauseated Miranda—any one of those jobs would become all-consuming.

"Doesn't even have to be law enforcement," Bianca continued. "NASA could find all sorts of uses for your new resilience and speed. This opens up so many doors."

"Those places all have bosses and bureaucracies."

"Welcome to adulthood. Besides, didn't Fantastic Man just appoint himself your boss? And don't you have directors telling you what to do in your shows?"

"That's different."

"Because you have fawning audiences to pat you on the back for a job well done?"

Miranda clenched her teeth. "Shut up."

"Such an intelligent rebuttal."

This was a mistake, Miranda thought. Maybe she should've taken the chance with Alyssa after all.

"Sorry I'm not a super-selfless medical student like you are," Miranda said.

"Miri, you're already showing you're not selfish. I just don't want you to limit yourself. Don't hide behind some mask, or goggles as the case may be. Sounds like this Fantastic Man is the one being selfish, trying to mold everything to suit his preferences."

"Well, he doesn't seem to mind taking on the weight of the world. Better him than me. See? Selfish."

Bianca sighed. "I'll come over to Olympus. I've still got a little more time before classes start."

"No, no. I don't want you to come all this way, especially after you were just here."

"Yeah. You could've told me then."

"I didn't know a tenth of this stuff then. But no—do not come here. You have your own life to worry about. I just needed to tell someone. I've told someone. Thank you for your service."

"I'm coming—"

"No. Someone might be trying to kill me." That sounded so weird to say aloud. Her hands were shaking. "I don't want you anywhere near me. Please, please promise me you won't come. I don't want to have to worry about you on top of everything else."

"*I'm* supposed to worry about *you*. Who else will? The boys hiding behind their masks?"

"I'm bulletproof. Are you?"

A long pause.

"Okay, fine," Bianca said. "I concede that you have the more compelling argument."

"And you promise not to tell anyone about any of this?"

"I'll promise that if *you* promise to eventually tell everyone. Let the world see who Ultra Woman really is."

That would be so anticlimactic for the world, Miranda thought. *Who's Ultra Woman? Oh, just this nobody.*

Bianca continued, "You deserve for everyone to see who you are."

"I can't even think about that now."

"I understand if you need to table it for the time being, but once you resolve the current crisis, think about it. Okay?"

Perhaps thinking couldn't hurt. Thinking obligated her to nothing.

"Fine," Miranda said. "So you're not coming, you're

not telling anyone, and I'll maybe rethink the secret identity at some later point."

"Not really an even deal there."

Miranda's instinct was to mutter something snarky. Sincerity won out instead. "Thank you for listening, Bianca."

"I'm glad you reached out. I truly am. Call me anytime you need me. You can promise that, right?"

Miranda hesitated. "Sure."

She didn't believe herself, but Bianca didn't press any further.

24

Ken picked exactly the wrong coffee shop. One block over, the street was closed off for filming of the movie Miranda had gotten fired from. It may not have been meaningful work experience, utterly trivial in light of recent events, but it stung and would continue to sting until she had achieved a sufficient level of professional success that she could gaze back upon it as an amusing little anecdote, a cute before-they-were-stars story to get a laugh from a talk show's audience.

The uncomfortable reminder served another purpose, though. Coffee with a friend was supposed to be Miranda Thomas time, not Ultra Woman time. The movie's proximity helped her revert to the proper state of mind. Instead of dwelling on an unidentified murderer who was still on the loose, she got to dwell on her looming failure.

Miranda doubted anyone would recognize her from that one partial day of background acting, certainly not on this crowded sidewalk, where many curious souls had stationed themselves just outside the designated filming area. They craned their necks for any glimpse of the action, for any brief celebrity sighting to add excitement to their day.

Tuck Lewis would be there, she realized. Would he recognize her? From that single half a minute of interaction? Nah, the big star probably forgot all about her two seconds afterward.

With effort, Miranda refrained from using her superspeed to more quickly distance herself from the onlookers.

She entered Mug Shots, delighted in the coffee shop's pleasing aroma, and found Ken waiting at a small table near the window façade.

He stood up and smiled gently. "Miranda. Good to see you again."

"So sorry I'm late. The movie's made a mess of this whole area. I had to walk all the way around the block with a whole bunch of slow people. I'm really not sure how they could have been any slower."

Miranda realized she was overplaying her tardiness. This was just Ken. He was safe and nonjudgmental. She could relax.

"It's okay," he said. "It's been nice and peaceful in here."

It was relatively quiet, just a few lone coffee drinkers working on their laptops or scrolling through their phones. Mug Shots, though not vast, was roomy enough to give everyone the illusion of personal space.

As they took their seats, Ken said, "I'm surprised you're not involved in that movie."

She thought about mentioning her random firing. It

might break the ice. Or depress the mood. She erred on the side of not being depressing.

"Well, I can't do everything, now can I?" She pointed at the barren table surface between them. "We have no coffee, which means we're basically stealing this table."

"Then I guess we should order something and restore our innocence."

They went to the counter and did just that. While they awaited their beverages, Miranda noticed that Ken seemed rather tense compared to last time, verging of stiffness. His jaw tightened, like he was about to say something but couldn't bring himself to speak.

"So what's going on with you?" Miranda asked. "The other day it sounded like things were looking up."

"Oh, well, I thought I had figured something out. Turns out it's a little more complicated than I initially figured."

"And what was this something?"

He looked into her eyes, saying nothing.

"Ken? You okay?"

A barista set their drinks on the counter.

"Yeah, sorry," Ken said as they grabbed their espressos. "It's, um, just a tutoring gig. I thought that would be my ticket, freelance tutoring. But it's hard to string together enough hours to make it profitable. So I'm sort of back at square one."

"I'm sorry."

They returned to their table, silently. Was this a lull already?

"What about you?" Ken asked. "Any major developments in your life these past few days?"

Miranda contemplated an honest response. "Nah, I'm pretty boring. Just got my show, and I'm always looking for the next one."

And ... silence. Such awkward silence, and so soon.

She needed to say something. But what? They had already covered all the basics earlier in the week, and all interesting new developments were off limits.

Why did she have to carry the conversation, though? Ken could contribute. But he kept glancing out the window, an intense expression creeping across his face.

So Miranda followed his gaze. "Something fascinating out there?" She saw many of the same people as before, still gawking in search of anything thrilling.

Ken turned away from the window. "Sorry. Shiny object distracted me, but it's nothing. So, um, I saw in the news something about an electrical man exploding in the middle of a street. Were you anywhere near there?"

She quickly shook her head. "Um, no. You?"

"No, I only saw it in the news." Which he had just said. "Miraculously, he didn't kill anybody. Several injuries, according to the report, lots of property damage, but all victims are expected to pull through. And it seems it's all thanks to Ultra Woman."

Miranda had kept up with the news and already knew the victims were recovering, but hearing it again, she nearly smiled.

She stifled her relief, then stifled her guilt as she recalled the sole fatality of that day. A poker face suppressed it all, leaving only a generically pleased reaction, the same that anyone with a heart would show. "That's so good to hear."

More awkward silence followed. Ken's eyebrows lowered, and his pupils shifted toward the window, then back to Miranda.

"What do you think of Ultra Woman?" he asked, appearing genuinely curious.

She took a sip to stall. Did he suspect? Ken wasn't one of those "self-centered" friends Bianca had alluded to. If he saw a clear picture of Ultra Woman, he could very well have noticed the resemblance, just as Bianca had. Miranda needed a better disguise, or she needed to be honest. Was this a test? It was possible he was just grasping for something to talk about.

"She seems tough." Miranda felt so immodest. "Glad she's not evil."

"That would be unfortunate," Ken said. "I get the impression she's a good person, though. From the footage I've seen."

"Then let's hope you're an excellent judge of character."

This was her last chance. All she had to do was whisper *Because I'm Ultra Woman.*

But the killer was still out there somewhere. What if he hurt Ken trying to get to Ultra Woman? What if he was in this coffee shop, one of these random people working on their laptops? That barista with the fuzzy goatee looked kind of shifty—was he the killer? It could have been any guy in Olympus except for Ken. Maybe even a woman with a disguised voice.

Ken was looking out the window again. Miranda feared she was simply that engaging.

The Mug Shots doors opened, and a commotion flooded in, led by a familiar, boisterous voice.

"Caffeine's on me, boys and girls," the man told his group. "Get whatever you want."

Tuck Lewis had entered the coffee shop with an entourage of the film's crew, at least twenty in total. They formed a line from the counter to the door, filling the place with their bodies and their chatter. Miranda recognized a few; no reason they'd recognize her, she hoped.

Thus, the peaceful atmosphere died, but now Miranda and Ken had new conversational fodder.

"You see who that is, right?" Miranda said, keeping her voice low.

It took Ken a second. "Oh, yeah. That guy."

Miranda grimaced. "'That guy'?"

"I think I've seen him in a couple of things."

"He's been in a whole bunch of things."

"I don't watch many things."

Miranda wagged a finger. "Shame."

Without looking directly at him, they observed as Tuck bonded with the crew and charmed the baristas. The man knew what he was doing. His posture was relaxed enough to lessen any intimidation factor, and he occasionally established brief physical contact—a quick touch to the arm or friendly shoulder pat.

He was improving the day of everyone around him, and doing so involved not a single life-or-death struggle. It was a power Miranda wished she possessed.

At least she had something to talk about now. She was about to rattle off a dozen or so movies Ken needed to see at the earliest opportunity. She opened her mouth, then saw he wasn't paying attention. Again.

"I'm sorry. I just remembered—I have a tutoring job across town." He glanced at his cell phone. "Have to be there very soon."

"Oh." Miranda had no idea what to say. Absent-mindedness wasn't like him. Didn't used to be, anyway.

"Forgot I had to bump it up earlier—I am so sorry, but I have to go."

He was already going.

Miranda could have gotten him across town in plenty of time, if indeed he was rushing to a job. "Um, see you around, Ken," she said quickly. "Be careful getting there."

And he was gone, with only a barely sipped cup of

coffee remaining as evidence of his visit.

Miranda scared him away. She didn't know what else to assume. This coffee get-together was initially her idea, not his, and he was simply too nice to blow her off. And when it got too awkward, he choked up and bolted.

So, dating Ken—bad call, clearly not meant to be. Best to just stop right here, not try to push it any further, and maybe in a few months they might run into each other and pretend today never happened.

Ready to move on, she grabbed her cup, stood up, and nearly collided with Tuck Lewis.

"Hey, I know you," he said, with a casual, lopsided grin. "You were the jogger girl the other day, right?"

She was so very thankful she hadn't spilled her cup on him. "Um, yeah. Hi."

Everyone was staring at her—who was this random young woman Tuck Lewis decided to chat up? Or more likely, who was this *latest* young woman he decided to chat up?

He remembered her, though. Miranda decided to focus on that rather than the crew's judgment.

Tuck turned back to his people. "Go on ahead. I'll catch up soon."

They obeyed. Those who had their drinks started filing out the coffee shop.

"Are you in a hurry?" Tuck asked her. "I don't want to hold you up if you were rushing out with your boyfriend."

"Um, no. He's not—" She remembered how positively not witty she was last time. "I have a minute." She was off to *such* a better start.

He gestured to the table she had just vacated. "May I?"

"Yeah, sure."

Claiming Ken's seat, he slid the abandoned beverage aside and set his own latte there. "So, quick question. The other day, were you there for a hobby, a vocation, or a calling?"

"Calling," she said quickly, sitting back down.

"Okay." He pulled a business card from his pocket and set it on the table. "Give my assistant a call. Let's set up a meeting, see if I can get you a foot in the door."

Miranda slowly pulled the card toward her as she wondered, *Why me?* But she was afraid to ask. Mercifully, he answered the unspoken question.

"Look, I know how unfair life can be and how tough this business is, so I like to give back where I can. Don't think of it as charity—your success is ultimately up to you. All I can do is make sure you get a fair shot."

Miranda suspected this was simply Tuck Lewis's way of hitting on aspiring young actresses—be useful, earn gratitude, leverage that gratitude into a sexual relationship. If so, it struck her as an icky way to go about things. If he wanted to date her, all he had to do was ask. He was Tuck Lewis, after all.

From what she had read in the entertainment magazines, Tuck always seemed to treat people decently. The perennial bachelor had had a lot of girlfriends, but Miranda couldn't recall a single scandal involving the man.

Whatever his intentions, she needed help from someone with influence and she had no idea what better chance she'd get.

"Thank you," she said. "This is very generous."

"Eh, honestly, I'm being selfish." Tuck glanced out the window as he dismissed any possibility of altruism, then turned right back to her. "Got to feel like a decent human being somehow, don't I? So give my guy a call and help me feel like a productive good citizen. Truly, you'd be doing me a favor." He rose from his seat and, as an afterthought, said, "Oh, I never caught your name."

"Miranda Thomas."

He shook her hand. "Nice to meet you, Miranda. Hope to hear from you soon."

He left, and Miranda lingered for a few silent minutes, convincing herself that this had indeed happened. At some point, she had started smiling.

Some commotion outside. Police officers were arresting three people across the street. What the hell happened, and how had she missed it? Was she needed? Apparently not.

She stared at the business card and calculated the appropriate interval of time to wait before calling.

Her random firing might turn into an amusing anecdote after all.

25

The smell of burnt leather conquered the apartment.

Ultra Woman's shirt and jeans were easy enough to replace. Miranda had long ago discovered thrift stores to be an indispensable resource. But neon-green leather was hard to come by in her price range, especially if each jacket lasted only days. All of two minutes after she returned home from her awkward date, she marched up to the roof and threw on her costume.

First thing tomorrow morning, she'd call Tuck's assistant and get a meeting scheduled. The very thought propelled her off the roof. But was he sincere? Was he playing some cruel practical joke? Miranda tried to suppress all such thoughts. Her future was happening, provided she didn't screw it up.

Miranda embarked on a late-afternoon flight to blow the stink off her jacket, and during her aerial wandering she stumbled upon a few situations in need of ultra-help.

She saved a kid from drowning in the ocean, caught a falling steelworker, and functioned as a human version of the Jaws of Life to free a driver from a car wreck. Each good deed was straightforward. Malice played no role; the dangers resulted from mere accidents. Good clean wins, except that her jacket reeked the whole time. She didn't hang around anywhere long enough for people to inquire about the blatant scorch marks.

As long as she kept flying, the odor couldn't reach her nose, for she was Ultra Woman, faster than the speed of smell!

Soaring at her own pace, Miranda wove between buildings and swooped down to wave hello to excited pedestrians. She wanted to stop and bask in the attention, but not with the damaged jacket. Instead, she veered straight up, rising until she achieved solitude in the clouds.

She slowed down and savored the sky. Refreshing breeze, invigorating sunshine, total freedom of movement—like swimming in the most relaxing pool ever, one she had all to herself.

She turned her head exactly the wrong way, and the jacket's scorch marks appeared in her peripheral vision.

It was almost time to meet up at Hephaestus Enterprises. Being early couldn't hurt, and if Fantastic Man and Mr. Amazing were early, too, they could wrap this up quickly. She was also curious to meet Fantastic Man's "friend." Most importantly, though, she did need to be at the theater in just over an hour.

Miranda took off her jacket, and it flapped in the breeze as she held it at arm's length. Was the jacket a necessary costuming element? A more traditional superhero look *was* an option ...

Or why not streamline? Ultra Woman could be the casual lady in red, one with an affinity for distinctive eyewear.

A municipal landfill was directly below, on a peninsula at the city's northern tip. She could drop the jacket there and be rid of the unpleasant stench forever.

The scorch marks pulled her eyes toward them, and a pinching sensation developed on her abdomen where the robot's laser had struck.

She let go.

The jacket tumbled through the air, its sleeves coming alive as the wind filled them. It descended toward the garbage, sinking deeper through the sky, shrinking out of view ...

Flames engulfed the jacket—flames spewed from the mouth of a dragon.

Miranda lifted her goggles.

Green. Scaly. Reptilian. Winged. Twice the size of an adult human. Possessed of four meaty limbs, plus a plump tail. Internal combustion system included.

Dragon.

Miranda had a few questions.

She dove down and aligned her flight with the dragon's. Maintaining a respectable distance, she waved hello at the beast.

"Um, hi!" she shouted, though she felt stupid trying

to speak to a creature that was supposed to be mythical. What to say to a dragon? "Can I help you?" Probably not that, she decided after the fact.

The dragon turned its long head. Its deep-set, ruby eyes locked on to her. The snout opened. A furnace burned within.

Miranda evaded the flames but swerved directly into the dragon's second attack. The tail whipped forth and slammed into her stomach.

Pain, wind, a splash, and she was underwater without much air in her lungs.

Finding the light, Miranda swam up and gulped the oxygen. The coast was farther away than she had expected, maybe a full mile.

The dragon's fluttering, bat-like wings carried it farther inland.

Huh. So that just happened.

It simply didn't feel real. A dragon. Like a fairy tale, but one starring Ultra Woman as everyone's knight clad in an armor of super-powers.

She launched herself from the water and into the city. The dragon was easy to find. It had perched itself atop Mount Olympus, where the creature spread its wings to full extension, a span the length of a house. Craning its neck toward the sky, it vomited fire at the clouds, then bellowed an inhuman roar, all of which impressed the crowd below to the point of terror.

The park's many visitors gaped at the dragon. They stood in a collective, dumbfounded trance until the first among them began to rush away, influencing others to flee, then more. The domino effect soon encompassed everyone on the ground, propelling them in all directions from the tower. A few runners kept glancing back, but fear ultimately overrode all curiosity.

The observation deck was a different matter. The dozen or so people seemed uncertain whether to stay put behind the protective grates or hop on the elevator at once. The decision was not unanimous.

Miranda, unaware of any protocol for dealing with fantasy creatures, advanced cautiously. She worried her clothes would drip onto the fleeing people, so she was relieved to find she had mostly dried out during the flight over. It was much easier to think about courtesy than contemplate a dragon battle.

"Ultra Woman."

"Who the hell?" Miranda spun around, throwing her hands up in a defensive posture.

"It's just me," Mr. Amazing said, floating toward her. "Please don't attack again."

Miranda lowered her arms. "Sorry. Not used to company up here."

Mr. Amazing wore the same blank mask and tweed suit jacket as last time, but over jeans and a nondescript tee-shirt. Hard to dress up on a moment's notice, it seemed.

"Where'd the dragon come from?" he asked.

"Its parents maybe? Oh, God. I hope we don't meet its parents."

"Should we ... confront it? How does this work?"

More flame cut across the sky, and dark smoke dissipated in its wake. But nothing caught fire. The dragon wasn't attacking—it was posturing, as far as Miranda could tell. However, she wasn't all that confident in her ability to evaluate such a creature's motives.

"All I know is I don't want to be the one to make it mad," she said.

Tightening its grip, the dragon twisted hard and tugged at the structure. The beast grunted, and the metal screeched. The horrific sound impaled Miranda's eardrums, and her teeth became tuning forks.

She shot forth, hoping to wrestle the dragon off its perch, but it blasted fire from side to side, forcing her to abort the attack.

The dragon again wrenched the tower. The upper quarter of Mount Olympus bent toward the sun, like a flower, and everyone on the observation deck slid toward the grate. The roof ornamentation, a pointed metal spire that resembled a giant spear, broke off in the dragon's claws.

The elevator's pulley system snapped; the car plummeted.

Ultra Woman and Mr. Amazing sprang into action—

and into each other, eliciting a loud groan from the latter. Miranda inadvertently elbowed her new colleague in his side, knocking him into a downward spiral. She feared she sank the poor guy—feared she'd have to choose between him and the people in the elevator.

"I'm fine!" he yelled up as he stopped his own fall. "Go!"

Those people had no time for her to do otherwise. She hoped it was still enough time.

Against all common sense, Miranda swooped in and positioned herself beneath the crashing elevator car. Lighter than plastic, it fell into her flat hands, and she slowed its descent, well aware that if only she had acted faster, she could have saved Mount Olympus and averted this entire calamity. She berated herself as she lowered the elevator to the ground.

Right before reaching the bottom, Miranda kicked open the outer doors—one thrust of her leg, and the crumpled metal blew outward. What was a little more damage?

The city's skyline—forever altered. Even if the municipal government repaired the tower, it would never look quite the same again. Something would be different.

The elevator's three frazzled passengers hopped out and rushed down the brick path.

But one, an older man, paused for a second and shook his rescuer's hand. "Thank you, Ultra Woman."

A tower could be rebuilt, Miranda realized.

She was about to check on the observation deck, but that proved unnecessary.

Mr. Amazing floated toward the ground, and eight people floated in front of and around him, his telekinesis carrying them to safety.

The spectacle entranced Miranda. This feat should have been impossible—it only recently *was* impossible. She wondered if she looked that incredible in action.

His younger passengers, a few elementary-aged children, laughed and waved their arms high. Mr. Amazing had turned a frightening experience into a ride superior to any amusement park's. The adult passengers, the ones more familiar with the basic rules of reality, appeared considerably more nervous as their legs dangled over nothing, but relief swept over all faces as they reconnected with a solid surface.

They stared at him, and their expressions were mixed—awestruck, skeptical, frozen with terror. And he stood there, hardly more animated than a cardboard cutout.

"You're all safe now," he said, matter-of-fact, almost gruff.

Not a single expression changed. Saving their lives didn't automatically earn their trust. Granted, the past few minutes gave them much to process.

Miranda stepped in. "I see you've all met my new

buddy Mr. Amazing. He's still working on his social graces, but he's one of the good guys."

She was vouching for someone she barely knew— someone she didn't know at all, come to think of it—just like Fantastic Man had vouched for her. But given that a dragon was on the loose and making off with a piece of a significant landmark, now was not the time to wallow in feelings of hypocrisy.

"He's going to help me tame the dragon," Miranda continued, "which we really need to get on, like right now. Can't have creatures like that flying around thinking they can just tear up our towers. Mount Olympus will not go unavenged!"

She lifted off, and Mr. Amazing took the cue to follow.

"Are you okay?" she asked him. "Sorry about the elbow."

"Think nothing of it."

The structure didn't look like it was about to topple— no sounds of creaking metal or anything else that signi-fied an immediate hazard. But it would be a long time before anyone once again enjoyed the view from Mount Olympus.

"I always liked coming here," she said.

"Yeah," Mr. Amazing said. "So did I."

26

The dragon dipped toward the traffic, swerved skyward, and leveled itself between office windows fifty stories up. Fender benders trailed its path, though the creature gave no reaction to the thuds and crashes. Nor did it pay much attention to the spire's proximity to the buildings. So far, the tip came no closer than a few feet from the glass. The workers on the other side, however, might have appreciated a wider margin.

As she flew after the dragon, Miranda wondered how much thought she should put into this. Did fighting a dragon require a detailed strategy? Or would it be better to dive in and run on instinct before giving herself the slightest chance to contemplate the danger?

She turned to Mr. Amazing to get his opinion but found him lagging a full block behind her. She considered waiting for him to catch up. Then the spire veered toward another window, swinging within inches of catastrophe.

No more time for thinking.

Miranda zoomed forth, wrapped her arms around the dragon's long neck, and squeezed.

This was the way to go, she decided—don't think, just act.

The dragon bucked and flung her off, sending Miranda flying through an office window and crashing against an interior wall.

The wall sustained more damage than Miranda did, and she was thankful she hadn't collided with a person. That hypothetical fatality paralyzed her, until she noticed the heads poking up from their cubicles and staring at her. They, too, were rigid in their fear, unwilling to move until someone provided clear guidance on what was happening and what to do—that someone being Miranda, who had yet to figure out what she herself should do.

As they were focused on Miranda, the employees failed to see the dragon flapping toward their long window.

"Everyone down!" Miranda yelled, and just in time.

The spire smashed through. Still in the dragon's grip, it sliced across the window at head level. The screams nearly drowned out the shattering glass, but everyone ducked in time, thereby avoiding serious injury.

Then the dragon chopped straight down, slicing the spire through a few floors. As their surface bent inward, a pair of workers tumbled out the newly open window.

Miranda rushed across the room and leapt after them, face-first. She saw a young man and young woman in freefall, neither much older than herself. Further beyond, the sidewalk.

The wind picked up as she boosted her speed. Her

screaming targets grew closer, as did the pavement, but Miranda preferred not to dwell on the latter just yet.

She grabbed their wrists and carefully reduced her speed, angling their descent to lengthen the deceleration as they flailed in her grasp.

"Easy!" Miranda said. "I've got you!"

They screamed nevertheless.

Miranda gently deposited them on the sidewalk, which was littered with debris. Thankfully, most pedestrians had already sought shelter. She checked that the pair were okay, then looked to the sky.

Mr. Amazing and the dragon were faced off, slowly rotating while locked in a tug-of-war over the spire high in the air. His telekinesis failed to pry it away, but he kept the creature occupied.

"Clear the area!" Miranda called out to all remaining bystanders. To appear more authoritative, she increased her height by floating, and she again wondered who the hell decided to give her any authority whatsoever. Someone did *not* think that through.

The dragon spat fire at Mr. Amazing, forcing him to drop out of the way and break concentration. The telekinetic grip severed, the dragon recoiled and slammed against the corner of a brick building. A hefty chunk of masonry, about the size of a person, plunged toward the sidewalk.

Miranda swooped in and caught it. Her first instinct

was to throw it at the dragon, but she worried about it breaking into smaller pieces and hurting people below. That momentary indecision curtailed all action, reducing her to an easy target.

The dragon's tail whacked her across the head, and she dropped the debris. Before she could lunge for it, the dragon pounced on her. Though she was fending off talons, all she could think about was accelerated brick squishing someone.

Mr. Amazing prevented that scenario. His telekinesis played catcher's mitt, then lobbed it onto the nearest available rooftop.

Miranda punched the dragon in the snout and pulled away, knowing she'd have to reengage soon. First they needed a strategy. No, first they needed *time* to strategize.

Light flashed on a rooftop. Miranda was wondering when he'd finally arrive. She flew right over, and Mr. Amazing followed.

Fantastic Man stood confidently, a foot planted on the ledge and cape flapping to the side as he studied the angry dragon down the street.

"Let's make this snappy, team," he said the instant they landed. "My task will be to lure the dragon upward, away from collateral damage, at which point I'll blind the beast. Then, Ultra Woman, you attack it. Mr. Amazing, it will drop the spire—don't let it fall on any civilians. Go!"

Fantastic Man vanished. A pool of shimmering light

appeared before the dragon's eyes, then shot straight up. The dragon chased after it, rising higher than the skyscrapers.

Happy to have a plan to follow—one she didn't have to concoct herself—Miranda flew up, watching for her cue to strike.

Fantastic Man's glare enveloped the dragon's head and kept pulsing at irregular intervals. The dragon thrashed about, its eyes squeezed tight. It roared and, as predicted, dropped the spire.

Mr. Amazing dove for the catch, and Miranda barreled into the dragon.

The dragon retaliated by whipping its tail, but Miranda was prepared for it this time. She evaded, then clocked the dragon on the snout to discourage any flame attacks.

But she neglected its arm, which was half as big as she was. The dragon batted her away, rattling her jaw, but she swung back around, her fists leading the charge.

The glare intensified, distracting the creature long enough for Miranda to deliver her strongest blow.

The impact boomed like cannon fire, and though the dragon shrieked in pain, its leathery skin was dense enough to send a painful jolt up Miranda's arm.

It felt great, felt like progress.

Miranda battled the dragon high above the city. It continued blindly throwing fire, huge arms, and a tail at her, and she maneuvered away from each attack, then returned with a mighty punch. Strike, withdraw, strike, withdraw.

Her arms were getting sore, but she had this.

This dragon thought it could just come into her city and do whatever the hell it wanted? Endanger lives without consequence? Put itself above everyone and everything else?

POW!

The dragon fell.

It took her a moment to accept the fact that she punched out a dragon. Then Miranda slipped beneath the limp, plummeting body and caught it. The bulk handled awkwardly, but she managed.

Mr. Amazing had set the spire in the middle of the road, blocking all traffic behind it but creating a still-lengthening stretch of vacant pavement in front. Miranda dropped the unconscious dragon there.

Floating before it, she admired her handiwork and had to laugh. That defeated dragon right there? She did that.

She landed near Mr. Amazing, and Fantastic Man materialized between them.

"Great work, team!" he said, clasping each one's shoulder. "A stellar debut for the Terrific Trio!"

Miranda flexed her sore hands to relieve their stinging. The name didn't feel right to her. It felt limiting.

She started to ask, "Are you sure that's—"

Bystanders cautiously emerged from buildings and vehicles, and Miranda wasn't sure what reception these people would give.

The people aimed their cell phones at the three oddly dressed individuals standing before the unconscious dragon and Mount Olympus's spire. The superhero equivalent of the red carpet, apparently.

Miranda feared the dragon might wake up. It didn't— yet. Its chest was rising and falling, but the eyes were shut tight and the creature didn't so much as fidget. Did it? No.

"Citizens of Olympus City," Fantastic Man called out. "You have nothing to fear. No matter what peculiar menaces threaten our home, the Terrific Trio stand ready to defend you! You can always count on Ultra Woman, Mr. Amazing, and myself to fight for your safety!"

Miranda succeeded in not cringing at the name. She hoped it would serve merely as a starting point. Surely they would find a fourth member before long and need to revise it.

With a flourish of his cape, Fantastic Man turned toward his teammates and whispered, "Let's rendezvous at Hephaestus Enterprises as planned. Bring the dragon and spire. We must set a good example and clean up our messes."

Miranda wondered how this was her mess. She defeated the dragon, so she won responsibility for it?

Fantastic Man waved at the crowd and dematerialized into a glittering luminescence that ascended
skyward.

Miranda also smiled and waved. Mr. Amazing instead
faced their cargo.

"I could try to carry both," he said, though he didn't
sound confident about it.

"It's okay," Miranda said. "The dragon's mine."

27

Plenty of daylight remained. Nevertheless, Fantastic Man illuminated a landing strip along the Hephaestus Enterprises parking lot. Only two cars remained on the premises, so it would hardly inconvenience anyone if the lot doubled as a dragon's bed.

Miranda gently set the creature down on the pavement, and she checked to make sure it remained asleep.

It snored. It smelled like burnt fish. But it didn't awaken.

The spire thudded as it landed, creating another pothole. The dragon stirred, the eyes opened halfway, Miranda started to panic—and it continued sleeping.

"Sorry," Mr. Amazing muttered.

"If you wake it," she said with a crooked grin, "then it's your turn to put it to sleep."

The extra lighting congealed into Fantastic Man, marching straight for the main entrance.

"This way, team," he said. "There's someone I'd like you to meet."

Miranda pointed at the dragon. "Um ..."

"We'll keep it within our line of sight." Fantastic Man proceeded forth.

The Terrific Trio entered a tight, utilitarian lobby, which contained little more than a few plastic chairs and a receptionist's desk that had already been vacated for the night. On the far side, a security keypad was affixed to a door, beneath a small window.

"I'll go fetch Dr. Luna," Fantastic Man said, right before disappearing through that window.

Miranda and Mr. Amazing stood awkwardly in the lobby. Both immediately turned to the exterior window to check on the dragon. Still out.

"So how much do you want to bet," Miranda said, smirking, "that this Dr. Luna winds up bearing a striking resemblance to Fantastic Man?"

Mr. Amazing's chuckle sounded more like a grunt as it filtered through his mask. "Yeah, I've been wondering how he expects to fool us," he said.

"Maybe we won't notice that only Dr. Luna walks through that door."

"And we'll think nothing of it when Dr. Luna goes to get Fantastic Man, and only Fantastic Man returns."

"Of course not. Why on earth would that seem suspicious?" Miranda checked outside. The dragon hadn't moved, but the longer she stared at it, the more her smile eroded. "He may be counting on the dragon to distract us from the obvious. That actually could be an effective ploy."

A hand landed softly on her shoulder. She flinched, and Mr. Amazing removed it at once.

"We can stop it again if we need to," Mr. Amazing said. "I'm sure Fantastic Man has a reason for bringing it here. I doubt he's that divorced from reality."

"But how do we know he's not?" Miranda asked.

The door clicked as it opened, and a bespectacled woman in a lab coat entered, smiling warmly.

"Hi, I'm Cadelaria Luna, but please call me Cadee. Welcome to Hephaestus Enterprises."

Fantastic Man was nowhere to be seen. Miranda wasn't sure which would make her feel stupider—suspecting that this woman was somehow Fantastic Man, or *not* suspecting it. She was rapidly losing track of what was and wasn't possible.

Noticing Miranda's confusion, Cadee explained, "Oh, your ... associate, or whatever you'd call him, he said he wanted to check on something. And then he disappeared. It's really annoying when he does that. Anyway, I have something for you."

Cadee handed flip phones to Miranda and Mr. Amazing. Miranda tried not to look too underwhelmed. Outdated though it was, the phone displayed the time. Miranda still had half an hour before anyone at the theater would miss her.

"Don't let him make up any cute nickname for these," Cadee said. "They're basic old cell phones, nothing fancy."

"Thanks. And it's nice to meet you." Miranda glanced out at the sleeping dragon, then turned back to Cadee.

"So how do you know Fantastic Man?"

Cadee's eyes widened as she followed Miranda's out the window. "What is *that*?"

"The dragon?" Miranda said. "Did he not mention the dragon?"

Mr. Amazing's face fell into his palm.

"No," Cadee said, adjusting her glasses and sucking in a sharp breath. "He most certainly did not."

The two superheroes followed her as she stormed outside.

In a flash, Fantastic Man appeared beside Cadee. She didn't flinch, but she did clench her fingers like she wanted to wring a certain someone's neck.

Fantastic Man started, "Dr. Luna! I—"

"You brought a dragon here? How? How is there a dragon?" Her eyes landed on the large spire. "And what's that?"

"The spire of Mount Olympus," Fantastic Man said casually. "My apologies for the inconvenience, but we—"

"What happened to Mount Olympus?"

"The dragon happened."

Cadee flung her arms up, and she continued approaching the creature. "How does a dragon happen to anything? Did it hurt anyone?"

"We ensured it did not. Now be careful," Fantastic Man advised. "It's merely unconscious."

"Then good thing I've got 'Fantastic Man' standing guard."

She said his name so sarcastically that Miranda had to stifle a chuckle.

Standing closer than Miranda would have dared without powers, the scientist examined the scaly skin and observed the dragon's breathing. Her expression oscillated between bewilderment, neutrality, and awe.

Fantastic Man watched Cadee closely. The corner of his mouth curled up, then flattened as he noticed Miranda looking his way. Miranda made no effort to flatten her own amused smirk.

Cadee seemed age-appropriate for Fantastic Man and in decent shape. Her skin was clear other than a mole on her cheekbone, and she had a cute bob cut. Combining her physical attractiveness with her evident comfort around dragons, Miranda concluded that a thirty-something dude would definitely go for her. So, they probably weren't the same person, but was Fantastic Man her boyfriend, husband, or male friend who was secretly in love with her?

The dragon was still asleep, right? Miranda stepped closer and watched its eyes. They remained shut, but she knew that was only temporary.

"So why did you bring the dragon here?" Cadee asked.

"Because, I regret to say," Fantastic Man said dramatically, "the dragon's origins can be traced to someone in this very facility!"

Cadee glowered at him. "We've had our share of

oddities lately, but there is no way anyone here accidentally made a dragon."

"No, I don't believe the dragon was made 'accidentally,' as you say. Its birth was a deliberate act for nefarious purposes!"

Miranda nudged Mr. Amazing, pointed at the dragon, and whispered, "You don't think it's waking up, do you?"

He stared at it for several seconds, so Miranda prodded him along.

"This is when you're supposed to say, 'No, everything's fine, nothing to worry about.'"

"The eyes are still closed. I guess that's a good sign."

Miranda was not reassured. She thought Cadee's berating of Fantastic Man would prove suitably distracting, so she tried to focus on that.

"—absolutely unacceptable," Cadee said. "We need to have a word in private—after we figure out what to do with your dragon."

Impervious to her criticism, Fantastic Man beamed with confidence. "I don't suspect the dragon will be a problem for much longer."

Miranda almost pulled out her new flip phone to check the time but didn't want to appear rude. Though she knew there was no way a full thirty minutes had passed, she wouldn't have minded confirmation.

A lanky scientist rushed outside, but he stopped and went pale at the sight of the dragon. Miranda recognized him. The blue car fire guy. Pinkney.

Fantastic Man shone a light on Pinkney, whose beads of sweat glistened. The scientist squinted and raised his hands to shield his eyes.

"Dr. Warner Pinkney," Fantastic Man said, "would you care to illuminate us about your extracurricular activities?"

Pinkney squinted through the glare. "What the hell are you talking about?"

"A common refrain among scoundrels with something to hide!"

"Turn that light off!" Pinkney shouted.

Fantastic Man did, but only after Cadee smacked his arm and insisted. However, he maintained a glow over his face, a cover he hadn't needed with Cadee.

His hands in his lab coat pockets, Pinkney pointed at the dragon with a nod. "That's what you wanted me to see? This creature? Are you accusing me of something?"

Cadee grabbed Fantastic Man by the cape and sternly whispered ... something. Miranda strained to hear, unsuccessfully.

"The proof will assert itself momentarily," Fantastic Man said, straightening his cape after Cadee released. "In the meantime, if Dr. Pinkney is feeling tight-lipped, I'll share my findings."

Fantastic Man paced back and forth, like he was acting out the climactic scene of a mystery film. "This afternoon, my suspicions aroused, I slipped inside Dr. Pinkney's home to investigate—"

"You what?" Pinkney yelled. "You had no right!"

"I remained in my photonic form the entire time," Fantastic Man said calmly. "Technically, I never stepped foot in your residence."

While the two men quibbled over the legality of sentient photons conducting a warrantless search, Miranda stared at the dragon, noting its bulky frame, thick skin, and powerful limbs. It existed. She defeated it, somehow. Her hands weren't stinging anymore.

Faint sirens emerged in the background.

"You are not above the law!" Pinkney barked, flecks of spittle flying from his mouth. "Someone needs to put you in your place."

Cadee stepped between them, raising a hand toward each. "Calm down, guys. Both of you." She pointed at Fantastic Man. "But you're the one who really needs to explain yourself. Right now."

If Miranda were to wear a watch, she wondered, how long would it last before breaking? How would she keep the phone in one piece?

"As I always intended to," Fantastic Man said. "Pinkney's basement held three most alarming discoveries. This dragon, for one, in a cage that ultimately proved inadequate. Two, an inert but fully assembled humanoid robot. And, most concerning, a corpse."

Miranda snapped to attention. "Wait, what about a robot?" The final part registered. "And a corpse? Who—whose corpse?"

"I'm hoping Dr. Pinkney can enlighten us as to the identity of his victim." Fantastic Man cast another spotlight on Pinkney. This time, the scientist hardly winced as he stared into the brightness. "Whom did you kill, Pinkney?"

"That can't be right," Cadee said. "Warner, tell him he's mistaken."

Fantastic Man solemnly shook his head. "If only I were."

"I don't have to say anything to you." Pinkney looked the superhero straight in the eye. "You have no legal authority."

The sirens grew louder, and Fantastic Man smirked. Police and rescue vehicles were pulling up, as well as news vans.

"I may not," he said, "but Olympus's Finest do. Your neighbors reported a violent beast—this very dragon—bursting up through *your* home."

Pinkney's arms were shaking in his pockets. "Did—did this thing destroy my home?"

"Regrettably, yes," Fantastic Man said. "From the inside."

Fantastic Man unleashed several intense flashes at the dragon's eyes.

The dragon stirred and grunted, expelling a forceful gust from its nostrils.

Miranda readied her fists and resisted the urge to throw the first punch at Fantastic Man. "What did you do that for?"

"Don't touch it!" Fantastic Man shouted.

Miranda turned. "But—"

The tail whacked Miranda and smashed her face-first into the pavement. The dragon stretched its neck, reclaimed the spire, and cocked it, aiming the tip at only one of the assembled humans—Pinkney. Miranda prepared to intercept, but the spire never launched.

Pinkney whipped out a small remote control from his coat pocket, hit its sole button, and fried the dragon.

Mr. Amazing caught the falling spire with his tele-kinesis, sparing the cars it would have pulverized, and Miranda grabbed the dragon before it crashed onto the police officers hopping out of their vehicles.

The dragon was hot to the touch. Steam rose from the creature's body. It wasn't breathing.

Miranda laid the body down and pointed at Pinkney. "You killed it." Who else had he killed?

Fantastic Man strode toward the guilty party. "But why would Dr. Pinkney have prepared a failsafe for the dragon unless he was aware of its existence?"

"Warner," Cadee said nervously, "this makes no sense. What's the purpose of creating a dragon? Can you explain any of this?"

The police were approaching, and Pinkney took a deep breath and shook his head. "The dragon resulted from a synthetic fuel I was trying to develop. You're right, Cadee—it makes no sense. I've been trying to make sense of the senseless, trying to save science itself. Its laws are falling apart."

"You could've come to me for help."

"Then you'd be culpable."

Pinkney pulled another device out of his pocket, a golden box. He dropped it at his feet, and the box rapidly unfolded several times, then refolded around him, encasing him within a suit of sleek golden armor. It was a perfect fit for his frame, covering him from sternum to toe and shoulder to fingertips, everything except his head. The metal was immaculate—it was too perfect for this world.

Miranda recalled the unknown superhero Hoskins mentioned. The Golden Gladiator.

"I'm sorry, but my work is too important," Pinkney said, right before jet boots propelled him straight up.

This guy killed Officer Hoskins. He killed Dame Disaster. And he must have killed the Golden Gladiator, too. Nothing was important enough to let him escape.

Miranda grabbed the spire, leapt after him, and whacked the armor, batting Pinkney right back down. Instinct told her not to hold back against that alien metal.

She enjoyed the release.

Crashing onto the pavement, Pinkney bounced off newly formed cracks and rolled side over side, landing on his back as four police officers aimed their guns at him. One officer commanded Pinkney to deactivate and remove the armor. Since his head was exposed, he had little choice but to comply.

The armor, still spotless, not even dented, unfolded from Pinkney and collapsed into its previous box form.

Cadee stared at her colleague. She looked confused and hurt as she pointed at the box. "Help me understand. Where did that come from? You never said anything about … that—about any of this."

Pinkney slowly rose to his feet and placed his hands on the back of his head. "I don't think I should say anything else just now."

"As is your right as a citizen of these United States," Fantastic Man said. "Take him away, officers!"

One of the officers cocked an eyebrow at Fantastic Man and grimaced, as if silently questioning whether the guy was for real.

As much as Miranda wanted to mock her new team leader, she had to give him credit for his investigative work in exposing the culprit behind the random dragon attack … though it was more of a frolic than a deliberate attack. A destructive frolic, but one without casualties, thanks to the Terrific Trio.

What else was Pinkney up to?

The police handcuffed Pinkney and escorted him into the back of a car. They'd interrogate him and piece together the extent of his activities. *Better them than me*, Miranda thought, since she found herself tempted to dangle him over a few thousand feet of empty air until he answered her questions to her satisfaction. For now, at least, there existed the possibility that Hoskins's killer was off the streets.

The reporters rushed toward the superheroes and launched into questions about the Terrific Trio.

They already knew the name.

Miranda let Fantastic Man do most of the talking. Mr. Amazing, with his arms crossed tight, didn't seem to mind either.

Fantastic Man offered up the same platitudes as before, and the media devoured it, eager to regurgitate it all at their viewers and readers. No one raised a question that sounded even remotely critical.

Miranda basked and smiled at the positive attention, content to soak it all in. Dragon defeated, suspected murderer in custody, and Fantastic Man possibly decent at this whole crimefighting thing.

She noticed Cadee on the sidelines, resting her chin on her hand as she studied the scene, her eyes unblinking. Miranda felt bad for her, and she desperately wanted to know what her relationship to Fantastic Man was.

What time was it? Miranda hoped her split-second panic didn't appear on any footage. She probably still had plenty of time. Probably.

"Thank you again for coming," Fantastic Man told the press. "I'm sure we'll be seeing plenty more of each other as we all work for the betterment of our fellow citizens!"

The Terrific Trio waved goodbye, and each lifted off in a distinctive manner—Mr. Amazing telekinetically, Fantastic Man photonically, and Miranda effortlessly.

Fantastic Man disappeared. Miranda bid Mr. Amazing farewell as their flight paths diverged, and it occurred to her that no one said goodbye to Cadee after they left a dragon corpse on her property. Felt wrong, but Miranda was already halfway to the Aeschylus Theater and didn't want to risk any delays.

To her surprise, she arrived a few minutes early. Reminding herself to slow down to a normal speed, she greeted her castmates, got into costume, and prepared for the show.

And everything clicked. Energy was high, crowd frequently roared with laughter, and director Heather was in attendance and praised Miranda's performance afterward.

Miranda flew back to her apartment, planning to spend the rest of the night relaxing and checking out the Terrific Trio's news coverage.

But she had a visitor. Bianca was sitting on the couch,

reading a book.

"You need some air freshener in here," Bianca said. "Did something burn?"

Miranda looked at her, eyes wide as she awaited an explanation.

"I only conceded that you had the better argument," Bianca said. "I never explicitly promised I wouldn't come over."

So much for relaxing.

28

The brilliant, selfless medical student neglected to book herself a hotel room. So, Miranda and Bianca clung to opposite sides of her couch's narrow pullout bed.

This sort of thing worked much better fifteen years ago.

"Your mattress is hard," Bianca observed as they stared at the ceiling.

Miranda inched further against her edge of the bed. "It's more comfortable with one person."

"Yeah ..." Bianca drew out the word. "So how are things with Ken?"

"There are no things with Ken."

Bianca rolled to face her. "That was quick."

"We went out for coffee and ran out of things to talk about." Miranda closed her eyes. She felt like she was being watched.

"But you convinced yourself you tried, and that's the important part, right?"

"I tried. There's no chemistry. That's the end of that. And he was the one who left first."

"I'm sorry."

Miranda's eyes popped back open, and she flipped

toward Bianca. "Sure you are. Now you're going to tell me I intentionally pushed him away or something."

"No. Usually you're so careful to end things on your terms, but this one got away from you."

Miranda stole a larger share of the blanket and turned onto her other side. "Good night, Bianca."

"I take it you didn't talk about your new hobby? I'm pretty sure that would have livened up the conversation."

"I couldn't bring that up."

"You didn't *want* to bring that up."

Miranda hadn't mentioned her encounter with Tuck in the coffee shop, but she didn't want to create any false excitement. It was entirely possible nothing would come from his gesture, which might have been just that—a gesture so Tuck could feel good about himself. He'd admitted as much, hadn't he? So why tell Bianca if it was nothing? Miranda could tell Alyssa about it, though.

She kept wondering about the corpse Fantastic Man found in Pinkney's home. Its identity was the paramount question. Dame Disaster was one possibility. Miranda hoped that was the case. Otherwise, a third person died. *At least* a third person. The Golden Gladiator? Someone else?

The police would determine the extent of Pinkney's crimes. Miranda reminded herself she wasn't a detective. Her theatre degree included no criminology courses. For the moment, Pinkney was behind bars, awaiting trial.

Or was he awaiting *charges*? Did the police have enough to hold him? What if Fantastic Man screwed up their evidence? What if the dragon destroyed everything incriminating? Was owning a dragon even illegal?

"I feel like flying," Miranda said, hopping out of bed.

Bianca sat up. "That must be nice. You can escape into the clouds anytime you want."

"Come with me. I'll carry you."

Bianca stared at her blankly for a second. "Will you drop me?"

"You know you want to fly. Come fly."

Bianca took a hesitant step out of bed. Only the one foot made it out so far.

To prod her the rest of the way, Miranda resorted to juvenile pleading. "Do it," she said, stretching out the syllables.

A smile gradually formed. "Okay."

They threw on warmer clothes, and Miranda led her sister to the roof, where a harsh, cool wind greeted them. Bianca shivered slightly while Miranda remained comfortable.

Clouds and smog obscured most of the stars, but several peeked through.

"Pick a star," Miranda said, smirking.

"Why a star? You can't fly into space ... right?"

"Fine. I'll pick." Miranda pointed straight up and moved her finger two stars to the right. "That one."

She scooped up Bianca with both arms and, with her eyes on that star, took off.

The wind howled violently, and Bianca screamed, clutching her sister tight.

They climbed higher, higher … then Miranda abruptly curved into a loop. Midway through the second loop, the scream turned into laughter and Bianca eased her grip just a little.

Miranda slowed but maintained a brisk clip, and they sailed above the city.

Bianca dared to look down, flinched, then gazed at the city below, a wide grin plastered across her face. Miranda was happy to take credit for her merriment. For now, they were kids without responsibilities, with freedom greater than any adult's.

"Do you love it?" Miranda shouted as the wind kept trying to gag her.

"What?"

"Never mind. We'll talk la—"

"What?"

Miranda shook her head, and they resumed their aerial sightseeing.

Bianca's shivering intensified, which Miranda took as a cue to pause the tour. Arbitrarily selecting an office building's rooftop, Miranda landed and gently released her sister. Bianca rocked like she had just stepped off a long boat ride, but she soon steadied herself.

"That was incredible," she said. "Miri, you've received such a tremendous gift."

Miranda looked down the street and saw Mount Olympus's bent upper tier. Turning the other way, she recognized the office building she had crashed into. A tarp fluttered in the breeze as it covered the hole—the hole she contributed to. Her shoulders slackened.

"It is incredible," Miranda said. "The most incredible thing. Also the scariest. There's so much to do, and I'm—I'm just not good enough."

Bianca put an arm around her and squeezed for a sideways hug. "Hey. What's with this? You saved the city from a dragon. People are alive because of you."

"I have to succeed every time. Every single time. I don't get to make mistakes, can't slip up even a little. I mess up, people die. How can I live up to that? In what possible way am I qualified? I've already failed. That nice man—murdered right in front of me. I was too slow. I'm faster than anyone, and I couldn't react quickly enough."

Her head sank onto Bianca's shoulder. She sniffled.

"He's dead because of me." Her eyes leaked down her face. "If you had gotten these powers, you probably would have saved him."

"I doubt that."

But she would have. Miranda was certain of that. Bianca was the smarter one, the selfless one, the better one—the one who, beneath her sisterly concern, was judging the self-centered performer who hardly bothered to think about other people until she became stronger and swifter than everyone else. Miranda believed that, too.

"I can't do this." Miranda sobbed against the shoulder and hated herself for it. If anyone else saw this ... "I don't deserve this. I'm not Ultra Woman, I'm just not. Look at me! Crying like an idiot. Ultra Woman shouldn't cry."

"Ultra Woman is human. She's you."

"Who else am I going to fail? Who will I watch die next?"

Bianca gently hushed her. "You're focusing on the wrong thing. It's not who you fail; it's who you help. It's all the people who are better off because *you* were there."

"What about when people are counting on me and I don't come through?"

"No one can do everything. Do you think I'm expecting to save every patient who comes my way? I'm going to fail a lot, too. What's the alternative? Not even try?"

Miranda withdrew and wiped her eyes. "Why are you suddenly so interested in my life?"

"I've always been interested."

Because she had to be! Bianca only cared about Miranda insofar as shared genetics obligated her to care. They had long since stopped having much else in common, and no way would Bianca think highly of her if they met as strangers. And yet the virtuous future doctor traveled all this way on short notice to help someone who didn't deserve it—she came either out of obligation or a desire to feel like a decent person, but not because Miranda warranted it on her own merits.

Miranda didn't intend to say any of that out loud, but it all spewed from her mouth nevertheless.

Throughout the rant, Bianca listened patiently, and she responded only after Miranda had fallen into embarrassed silence.

"But I do know you," Bianca said. "I know your potential, probably better than you realize. You deserve to have someone to talk to about all this, and I am glad to be that person."

"You've been pulling away for years now."

"No," Bianca said more firmly. "*You* were pulling away, and I took the hint. You've retreated into your own little world a whole country away, and you've compartmentalized your life. What are you afraid people will see?"

Miranda gave it a long moment's thought. She *was* afraid, she realized. She had been afraid since long before Dame Disaster. She was afraid people would see Miranda Thomas, and it wouldn't be enough.

"I'm going to disappoint everyone," Miranda said, staring ahead at the tower.

"I watched the news while I was waiting," Bianca said. "Seems to me you're the best superhero this city's got, which also means you're the world's greatest superhero."

"You're biased."

"Peyton never shuts up about you. It's getting kind of obnoxious."

If Peyton saw Ultra Woman crying ... "She's very young."

"Punching out a dragon gives us a fairly objective metric."

So does letting Officer Hoskins get murdered, Miranda thought. "Pretty sad for the world if I'm the best."

"You can always be better, but you'll never be perfect. Don't put that on yourself."

"Fantastic Man said—"

"I don't care."

More tears welled up, but Miranda resented them less this time as she hugged her. "Thank you for coming."

"Of course. I'm glad I could help."

They settled into a comfortable, quiet moment that ended sooner than Miranda would've liked.

"Something to start thinking about," Bianca said, "is who you want to tell next."

Miranda tensed, stepped back, and quickly shook her head. "I can't. I just can't think about that right now."

"Doesn't have to be right now. Just know you have options. Mom and Dad, Peyton, Alyssa, Ken—"

"Not now, okay?" Miranda snapped, pointing a quivering finger.

Bianca raised her hands in surrender. "Okay. We'll

discuss it later."

Miranda's shoulders slumped under the weight of the late hour. "I'm tired. Let's go back."

29

The next day started off great. Deeming Miranda's breakfast options not up to her nutritional standards, Bianca headed out in search of worthy food, creating the perfect window of time for Miranda to call Tuck's assistant.

The assistant was expecting her call, and Miranda somehow wound up with an appointment at Tuck's Beverly Hills mansion for lunch the following afternoon. She wondered if her ears were malfunctioning. He must really have wanted to feel good about himself.

Whatever his motive, Miranda intended to make sure her career benefited, so Ultra Woman would be taking a little break tomorrow afternoon. That was what the Terrific Trio were for, right? Divide the labor?

She needed to tell Alyssa about the whole Tuck thing, so she grabbed her phone. And her other phone lit up.

A text came through: *Come to the suburbs. You'll see which house. –FM*

Lack of "please" aside, Miranda was about to respond that she was on her way, but the phone had no keyboard. What manner of antique was this? Was she expected to keep pressing numbers until the correct letter deigned to answer the summons? Perhaps Fantastic Man's brusque tone was justified.

She got dressed and flew over, figuring that was quicker than replying. And she indeed had zero difficulty locating the house Fantastic Man was referring to. Former house, more like. It asserted itself as the reigning eyesore on the block, the only quarter-acre lot to host a sizable tent rather than a home.

A nondescript sedan was parked in front of the property, where three serious people were conversing. Two were dressed in subdued, professional attire; the other wore a cape. They paid no attention to the curious neighbors watching from their respective lawns.

Those neighbors, children and adults alike, now directed their attention upward and excitedly announced Ultra Woman's arrival. Their enthusiasm sparked a smile across Miranda's face, and her two-handed wave bolstered their excitement. She slowed her descent to prolong the experience, and she savored the opportunity to make each kid feel a little more special with a quick moment of eye contact. Their open-mouthed grins were a delight.

But as Miranda's shoes touched the pavement, it was time for business. After all, those nice people *were* expecting greatness from her.

"Ah, Ultra Woman, you got my message," Fantastic Man said. "Excellent. I'd like you to meet my esteemed acquaintances from the Olympus City Police Department, detectives Farley Wallace and Jeri Dunn. We assisted each other in my inaugural crimefighting escapade, 'The Case of the Diabolical Dentist.' "

"His description, not ours," said Wallace, a short, stocky man with a gravelly voice.

Miranda shook their proffered hands. Both had firm grips, and their focused eyes seemed capable of penetrating her goggles.

"A pleasure," said Dunn, who towered over Miranda. Her tone was businesslike, her expression neutral, and her volume soft enough to thwart any eavesdroppers. "We understand you were the last person to see Earl Hoskins alive?"

"Um, yes," Miranda said, wondering if she had become a suspect. "I'm sorry." She wasn't sure why she apologized, and hoped it didn't sound like an admission of guilt. Nor did she want to exhibit any discomfort with so many eyes on her.

"Something we need to show you," Wallace said, stepping under the police tape and toward the tent.

Dunn followed, casting a glance back at Fantastic Man. "Make sure no one wanders onto the property, okay?"

"Yes, ma'am. I'll await Mr. Amazing and the others," Fantastic Man said, fading from view. The suburban backdrop made him look like a kid's birthday party attraction, so invisibility was probably the least awkward way to go.

Miranda took the hint to join the detectives, and she had to ask, "The Diabolical Dentist?"

Dunn cocked an eyebrow. "A local dentist was poisoning his patients earlier this summer. You didn't hear about that? You must be new in town."

Or just in her own little world, Miranda realized.

Wallace parted the nylon door at the middle, and the tent's interior looked more like an archaeological dig than a forensic investigation. A few steps into the tent, the lawn gave way to a steep drop into what used to be Warner Pinkney's basement. Dunn explained how crews had already removed most of the debris so the detectives could examine what they believed to be the scientist's workstation.

Miranda stopped listening, though, after she saw the robot.

It stood by a wall, its eye slits dark.

She noticed more. The chalk outline of a victim. The broken bars of a wrecked cage that was almost large enough to hold the dragon. Various computers, parts of computers, and scientific instruments, plus residual debris all over the floor.

But her eyes kept returning to the robot.

Wallace and Dunn observed Miranda's reaction, and she was a little embarrassed. No fear allowed, she reminded herself, though she tensed as she watched for even the slightest movement from the robot. It appeared to be deactivated.

"Where do you recognize it from?" Dunn asked.

"The robot that killed Officer Hoskins—that's it. It looked exactly like that. Is it going to turn on? We have to destroy it—"

"Hold on, Ultra Woman," Wallace said. "For one thing, it's evidence. For another, we've got no idea how it works or what powers it. You start tearing into it, you might trigger an explosion. Fantastic Man has arranged to have it shipped to Hephaestus Enterprises for study and safekeeping."

Dunn added, "We just wanted to confirm that this is the same model you saw."

Miranda nodded. She never turned away from the robot. It remained inert. "It is, and ... I'm so sorry I couldn't save him. Did ..." She didn't want to ask, but the question surfaced regardless. "Did you know him?"

"Yeah. Good man. Damn shame, the whole thing." Wallace gazed into the pit, then locked eyes with Miranda. "Something else I know—he would've been thankful you were there to get him away from people. That would've mattered to him a hell of a lot more than his own well-being. Don't beat yourself up over things you can't control and never could've predicted. From what I heard, you did good that day."

"Especially since you're only, what, eighteen?" Dunn said.

"Twenty-two." Miranda instantly regretted telling the

detectives her age, but then she saw the chalk outline again and the slip-up hardly seemed to matter. "Do you know who that is? Was?"

"No," Dunn said. "Male Caucasian victim. Roughly forty. No fingerprint matches in the database. Whoever he was, he doesn't have a criminal record that we're aware of. All we can say right now."

Had to be the Golden Gladiator, Miranda suspected, but that only raised more questions.

"What about that armor Pinkney was wearing?" she asked, wondering whether Pinkney built it or stole it. "Have you figured out what it is exactly?"

"It's evidence," Dunn said.

"More to the point," Wallace said, "we need you to walk us through precisely what happened when you encountered the robot. Fantastic Man passed along your summary, but we're going to need it firsthand."

Dunn watched the motionless robot. "Then we've got a favor to ask."

30

Riding in the back of a police van was not fun. Perhaps it was the irregular bumping and jostling as the vehicle traveled across Olympus. Or maybe it was the deadly robot staring vacantly in Miranda's general direction.

The police had asked her and Mr. Amazing to stand guard in the back as they transported the robot to Hephaestus. The pair sat on benches on opposite sides, and both were reluctant to take their eyes off the cargo. The robot was sturdy enough to stay planted on its feet, no matter how bumpy the ride.

Fantastic Man already zapped on ahead. His uselessness against robots spared him the trouble of security duty. Miranda wished Mr. Amazing had also been excused. If he got shot right in front of her ...

The robot shifted, but it was just another bump in the road. The eye slits remained dark.

There was no reason it should come alive. Pinkney was in no position to activate it, no position to control it, no position to harm another soul. Miranda knew she was being paranoid. She was just there to put people's minds at ease. That was all.

"Are you okay?" Mr. Amazing asked, his head still

turned toward the robot.

"Huh? Yeah. Fine. Thanks."

The situation was not conducive to small talk. The proximity of a killer robot curtailed any pretense that the weather was a compelling topic of conversation.

"It's so weird that this is what we're doing with our day," Miranda said, still watching the robot. "I mean, a week ago, what would you have expected to be doing right now? You don't have to answer that. Might give away precious secret-identity details. But I'm guessing not this."

"I know what you mean. Things certainly took a sharp turn."

Silence resumed. Miranda clenched her hands into fists. Upon realizing it, she flattened her palms.

"We're basically coworkers," she said, "but we hardly know the first thing about each other. It doesn't seem right."

He looked at her, then back at the robot, and he spoke tentatively. "What do you want to know?"

"I'm not even sure where to begin."

Mr. Amazing lifted his hand to his mask. Miranda thought he was going to peel it off. But he simply scratched the fabric over his chin, set his hands on his lap, and spoke.

"I did nothing to earn my powers, and I'm terrified I'm going to fail to live up to the responsibility," he said.

Miranda nodded knowingly. She got the feeling he

had more to say, so she kept quiet.

"But that terror is a good thing," Mr. Amazing continued. "What if someone else had acquired our powers instead? They might go on a crime spree or start bullying everyone who ever bullied them. Or worse. I don't know if we're the best choices for the job, but if nothing else, the world is lucky we at least want to do the right thing."

"How can you be sure that's what I want?"

"From what I've seen, it's obvious you're a good person."

Miranda laughed, and she didn't know why. She focused on the robot, ready to pounce if it came alive. It didn't.

"Why is that funny to you?" Mr. Amazing asked. "You've saved the city twice in less than a week, and that's not even counting the hostage situation."

Still no movement from the robot. Her hands clenched again, so she laid her palms flat on the bench.

"Did you know Fantastic Man names his ... his 'escapades'?" Miranda said. "I heard him call his first one 'The Case of the Diabolical Dentist.'"

"He's a strange man." After a moment, Mr. Amazing's head perked up. "Oh, was that the dentist who was poisoning people? I didn't realize he was involved in that. I guess that would've been right before his big debut."

Miranda's fingers curled back up. "I haven't shared anything about myself yet. So here it is. I'm not a hero. I'm selfish, self-centered. Only reason I don't want to screw up is because I don't want people to hate me."

The blank mask stared at her. Miranda tried to imagine a facial expression beneath it, but she didn't have enough to go on.

"I don't believe you," Mr. Amazing said. "You're riding in the back of a van, entirely out of the public's view, with a killer robot. And with your strength, no one could've forced you to do it."

There was another reason, Miranda thought—*Peyton*. Ultra Woman couldn't be the superhero who disenchanted her. Miranda would not be responsible for the kid's cynicism.

She pointed at the robot. "It doesn't even look real, does it? It's like something out of an old sci-fi movie."

"I wouldn't know." He shrugged. "I don't watch a lot of movies."

She smirked. "There we go. Now I know something about you. You're uncultured."

"Not entirely. I enjoy live theatre. Know any good plays I should see?"

He said it nonchalantly, just making chitchat. Miranda hoped that was all.

"Olympus Repertory Theatre has a great production of *Measure for Measure*, if Shakespeare's your thing," she said.

"I'll have to look into that. Thanks."

They fell into a comfortable silence. The masks reduced the pressure to maintain constant conversation, so Miranda watched the robot and listened for any unusual sounds. That was their job, after all, and they couldn't screw it up.

This robot killed Officer Hoskins—or perhaps another like it did.

What if this wasn't the only robot?

She wanted to wreck it, the whole robot from head to foot, rip the metal to scraps. She wasn't sure she could. It might spring to life at the slightest provocation. Action could make everything worse.

So she and the masked stranger simply watched the robot, pretending they'd be of any use should the death machine attack.

31

The moment the van parked at Hephaestus Enterprises, Miranda opened the back door. A bomb squad was waiting to give the robot another inspection before handing it over to the civilian scientists. Everyone else was safely indoors.

"I'll go find Fantastic Man and Cadee," she told Mr. Amazing. "You're in charge of the robot."

She leapt out before he could acknowledge or protest, and into the big building she went, in a blur of speed.

A young receptionist stopped all activity, including blinking, upon Miranda's abrupt entrance into the lobby.

"Hi!" Miranda said with maximum cheerfulness as she hovered above the floor to establish her credentials. "Ultra Woman here to see Dr. Luna. I've got a robot delivery she's expecting."

The still-unblinking receptionist unlocked the interior door, which led to a long hallway full of yet more doors. The furthest was Cadee's office. Miranda greeted each scientist she passed along the way, and they all flinched upon finding an actual human floating down their hall.

Landing before Cadee's closed door, Miranda was

about to knock, but she heard muffled voices from the other side. Sounded like one female and one male voice. Sounded private. She strained to hear.

"—know how you feel about him," Cadee said.

Miranda checked behind her. The hallway was empty. She leaned her ear toward the door.

"I assure you, my judgment remains unimpeachable." The voice was unmistakably Fantastic Man's. "I've seen Pinkney for what he truly is—a mischievous malefactor, a reprobate who's reneged on his once-exalted ethics—"

"Oh, just stop it."

Wait, Miranda thought—*how exactly does he feel toward this Pinkney guy?*

Cadee's voice was scratchy and lethargic. "You do not get to take that tone with me. Not with me."

"You're right." His inflection changed instantly. Mumbly. Grumpy. The real Fantastic Man. "But I'm not wrong."

"I don't get it," Cadee said, beyond exasperated. "Why would he work in some secret basement lab? *I'm* his partner. *This* is our lab. And you obviously regret that it's not yours."

Miranda glanced behind her. Hallway still empty.

Should she feel guilty about eavesdropping? She could always apologize later.

"How has he been?" Fantastic Man asked. "Any odd behavior lately?"

"No." Cadee sounded firm. "Well, he'd been in a rut for a while and was getting frustrated, especially when everything started acting wonky. But he wouldn't—what does he have to gain by letting a dragon loose? And he would *never* kill people. I am absolutely positive about that. Maybe he built that robot as an experiment, maybe he thought he was on to something worthwhile, but no way in hell did he pull the trigger."

"You might not know him as well as you think."

"I could say the same about you. How's Natalie?"

A long pause, long enough for Miranda to brainstorm several possibilities about who this Natalie might be. She checked behind her. The hallways remained clear. She tried hard to feel guilty, but nope.

"The robot should be arriving any moment now," Fantastic Man said. "We should get out there."

"Right, and thanks again for having the *lethal robot* delivered to my doorstep." A loud sigh. "You cannot keep doing this."

"No one is better equipped to—"

"Is that the only reason?"

A pause. "We have more pressing matters to attend to." Fantastic Man's voice grew louder, nearer.

Miranda raced halfway down the hall at super-speed, then strolled forward as though she were only now arriving.

Fantastic Man emerged from the office in full

costume, Cadee right behind him, both appearing sullen for half a second. But when their eyes landed on Miranda, they perked up and sprouted chipper smiles.

"Ah, good, you're here!" Fantastic Man said. "I trust you encountered no complications in transit?"

Miranda smiled back. "Nope. All good. Got a big ugly robot for everyone to play with."

"Ooh, I can't wait to dive in and see what's inside." Cadee practically salivated at the prospect of robot dissection. All vocal scratchiness disappeared, and any traces of weariness or frustration had receded from view.

The three headed for the parking lot, all acting as though the previous conversation didn't happen.

32

The scientists spent a long afternoon disassembling the robot, aiming to reduce it to harmless parts. Having nothing better to do while playing security guard during a smooth operation, Miranda people-watched. Everyone acted strictly professional and cordial on the surface, and she observed the effort.

Cadee had bags under her eyes, and Miranda couldn't tell whether her movements were methodical or sluggish—or both.

Fantastic Man, also relegated to guard duty, maintained his standard phony grin, but the stress lines had deepened. Miranda wondered how much fatigue his mask concealed.

Weariness also afflicted Hephaestus's subordinate scientists, and they cast the occasional suspicious glance at each other, unsure if the person standing beside them would turn out to be the next Pinkney.

They got the job done without so much as a brusque remark, but Miranda found it draining to watch.

Seeing a heap of disassembled robot parts, however, proved far more refreshing. At least this robot couldn't hurt anyone else. But they couldn't know if this was the only robot Pinkney built. Then again, building even one functional robot must have been a time-consuming, expensive endeavor, right?

The bomb squad examined the parts one more time and deemed none to be a threat. The metal was an unknown alloy, so the police and scientists agreed the pieces would remain at Hephaestus for further study. For now, the police had the evidence they needed for their homicide investigation—a tiny, double-barreled laser cannon extracted from behind the robot's eye slits.

Miranda flew home and told Bianca about the whole day. A weight lifted as the words came out, and for the first time in a week, she didn't feel alone.

"So Cadee definitely knows who Fantastic Man is," Miranda said, pacing on the ceiling while Bianca rested her head on the couch's armrest. "After he made such a big fuss about me not telling anyone."

"You don't know how she found out. It might not have been intentional." Bianca's forehead creased as she thought aloud. "And perhaps this explains why he's so insistent on secret identities. He sees how taxing it's been on his friend." Rolling her eyes, she mocked that logic. "There's an obvious way to free her of that burden, though—he could just tell everyone."

Or, Miranda considered, perhaps Pinkney's betrayal was far more taxing on Cadee than knowing the real Fantastic Man.

"Who do you think Natalie is?" Miranda asked.

"Probably someone who needs to learn who Fantastic Man is."

Miranda paced faster, thinking about all the people Fantastic Man may have been lying to on a daily basis.

Bianca asked, "Have you given any thought to who you might want to tell next?"

The pacing stopped. Miranda considered the possibility of letting someone else in on the secret. But she recalled Cadee's fatigued voice, talking to Fantastic Man in a tone no one else did, totally unimpressed because she knew the man. Honesty diminished Fantastic Man, and it could very well diminish Ultra Woman.

"I have to get ready for my show," she said abruptly, expecting Bianca to call her out on the evasion, which was so obvious that it embarrassed her.

Saying nothing, Bianca simply watched Miranda hop off the ceiling and reorient herself for the floor.

Miranda continued, "Um, while I'm gone, I guess just … do whatever you want?"

"Like I've been doing all day, after I've traveled all across the country."

"Robot—"

"I know. But how about I come watch the show? I figure I'll probably miss a bunch, so I might as well see this one again."

"I'd like that."

The response was automatic. Bianca would be a guaranteed friendly audience member—but also unearned applause. Then again, the theater wasn't expecting a sold-out house, so why let the seat go empty?

Miranda realized—Bianca wanted to be there, after she had already fulfilled her familial obligation. Maybe the applause wouldn't be entirely unearned.

"And tomorrow," Bianca said, "if Ultra Woman isn't needed, maybe we can hang out somewhere in the city. Show me any part of Olympus I haven't seen yet."

The appointment with Tuck. Miranda's smile faded. But why not simply tell Bianca about it?

"I forgot to tell you ... I have an audition tomorrow. Not sure how long it will take, but afterward, I'm all yours."

It almost wasn't a lie.

33

Olympus City faded into the distance as the car rode along the bridge. Tuck had even sprung for the transportation—no limo, nothing fancy, just a clean sedan and a professional driver. Still too nice of him. He probably remembered how poor he was at the start of his career, Miranda figured. If he felt the need to overcompensate for anything, she was more than happy to take advantage.

The driver was courteous enough and neatly groomed, but his taciturn demeanor did not encourage conversation. Content to play with her phone in the back seat, Miranda reached into her purse and swiped across the screen.

And she made the mistake of checking the news.

Pinkney escaped jail. Somehow, he reacquired the golden armor and blasted his way to freedom.

The Olympian Herald presented this as breaking news. It happened within the past hour, so no other details were available, no indication that Pinkney was posing a threat to anyone, no mention of his robot. He fled; that was all.

Odds were, a text from Fantastic Man awaited on the flip phone, which she had already set to silent. If Miranda saw the text, she'd have no excuse for not dropping everything and rushing into battle—with "everything" including an opportunity she had waited her entire life for.

She was halfway down the bridge, and the car was right on schedule, even accounting for traffic. She could pretend she hadn't seen the news, and the news didn't mention any actual threat under way. Ultra Woman ultimately wasn't needed against the robot yesterday, and Cadee said Pinkney never seemed like a killer. Maybe he just wanted to get away from this whole mess and start over elsewhere.

Miranda buried the flip phone at the bottom of her purse. Out the window, ocean waves rolled gently while boats of various sizes rode to and from Olympus.

The car advanced slowly, but it was advancing. And the pit in her stomach kept nagging.

She *could* check with Fantastic Man, see if he had any additional details. Perhaps he could confirm that Pinkney was laying low at the moment, no need for the Terrific Trio.

Or he might want them to patrol the city, or meet up to chart a plan of action, or do something else that might feel productive without accomplishing a thing.

Sticking with her smartphone, Miranda opened her text messages. She tapped Peyton's name and reread several texts from the past few days, most of them gushing about superheroes.

One text included a link to an article about the

Terrific Trio's debut after the dragon attack. The preview image showed Ultra Woman, Fantastic Man, and Mr. Amazing standing before the thwarted creature in the middle of the street. Ultra Woman was the only one not looking ahead; the photographer caught her glancing back at the dragon.

Peyton's accompanying note said, *So cool! Like a crossover! And another superhero! Telekinesis is an awesome power.*

Miranda imagined Peyton reading a report about only Fantastic Man and Mr. Amazing apprehending the fugitive scientist, no Ultra Woman in sight. What would she think of her? Would she think anything of it? Ultra Woman could be the hero tomorrow and several consecutive days afterward. Let the guys have their turn in the spotlight.

She leaned forward. "Hey, isn't the weather gorgeous today?"

The driver stared ahead at the traffic. A few seconds later, he glanced in the rearview mirror and responded, "Yes, ma'am."

Miranda deemed him useless, and she wondered why her resistance to pain did nothing to alleviate her unsettled stomach.

Her business-casual attire was not action-ready. She went with a knee-length pencil skirt and summery blouse. She hoped she struck the right balance between professional and relaxed. She didn't want Tuck to misread her intentions, though she wasn't certain she hadn't misread his.

The *Herald*'s article contained no further updates. Nothing about robots or another dragon or anyone else developing super-powers. No active robbery or bomb threat or hostage situation either.

She thought about Bianca pestering her to dispose of the secret identity, but that felt premature. If she was ever going to reveal herself, then Miranda Thomas needed to be someone worth revealing.

Miranda silenced her smartphone and stowed it in her purse.

34

Miranda attempted to calculate how many times her apartment would fit inside Tuck's mansion, and she remembered why math was never her thing.

The car pulled around an opulent fountain, then stopped at a set of brick stairs leading to the imposing front doors, both tall enough to accommodate any visitor up to twelve feet tall. The driver abruptly wished her a good day. She thanked him, approached the four-story structure, and knocked.

A butler answered, his posture impeccable but his eyelids droopy.

Miranda smiled. "Hi. I'm Miranda Thomas—I have an appointment with Tuck ..." Had she earned first-name privileges? "... Lewis. Here to see Tuck Lewis."

"He's expecting you."

The butler led her into a vast foyer, with a high, curved ceiling and a symmetrical pair of staircases snaking down on both sides. Paintings and a few small sculptures decorated the room, each piece of museum quality.

The room looked like it belonged in a movie. Miranda wanted a home like this.

The butler ushered her through another set of doors,

down a hall, and into a dining room that also had plenty of flying space up top.

Don't even think about super-powers, Miranda thought. *What's Pinkney—stop.*

A table stretched along a series of tall windows. The spotless glass filled the room with natural lighting and showcased an extravagant pool outside, its pristine water sparkling under the sun.

Tuck rose from the far end of the table. He, too, went the business-casual route—a polo shirt and khakis, but also a day's worth of stubble. The unshaven look suited him, Miranda thought, and maybe that was the point.

He looked vaguely surprised to see her, and Miranda got nervous for a second. But the look passed, and Tuck shook her hand, looking down into her eyes but no lower.

"Miranda. I'm glad you could make it."

"Thank you so much for having me." Miranda turned to thank the butler, but he had vanished, like a ninja.

"My staff's efficient," Tuck said with a crooked grin. "They'll have lunch out in just a minute. Come. Have a seat. Let's talk."

He pulled out a corner chair for Miranda. She took it, and he sat at the head, without so much as a passing glance below her face. Maybe he truly didn't have an ulterior motive.

"Your house is lovely," she said.

"One of my prized possessions. And you want all of

this, too, don't you?"

Miranda mixed a small shrug with a modest smile. "I mean, I wouldn't be terribly upset about it."

Tuck leaned back in his chair, crossed his legs, and draped an arm across the backrest. "How long have you wanted to act for a living?"

"Since forever."

"Why? For Miranda Thomas, what's the appeal?"

"Everything. I get to go into other people's heads and get out of my own and experience all these other perspectives. The more I learn about the craft behind doing that, the more rewarding the entire process is." The response flowed out, no need to hide a thing. "I also love that performer-audience connection. I get to make people happier, help them feel a whole wide range of emotions, and with theatre I get to see the reactions unfold right in front of me." Miranda inwardly scolded herself, remembering they weren't there to discuss theatre.

Tuck smirked knowingly. "The applause is pretty intoxicating, too, isn't it?"

Her head sank to appear both guilty and charming. "Well, yeah …" A more serious point springing to mind, she popped back up. Her hands came alive, gesturing pointlessly. "But only when it's genuine, when you know you earned it. I hear that, I know I accomplished something." She noticed the hands and clamped them to her lap.

"Not bad for the ego either."

Miranda laughed. "I suppose not."

A door opened, and a delicious smell wafted in. Four women entered, all wearing matching kitchen-staff attire. They carted in several large pizzas, freshly made and adorned with various toppings. A young lady set plates in front of Miranda and Tuck.

"This looks incredible. And abundant." Miranda smiled at the staff. "Thank you."

"Yes. Thanks, ladies." Tuck flashed a lazy smile at his staff. "Hey, know what? Take the rest of the day off. That goes for everyone. Spread the word."

The staff beamed and thanked him as they exited, and Miranda became fairly certain Tuck Lewis was going to hit on her before this meeting was over. She couldn't come up with a convincing reason why that would be an awful turn of events, though.

Tuck uncrossed his legs and set a napkin on his lap, and Miranda followed his lead.

"I've always hated California pizza," he said, "so I've had my chef perfect something closer to the New York style and taste. But judge for yourself."

He motioned to the pies, and Miranda grabbed a large, limp, greasy slice. As she bit into it, her taste buds cheered and demanded more.

"Oh, this is so good. I think we're in agreement when it comes to pizza."

Meanwhile, Fantastic Man and Mr. Amazing were

likely facing danger, doing her job.

She savored another bite.

"It's the best West Coast pizza money can bake," Tuck said. "Requires more than a theatre stipend to fund."

Miranda examined the slice in her hand. How many dollars per bite was she consuming? What would happen to the inevitable leftovers? What would *she* do with this much disposable income?

"Yeah, I'd imagine so." She chomped into the slice again and realized that any second now, she would be alone in a giant house with a former teen idol who had aged remarkably well. She could've sworn the room had gotten warmer.

Tuck shifted in his seat. He gazed out at his pool; the glistening water seemed to hypnotize him. "You should know ... this kind of money comes with a cost. Success of any kind comes with a cost." He turned and swept his hand wide, as though presenting the spacious dining room, perhaps the whole house. "What's missing here?"

Miranda paused, preferring not to wade into a trick question. She didn't want to insult him, but she was also ignorant of any correct responses. The sampling she had seen so far suggested the man had everything.

Then she realized where this was going. He was finally getting around to it. He'd show a smidgen of vulnerability, enough to humanize himself, and subtly convince Miranda she could rescue him from his lonely life, at least for one glorious afternoon. She recalled Ken's awkward rejection of her, and for now, at least, she didn't mind playing along.

"You have a lot," she said.

"A lot of empty space, too. I've tried to fill it with stuff. That helps a little."

"And people, too, right?"

"Everyone you've seen is staff. A great staff, sure, but they wouldn't be here if I wasn't paying them. Unless they were stalking me. That's happened." He locked eyes with Miranda and leaned forward, as though trying to connect his soul to hers. "This is what you have to be prepared for. This level of success isolates you from the world. The public's adoration reduces you to a commodity. Don't get me wrong—there are so many benefits. But when the workday is over and the spotlights turn off, you'll find it's harder than ever to establish genuine human connections, which was never easy to begin with."

His eyes drifted down, gazing within, wistful.

"Sure, I know a lot of people," Tuck said. "I've thrown truly spectacular parties. But even if I'm with someone, even if I'm surrounded by people, I always feel alone."

Miranda was confused. He was overplaying the sympathy card way too much, and he was far too successful to merit pity. Or was his idea of "helping" her to scare her straight?

"Are you prepared to be lonely?" he asked.

She considered her response as she finished a bite. Surely Miranda's success wouldn't take the same form as his. For one, she wouldn't spend her spare time inviting much younger actors she barely knew into her home.

Failure was no option, but what if success also led to misery? Better to be a miserable success than a miserable failure. She refused to aim for some mediocre middle.

What's Pinkney up to? Have the guys caught him yet? She unconsciously reached toward her purse, then stopped herself.

"I can't imagine anything else for my life," she said.

"Good," Tuck said, a broad smile forming. "Then I have a potential opportunity for you."

Miranda leaned forward, no longer wary about a sudden come-on. This felt more like Christmas morning. What special treat did he have for her?

"I know a producer who's working on a Robin Hood reboot. A television series this time, and a major network has just ordered a pilot. They're looking to cast unknowns—they worry if someone like me prances around as Robin Hood, no one will see Robin Hood."

Miranda was intrigued but had a hunch she wouldn't be up for the title role. Her best shot on any kind of Robin Hood show would be the one-dimensional romantic interest or perhaps another character's daughter—a damsel in weekly distress who could be saved only by thrilling swashbuckling. She held her hopes down at a low, reasonable altitude.

Tuck continued, "For this Robin Hood, they're thinking of shaking things up a bit, adding a young female archer who would act as a foil for the main guy. You might fit what they're looking for."

Her hopes floated straight to the ceiling, like dropped balloons, but she managed not to drool over the prospect.

"That sounds interesting," she said in what she considered a calm, professional manner.

"Be aware, though ... television is not the most glamorous work, especially hour-long dramas. Demanding schedule, twelve hours a day in many cases. But if this goes to series—which, knowing the people involved, it almost certainly will—whoever gets this role will have literally millions of eyes on her every week. You could have name recognition, eternal youth in DVD sales, digital immortality in streaming—not to mention a decent royalties paycheck on a regular basis."

How would Ultra Woman coexist with such a schedule? By being part of a team. Their current trio was just the beginning, Miranda hoped.

"I got my start in television and did my first films during the summer hiatuses," Tuck said, right as Miranda was recalling that same history. "My producer friend owes me a favor. I can get you an audition and an open mind. From there, it's all up to you."

"This is incredibly generous."

"It's really not. Think nothing of it. Just take the opportunity, and when you make it big, I can congratulate myself. Should I go ahead and set that up?"

Don't sound too eager, she told herself.

Her mouth was full, giving her a moment to contemplate acting on television. A moment was more than she needed.

She swallowed. "Please. That would be amazing."

"Great," he said, smiling. "If it works out, you'll learn a lot on set. Let me see if I can get ahold of my friend. Wait right here." Tuck wiped his mouth with a napkin, and he rose from his chair. "Help yourself to as much pizza as you like."

Tuck left to make the call, and Miranda, calm only on the outside, remained alone in the enormous room with the abundant meal.

And he really didn't hit on her, did he? Not even light flirting. Was he playing a long game, or was he sincerely trying to be helpful?

She'd figure out what it meant for Ultra Woman later, if it even came to pass. She was well aware the producer might hate her or dismiss her as one of Tuck's floozies, to be humored but not taken seriously.

She grabbed her smartphone, stared at the blank screen, and willed herself not to check the news. Still more pizza to enjoy. She wasn't close to full, and Tuck hadn't given her any specific details yet. This was not the time to go save the world, so she needed to not go online and—

The Olympian Herald's top headline blared, "BREAKING: ROBOT ATTACKS CITY"

The article was short and choppy. Several breaking news updates, but few details.

Pinkney was still at large. His robot, as if by magic, had reassembled itself and activated. Somehow, it came alive at Hephaestus, inflicted several thousand dollars' worth of property damage, ruined multiple projects, but killed no one. Nothing more than minor injuries reported there. That relaxed Miranda's heart rate only somewhat.

The latest update said the robot was flying over the city, shooting down random laser blasts. So far, it damaged only things—rooftops, empty parked cars, sidewalks. Not a single casualty yet. Nevertheless, police and rescue crews advised citizens to remain indoors, safely away from any falling debris.

A question came to mind as Miranda read, and she saw it mirrored in the article's list of related links.

One read, "City wonders, where are the Terrific Trio?"

Her hunger vanished, replaced by a heaviness. She opened the flip phone. No texts. No calls. Not one word from Fantastic Man about his nemesis or the menacing robot.

Tuck returned. He ambled down the long table, his face cordial but mildly disappointed.

"Well, he didn't pick up, but don't worry, he'll call me back." His smile faded and gaze narrowed as Miranda quickly shoved her phones back in her purse. "Is something wrong?"

She sprang to her feet. "I—I have to go. I'm really sorry. You've been so nice, but ... an emergency has come up."

"Emergency?" He sounded concerned. "Anything I can do to help?"

"Um, no. Family thing. I've called a cab. I'll just go wait outside your gate. I'm really sorry—I feel just terrible."

"I understand."

Miranda stepped toward the door—or she thought she did. Her foot didn't move. The entire leg *couldn't* move. Neither leg responded to her commands, nor did her arms. Stiffness overcame her, locking every muscle in its current position.

She tried to wriggle, wrench herself free, even fly—nothing. Total paralysis.

Tuck frowned. "Yes, I understand completely, *'Ultra Woman.'*"

35

"I knew you'd come," Tuck said, reclaiming his seat at the head of the table. "I considered holding off until you were here, but I had to see if I was right. And, of course, I was."

Miranda also returned to her seat, but not by choice. She trudged toward the chair, clumsy step followed by clumsier step, an invisible force posing and re-posing her like an action figure. It felt nothing like Mr. Amazing's telekinesis, which affected targets externally. Rather, this force invaded her and manipulated her entire body from within, lifting each foot, pulling the whole leg forward, and planting it back on the floor. Everything above the waist remained stiff, and her skin itched all over, nerve endings misfiring as they waged war against the infiltrator. They lost.

Attempts to speak failed, producing only mumbles. She was bent into the chair, and her face was turned toward Tuck, who appeared not the least bit concerned about her awkward, involuntary mobility. He took another bite of pizza.

Miranda's heart thundered against her chest as she dreaded what else Tuck might be capable of, dreaded what her teammates might be up against, dreaded failing to prevent Pinkney from killing more people. She chastised herself for her own stupidity—allowing herself to be taken hostage by a former teen idol. Some superhero.

She mumbled again. Sipping a glass of water, Tuck lazily waved a finger and freed her mouth.

"How are you doing this?" she asked.

He shrugged. "How do you fly?"

"Stop it." Her skin was crawling, as if trying to scratch itself. "I want to leave now."

His face contorted in bemusement. "Do you really? Is that what you want to do? You *want* to go fight a mad scientist and his robot?"

Miranda half-expected her skin to explode. If that relieved the ever-escalating itchiness, she might not have minded. Miraculously, she managed not to scream out her frustration.

Seemingly oblivious to her discomfort, Tuck shook his head and continued. "No, you *want* to act in some mediocre television show. You don't want the responsibility—you want the fame, the fortune, the glory, no matter how much it cuts you off from the rest of the world. Not a very heroic aspiration." Enjoying another bite, he chuckled. "Come to think of it, know who typically shirks their responsibilities in the pursuit of power? The villains."

Miranda shot him her angriest sneer. "You're looking a lot like a villain right now."

"For what? Saving your life?"

She would have slapped him if she could. "*Saving?*"

"Look, I apologize for having to resort to ... this." Tuck hung his hands out palms-down and wiggled his fingers like a puppeteer. "I hate using this. It's so creepy. But you're going to get yourself killed, and for what? So you can feel like a decent person?"

"Let go. Now."

"But you don't want to leave."

Miranda forgot about her itchiness. She imagined throwing Tuck through a window, and it was the most alluring fantasy she'd had about the man in years. She channeled her full concentration into moving her arm, but it defied her.

Tuck swallowed another bite. "And to think, I was worried I was laying it on too thick." He recast his own words in a mocking tone: " 'You'll find it's so hard to establish genuine human connections.' Yet it didn't send you running. Your ego proved my point."

"What point?" Numerous questions kept shoving and tripping over each other, competing to leap out first. They emerged in a jumble. "What the hell is going on? Why do you have powers, too? What powers exactly? And you said—what did you mean 'holding off'? What did you do? You don't have anything to do with that robot, do you?" It sounded both possible and absurd.

"The robot?" Tuck shook his head. "No. Well, not

really. Hardly anything at all. I just helped the scientist get out of jail so he could do what he was going to do anyway."

"Why?"

He stared at her, studying her. "I had to see. I had to confirm. Superheroes—true superheroes—they can't exist in this world. Not even just this world, but this whole reality. No one can live up to that. No one is *that* super. No one in this universe would be standing around in some great Hall of Do-Gooders waiting for the call to action. No, they'd be tending to their own little lives. Given the right temptation, they'd put their own interests first. And that's precisely what you did."

"What did you do?"

Tuck laughed. "You make it sound like I performed some horrible deed. Let me reiterate—" And he did, slowly, as if speaking to an idiot. "I'm saving your life. I'm putting a stop to this new trend before someone else dies."

"Well, you only have me, and I'm not the whole trend. Surely Fantastic Man—"

"He's not fighting any robot today." Tuck sounded so utterly confident about that statement, he caught Miranda off guard.

"But he's so—what are you getting at?" She repeated her initial question, slower this time: "What did you do?"

"Very little."

He explained how he didn't have to do much to distract Fantastic Man—or "Captain Flashlight," as Tuck called him. Fantastic Man had visitation with his daughter today, which decided the date for this experiment.

"His daughter?" Miranda said. "He has a—? How do you know this?"

"I have two powers."

The first, he said, was that he could control the movements of living organisms. Didn't matter how big or small—he could commandeer the muscular system and skeletal structure, animating the animal or person however he saw fit.

"Not exactly a power that inspires one to don tights and rescue puppies," Tuck said, cringing. "Using it feels ... icky."

His second power, he explained, was perhaps a side-effect of the first. Whatever the case, he could sense the presence of other super-powered people. He detected Miranda's powers the moment she arrived on his movie set, before even seeing her. That, in fact, was the moment he discovered he possessed that extra ability, and at the first opportunity he went about tracking down Fantastic Man—and he found him.

"Who is he?" Miranda asked.

"Nobody," Tuck said. "That is, nobody you'd know. Trust me, it's an underwhelming reveal."

Tuck returned to his plan, describing it in a sober, rational tone, without any hint of malice or glee. The idea was to let a "supervillain" loose on Olympus City ...

and the Terrific Trio wouldn't show up to save the day. Pinkney was perfect for the role, as he wouldn't harm any innocents, Tuck insisted. The scientist cared only about neutralizing superpowered people and had total control of the robot. But the public would learn the truth—that they couldn't depend on superheroes.

Fantastic Man's visitation would take him out of Olympus for the day, and Miranda, Tuck correctly guessed, would not refuse an invitation from an A-list celebrity.

"There's still Mr. Amazing," Miranda said.

"No, there's not."

For the bland, faceless Mr. Amazing, Tuck needed to get more creative, so he hired an overly vivacious escort to "randomly" meet the young man and keep him distracted.

"Poor boy probably thinks he's met his dream girl," Tuck said, both laughing and cringing. "It's so mean. I'm going to hell for that one."

"Just that one?" Miranda said, gritting her teeth—still about the only movement she could muster. She was growing claustrophobic in her own body, convinced she was condemned to eternal itchiness, certain her nerve endings were about to erupt through her skin.

"I fully intend to follow through about that pilot," Tuck said. "You're getting that audition. I meant everything I said."

"That's not the point!"

"Helping you *is* the point."

"I came for help about *acting*! When it comes to saving lives, I'm the one who's actually done it. We may both have powers, but *I'm* the only superhero here and *you're* getting in my way. And what the hell have you been doing with your powers? How did you even get them?"

Unfazed by the outburst, Tuck wiped the pizza grease off his hands and stood up. With a flick of his finger, Miranda was also brought to her feet.

"I'll take it from the beginning," he said. "Let's walk and talk. There's something in my garage you should see."

36

"Sorry if this all seems overly dramatic," Tuck said amiably while he manipulated Miranda into shuffling along the edge of his pool. "But you should see the other world, the one the actual superhero and super-villain came from. Everyone there lives in this state of never-ending melodrama. It's almost charming."

Tuck nattered on about an alternate reality, a world full of superheroes and supervillains, and he described them as a bunch of cartoons made flesh, simplistic beings, either all good or all evil, but sharing the common traits of utter ridiculousness and zero subtlety. Though he poked fun, undercurrents of reverence occasionally surfaced, particularly when he detailed the epic interdimensional fight between the Golden Gladiator, Dame Disaster, and her robotic henchman.

Miranda's ears perked up at the mention of those names, but distractions prevented her from properly paying attention—namely, her full-body itch and her numerous failed attempts at breaking free of Tuck's hold. He steered her across the back lawn toward a massive garage, her muscles obeying him alone.

She picked out the main points, though. Doomed

to perpetual failure in her own reality, Dame Disaster was coming to conquer this Earth. The Golden Gladiator pursued her. They battled. Tuck explained the fight in excessive detail—far more detail than he could possibly know, Miranda thought. He seemed to enjoy the telling, pausing their walk a few times so his hands could reenact key moments of the conflict, like an exuberant fan describing his favorite scene from a great new action movie.

While he spoke, Miranda again tried resisting his power. She tried not resisting. Nothing worked.

Her divided concentration gave her an idea, though. What if she could disrupt *his* concentration?

To start, she challenged his story. "You can't know any of this. What, were you there?"

"I wasn't there," Tuck said, flashing a calm, annoying smile. "I'll get to that."

They entered the garage and proceeded between rows of antique and modern cars. All the way in the back, a tarp covered an irregular shape roughly the size of a school bus.

Tuck resumed the tale, not bothering to mask his admiration as he detailed the Golden Gladiator's last-minute triumph over the villain's world-domination plot. He gushed over the hero, impressed by his ingenuity and technical prowess in turning the tide of battle.

"He saved us all," Tuck said, giving a nod of respect. "A

real superhero."

Miranda recalled the chalk outline in Pinkney's basement and the golden armor he wore, and she hated the idea that followed. But she needed to seize any opportunity to rattle Tuck.

"You should know … he's dead," she told him.

"Yes. Yes, I do know." He was somber as he said it, but his focus remained intact. "Things went wrong for both hero and villain."

As Tuck explained it, a cosmic storm separated the combatants, plunging them into this alien universe at different points in time. The Golden Gladiator and the robot arrived a few months ago. They crashed into Warner Pinkney's backyard, both dead on arrival.

"It was a loss for everyone, that's for sure," Tuck said, shaking his head. "Our world could've used someone that purely good. Instead, his corpse winds up a specimen for some desperate scientist to study in his basement. Such a damn shame."

He brought them to a stop in front of the tarp.

"Take a guess where the ship landed," he said.

"In the wrong place, apparently."

Tuck yanked off the tarp to reveal a rocket ship. Its hull was in rough shape. Scorch marks and dents marred the retro-futuristic design. The tailfins were crumpled in a few places.

"I was simply roaming around Mount Olympus late

one night, or early one morning. There was a big flash of light. A hole in the air. And this came crashing through. Almost crashed *on* me. I wasn't hurt ... but I was changed."

"Yeah," Miranda said. "From a great actor into a creep who lures young women into his home and doesn't let them leave."

Tuck's nostrils flared as he sucked in a sharp breath. Then he closed his eyes and exhaled for several long seconds.

"I'm keeping you safe." He said it like he was reciting a mantra. "And you're not just any young woman."

Miranda wiggled a finger without Tuck's consent. She scratched an itch on her palm, but the nuisance returned immediately. Meager progress, but enough to embolden her.

"You didn't mention when the ship arrived," Miranda said. "How long have you had these *creepy* powers?" She watched his face tense as she punched the word, and another finger gained a moment of freedom.

"Three months," he said, quietly.

"I didn't catch that," she lied, as she considered how handy his power would have been during the hostage situation at the C&P.

He repeated himself clearer and more confidently— so focused on presenting a calm front that he didn't notice Miranda clenching and releasing a fist.

"So," Miranda said, "you might even be our world's

first super-person. And yet you've done absolutely nothing with your powers. Nothing. You've helped not one person."

He started to reiterate how he was helping her and her teammates, but he changed course.

"As a kid, I dreamt about becoming a superhero someday," he said, chuckling at the memory. "I thought it'd be so cool to soar through the air, run faster than a train, lift a truck like it was nothing. And, of course, such gifts would require me to put on colorful tights and become the ultimate Good Samaritan. According to any child, there would be no other rational choice."

Miranda felt her arms slowly loosening. A little more, and she could manage a light shove, hopefully sever the remainder of his concentration.

"But then I grew up," Tuck concluded, "and I got a power."

With a flourish, he waved a hand, renewing his grip on Miranda's muscles, halting even the minor finger movements she had achieved. He marched her toward the vessel.

Tuck asked, "What does it feel like?"

"Like I want to rip my skin off."

"I'm sorry." He sounded sincere. "It won't be much longer. I promise."

Tuck opened the side door and walked Miranda inside. The lights activated immediately, showing a mostly hollow interior and an immaculate cabin floor. The only seating was behind the cockpit, where several computer screens also lit up. At the rear, clothing hung off a rack. Green-and-red tights and capes, several identical sets, exactly what Dame Disaster wore as she died, plus matching masks.

"I couldn't tell you how," Tuck said, "but this ship somehow imprinted on me when it arrived. It granted me full access to all its data, its footage from the other world, any answer to any question I could throw at it. I'd almost swear this thing was alive. It's far beyond anything we've developed in this reality. It could start a whole new cold war. Then again, so could the existence of people like us. It's only a matter of time before militaries start trying to create their own super-powered soldiers."

"Is that the excuse you keep telling yourself?"

Tuck gazed out the ship's large front window—not that there was much to look at, other than his automobile collection.

"What works there won't work here. I'm doing what's necessary," he said, with determined focus.

Miranda could wiggle her fingers again, so she doubled down: "Is it necessary to have people looking up in the sky and seeing a dangerous robot? A robot that's already killed? A robot that, as you said, originally belonged to a supervillain? You're saying it's necessary for people to expect superheroes to show up to save the day, but then be disappointed by their absence? You think that sort of lesson's okay for kids to pick up on?"

"It's honest. It's how the world is." His speech slowed down, as if he was trying to remember his own arguments. "When this ship cut into our reality, it changed all the rules—but it didn't change people, not below the surface. We can do things that were previously impossible, but beneath that, we're still the same. Powers or no, we're human. We're corruptible."

Miranda's elbows were no longer locked in place. Her legs were beginning to lose their rigidity. The itch was fading.

"You're just upset that you could've been the world's first superhero, but you didn't do anything." She was almost able to lift a heel. "You're embarrassed. I embarrass you, don't I?"

A flash of anger swept over Tuck's eyes, but he calmed himself with a deep breath. "If you got my powers instead, you wouldn't have done anything either. No, you won the super-powers lottery. The best of the best was granted to you, unasked and unearned. Honestly, if I had your powers, I would have given in to the temptation, too. And like you, I would've been blinded to the harm I was doing. My ego would have blinded me, just as yours blinds you. You've got an ego just like me. You can't deny that. If you were like the Golden Gladiator, you would've leapt into action the very second you heard about Pinkney's escape."

"So I'm just like you," Miranda said, suppressing a smirk.

"All that separates us are a few lucky breaks."

"Interesting. So then, earlier, in your dining room, why did you compare me to a villain?"

"I never called you that." He said it too quickly, as if actively barricading any such recollection.

"You said I was avoiding responsibility and pursuing fame and glory—like a selfish villain."

Tuck held up a finger and opened his mouth, but words escaped him.

Miranda shoved him in the chest. A light tap, but enough to send him crashing against the ship's sleek metallic wall.

Tuck groaned and slumped to the floor. Miranda stumbled as mobility returned, the pressure on her muscles easing and the itchiness fading. Stiffness remained, but she could move. She lunged for the exit.

"I'll make sure you never get work!" Tuck shouted. "You'll be yet another failed actress! I can do that!"

Miranda froze—she froze herself this time. But, remembering that Ultra Woman was presently disappointing an entire city, she shook it off.

Too late. A second's hesitation was enough for Tuck to renew his grip. Miranda cursed out loud, scolding herself as much as him.

"I'm sorry." Tuck sounded exhausted. A hand on the

wall, he pulled himself up. "I didn't mean that. I would never sabotage anyone's career, but I knew it'd scare you."

He tapped a computer screen in the cockpit.

"I don't want to immobilize you the entire time either. Still, I could never live with myself if I let someone rush off to their death. There's another solution to keep you safe, though. You'll return when it's all over."

"This doesn't make you a good person!" Miranda shouted. "I can't believe I admired—"

Her mouth tightened, and she could speak no more.

Tuck exited the vessel and shut the door, sealing Miranda inside. The engine hummed.

37

A dazzling mist blew across the vessel's front window, obscuring everything except multicolored lightning. The cabin lurched, metal groaned, and Miranda toppled, banging her head on a metal box. It hurt a little.

When she rose, the mist had dissipated, storm had cleared. In the distance, Earth.

The entire planet appeared hardly larger than her fist, and it was gradually receding further.

I'm in space? Her face went from contorted to stunned flat. She felt truant.

The cabin lights cut off. The engine's humming died out. Each computer screen displayed a simple timer, which started counting down from three hours—the length of Miranda's time-out, presumably.

She tapped the screens. She looked for a console or any buttons she could try pushing. Finding none, she attempted to give the computer verbal orders. The computer didn't care, and it proceeded with its countdown.

The ship was indeed safe. The air tasted no different than it did on Earth, and the temperature was neither warm nor cool, but perfectly comfortable. Nothing would hurt her over the next few hours if she remained here.

She wondered how many miles lay between her and the Earth. Too many for her to fly without air. That would be a safe assumption.

The chairback crumpled within her grip as she leaned on it. Miranda wanted to rescind all her idolatry of Tuck, retroactive to her youth. The real man turned out to be not the least bit impressive, utterly contemptible, a coward.

Am I that scary? she wondered.

The Earth drifted further from view. Everyone and everything she ever knew, all packed within a single image. The situation she so desperately wanted to return to? It equated to a microbe on that diminishing orb. So much more going on, so many people in need. Miranda feared she had stumbled into responsibility for the whole thing.

It's all scary.

In no way was she qualified for planetary responsibility, but even scarier would be letting a murderer like Pinkney influence its future. Fantastic Man was right, she realized, at least about what he said on that island after Hoskins's death. If Pinkney and Tuck won, future generations lost. If the Terrific Trio failed to even show up for a public robot battle so soon after their debut—or worse, they straggled in late one at a time and got beat—who would trust them? Who in their right mind would attempt anything similar? And if anyone else did try, Pinkney would have the robot kill them, too, just like Dame Disaster, just like Officer Hoskins. He might even experiment on their corpses, like whatever he did with the Golden Gladiator.

This couldn't go any further.

Miranda rushed around the cabin at super-speed, looking for any useful tools or equipment, knocking on walls and computers, hoping to activate something she could work with.

Aside from the countdown, the computers remained asleep. Nothing was hiding behind the costumes in the back.

She paused and stared at the empty costumes—so brightly colored with their red and green, but also so sad and ghostly as they hung there, never to be filled again. The bird of prey symbol must have meant something to the people of Dame Disaster's world. Something terrifying.

Miranda turned to the window, assessing the distance between her and Earth, which continued to dwindle away. Could she ...?

Maybe she *could* ...

It was outer space, a distance many times greater than the entire world that encompassed her reality. She doubted her abilities were sufficient.

If she were wearing her Ultra Woman costume, she could have gotten into character, fooled herself into thinking she was good enough to make it.

There was another costuming option, however.

Miranda ran her fingers down a sleeve of Dame Disaster's costume. The fabric was stronger than any she had felt, but still remarkably soft.

She worried this might be ghoulish, but then remembered the woman was evil and therefore owed a great debt to society. Maybe another universe's society, but Miranda decided to collect on their behalf.

In a rush of super-speed, she flung her own clothes off and replaced them with the costume. Dame Disaster had seemed taller, but it fit as if tailored for Miranda alone. The comfort exceeded her expectations. It was perfect, as only something from another universe could be.

The last piece was the mask. Miranda picked one from the rack and attached it to her face around her eyes. It dyed her hair a bright red to match the cape.

Taking a moment to inhabit this perfection, she felt her sense of Ultra Woman return and sharpen.

Miranda focused through the window, beyond the tremendous distance, at the tiny Earth.

Ultra Woman could make it.

She launched herself at the window. The booming crash immediately vanished into silence as glass shards dispersed in the void.

The initial stretch of her journey was tolerable, temperature-wise. Cooler than she'd like, but not what she'd expect from the vacuum of space. The costume, whatever it was made of, seemed to help, as the exposed parts of her face were by far the most frigid. Not frigid enough to stop her, though.

Her lungs began to burn several minutes later, when she was countless miles from anything. Nowhere to retreat; forward was her only option. As her chest ached, she doubted she'd make it.

The Earth swelled. It still fit within her field of vision, but the image was growing.

Thoughts swam across her head in various directions, struggling to piece together her present reality.

Was she flying through space under her own power, without a helmet or oxygen? She was. Was she dressed as a superhero? No, she was dressed as a villain. Could anyone tell the difference? Probably not. But what if they could? Oh God, what if they could?

She'd save them. Then she'd look like a superhero.

The robot was no doubt scaring people, those people straight ahead on that planet way over there. Miranda pushed herself to fly faster.

A mistake. Her hands snapped to her chest, and her gasps failed to produce results.

She was drowning in space, looking like neither a superhero nor a villain, and she feared she would never see another person ever again. They were all right there, but she was about to die. In outer space. No one would ever know what happened to her. Her family and friends would forever wonder why she disappeared, and the uncertainty would plague them for the rest of their lives. No one else would give a damn. She'd die a failure. Less than a failure—at least failures had gotten a chance to try. She had barely begun her life.

But if she could push herself a little further ... a lot further ...

Oh, here was the icy cold. Present all along, but now it decided to squeeze her and slowly grind her internal organs.

Her eyelids drifted shut.

She forced them open. The world was so big now. Almost there.

She wasn't consciously flying anymore, merely coasting, counting on her momentum to carry her the rest of the way.

Miranda's return to Earth was now a certainty, but she wasn't sure whether she'd return as a living person or a human-shaped meteorite.

She'd find out when she woke up. If she woke up.

Rushing wind woke her up, blistering at first but swiftly cooling off.

The atmosphere resuscitated her lungs, forcing her to gasp repeatedly, this time successfully.

All around, clouds and a blue sky.

Miranda was plummeting head-first toward a forest.

An oddly familiar sensation. She remembered that she had indeed plummeted through the atmosphere before, remembered how frightening the experience was.

This time, however, she knew what to do. This time she was Ultra Woman. Her breathing settled.

But who exactly was Ultra Woman?

She was the person who was going to stop Pinkney and the robot. That was enough for now.

So Miranda ignored her fatigue, leveled herself, and reoriented toward Olympus City.

38

The cape fluttered over Miranda's back as she soared toward Olympus. The mask, whose presence she was hardly aware of, clung to her face and obstructed none of her peripheral vision. The tights were impossibly comfortable, neither baggy nor restrictive. The material had substance but no weight. Peyton would undoubtedly approve of the more traditional look.

It all felt right, until Miranda thought about where it came from.

No time for that now. Ultra Woman had a villain to stop.

I'm Ultra Woman, she kept telling herself, hoping to believe it eventually.

From a distance outside the city, Mount Olympus came into view, bent at the top like the last time she saw it.

She flew faster. She thought she had already reached her top speed, but apparently not.

Property damage drew a jagged line across the city. Skyscraper rooftops had acquired cracks. New potholes dotted the sidewalks and streets. Several unlucky vehicles' hoods were bashed in.

The damage looked expensive but was restricted to

inanimate objects. Miranda spotted not one dead body, no injured civilians, nobody in immediate peril. Paramedics were on the scene in the hardest-hit areas, at the ready, but without any patients to transport. Not a single building had toppled. No fires raged. The atmosphere was tense, but quiet.

Miranda feared she was too late, that Pinkney and his robot had already terrorized the city unchallenged and left victorious, leaving people to wonder where their so-called "superheroes" were.

Then she noticed a shiny spot against Mount Olympus, and the drumming in her chest accelerated.

At the center of the city, a larger-than-expected crowd spread along the sidewalks and empty street for several blocks, keeping a cautious watch all in the same direction. In front of them, a police barricade. And in front of the police, the vacant Mount Olympus park.

Almost vacant, except for the tall, gaunt robot hovering in front of the tower, doing absolutely nothing else.

No sign of her teammates anywhere. Or Pinkney. Miranda paused above the park's border and, after the fact, realized she had become a floating spectacle.

Shouts rose from the street, the individual words unintelligible but the excitement unmistakable. Miranda glanced over her shoulder, but the flapping cape obstructed her view. She grabbed its corners, tugged it to her sides, and saw the mass of curious onlookers pointing up at her.

She hadn't made it easy for anyone to identify her as Ultra Woman. These people couldn't know for sure who she was or why she appeared. She hated the thought of adding to anyone's anxiety.

Miranda slowly lowered herself so more people could hear her—particularly the police officers casting suspicious looks her way.

"Yep, it's me." Feigning a confident smile, she projected to the cheap seats, hoping she convinced the crowd more than herself. "Ultra Woman reporting for duty and dressed for success! Don't worry, folks. I got this one."

The crowd cheered, either forgetting her tardiness or forgiving it. She hadn't earned that yet, but being everyone's best hope granted her an advance.

Feeling that weight, Miranda sank onto the paved path between the topiaries, and she gazed up at the robot. Its eye slits remained dark. It didn't move, didn't react to her presence—until she advanced.

As Miranda took a single step, the robot shifted an equal distance toward her. The crowd gasped, and Miranda almost slipped and did the same.

The robot did nothing else, so far. When she stopped advancing, it stopped. She couldn't pause for long, though, not with people watching, counting on her. Part of her wished this thing would just attack already, instead of trying to overwhelm her with dread.

She realized she had no plan whatsoever, but how could anyone plan for something that had never happened in all of human history?

Light shimmered beneath the tower, in front of what used to be the elevator entrance. Miranda hoped it was Fantastic Man, but she knew she couldn't count on him or anyone.

Another step. Another slight advance from the robot. And a slightly brighter, wider shimmer. Hints of three murky silhouettes developed within. Miranda backed up, and as suspected, the silhouettes disappeared. When she stepped forward again, they returned.

Mindful of the eyes on her—human eyes behind, robotic ahead—Miranda marched several more paces down the path, holding her head high as her palms grew sweaty. The robot continued to creep toward her.

Still no attack, only movement, like a monstrously large bee hanging out nearby, reserving the right to sting if the mood struck.

Breathe, Miranda reminded herself.

Each step brought greater clarity to the silhouettes beneath the tower. Two of them were squirming but unable to move their arms or legs. The third figure barely moved at all except to tap his wrist.

As Miranda reached the path's midpoint, the three figures sharpened into recognizable forms: Pinkney, decked out in that golden armor, was studying Fantastic Man and Mr. Amazing.

Her teammates were strapped within full-body braces, immobilized from the shoulders down, propped up against slanted metal beams that protruded from the backs of their restraints. They both wore blinking headbands over their masks as they tried, and failed, to wriggle free. Fantastic Man was gritting his teeth and recoiling from a source of light he didn't create, as Pinkney's wrist gauntlet bathed him in an eerie green glow. Fantastic Man had never looked more human, or more vulnerable.

But they were there, in costume. Two-thirds of the Terrific Trio showed up. Maybe they hadn't waited around idly for the call to action, maybe their personal lives preoccupied them as much as Miranda's had her, but they eventually responded to the danger. She was pleased to see Tuck was wrong, and all the more annoyed that he meddled, that he delayed her arrival. She wondered what difference she would have made in the initial confrontation.

Pinkney pressed buttons on his wrist and examined a holographic computer screen that Miranda couldn't read from this distance. She doubted a closer look would clarify much.

Miranda took a longer step, and the robot's eyes sparked a bright red.

She stopped. The robot hovered above and in front

of her, poised to strike should she take one step further.

No fear allowed. The slightest display of terror would erode people's confidence in her. Peyton might be watching this on the news. Had the kid already seen Fantastic Man and Mr. Amazing's defeat? Was she wondering where Ultra Woman had been all this time?

Miranda clenched her fists to stifle any quaking, and she directed her focus beyond the robot, on Pinkney, hoping she could pretend the humanoid machine wasn't right there within killing range.

I already almost died today, she thought. *Is this my life now?*

Her foot unconsciously shifted back, but she stopped herself.

No flinching.

"Dr. Pinkney," she called over, "what are you doing?"

"Attempting to conduct my research without harassment."

He was mumbling, his attention elsewhere, but Miranda heard him clearly enough.

"You're scaring a lot of people." She glanced up at the fiery-eyed robot and stiffened her whole body, willing herself not to shudder. "Well, *that* is, and you'll get the full blame."

Pinkney shook his head, his eyes on his screen. "Everyone should be scared. The data are ... alarming."

Miranda heard faint electric humming above her.

Power was charging within the robot, building, intensifying, preparing to erupt. A more sensible person would have flown away already. Miranda hoped she could resolve this without violence, but knowing the man was capable of murder, even from afar, she didn't get her hopes up.

"Tell me about that data," she said.

He sighed loudly, then spoke in a monotone. "It's over your head. So, I'll oversimplify the matter for you. The rules of reality are broken. I need to figure out how to fix them. Understand? You probably don't, but leave me be."

Miranda wanted to rail on him, tell him how the world had already changed and now they simply needed to adapt—how for better or worse, there was no going back to the way things were.

But with a deadly, autonomous weapon targeting her, its humming escalating, setting her nerves on edge, she proceeded straight to the point.

"The way you're going about 'fixing' things," she said, "you're not a hero. No one will see you as the good guy. You've let yourself become a supervillain, especially with your fancy armor—stolen off a corpse, right? World's first supervillain. Congratulations."

For the first time, Pinkney looked at her, his cold eyes full of contempt, and with a snort he turned right back to his work. He pointed his gauntlet's scanner onto Mr.

Amazing's dark, blood-tinged hair, revealed through a small tear in his mask.

"You like being a supervillain, Warner?" Miranda said, glaring at him, challenging him.

Pinkney ignored her. He pressed another button, and Fantastic Man and Mr. Amazing received a jolt. Miranda winced in sympathy.

She wished she could join the spectators behind her, blend into the crowd somewhere in the back, maybe hang out with Bianca and speculate about what bizarre things were happening inside the condemned park.

But no, she never did want to blend, did she? She always resisted the crowd—the crowd was supposed to watch her, admire her, validate her life choices with their applause and adoration. Any second, though, a laser could impale her, and then what would it all be for?

She understood Pinkney's fears. Recent, drastic changes rendered much of his professional expertise obsolete. For how many years was he building that knowledge base? How close was he to a career-defining breakthrough before the rules changed?

The world's possibilities expanded, and it had to be daunting.

But it was no excuse for killing. If fear reduced people to this, Miranda decided to err on the side of bravery.

She looked the robot in its deadly, blazing eyes, acknowledging the source of terrific pain within, also acknowledging that if anyone might be fast enough to evade its attack, she was that person.

Miranda took a breath, lowered her gaze to the headbands neutralizing her teammates, and, despite all common sense, dashed forward.

Scarlet lasers erupted from the eye slits and pounded against her legs, slamming her knees into the pavement. She tasted sediment as her face, too, hit the ground.

Miranda pressed her hands down so she could push herself up, but the robot stomped her back and clamped its cold hand around her neck, with enough pressure to restrain but not enough to choke.

As she reflexively clenched both hands, her fingers dug into the pavement.

Her first thought was that she had two handfuls of pavement chunks to throw at Pinkney's exposed head. But she didn't want to risk killing him. Nor did she want to hit the gauntlet and risk activating anything lethal.

Aiming to free her teammates, however, entailed less risk. Not none, but less.

Fantastic Man locked eyes with her, imploring her to take any chance available. Miranda focused on the beam propping him up, and she pitched a handful of pavement at it. It was an awkward pitch, thanks to the robot pinning her flat on her stomach, but super-strength compensated for the restricted arm movement.

The chunk kicked out the beam, sending Fantastic

Man crashing onto his side. Miranda panicked when his head also struck the ground, but then she realized *how* it struck. Fantastic Man, in mid-fall, whipped his head against the pavement—smashing not his skull, but the electronic headband, which now sparked and crackled.

Still looked painful, and in the aftermath of the fall, Fantastic Man continued lying there, not moving.

Pinkney went pale as he stared at his fallen captive, possibly dead captive for all he knew. Miranda watched the scientist's eyes—they widened, making room for reality to enter, for guilt to sink in, for sanity to take control.

But then Fantastic Man vanished from his bonds. The damaged headband rolled across the ground until it fell over. And a flare burst in Pinkney's face, forcing his eyes into a tight squint.

Pinkney struggled to locate his enemy, who kept dematerializing and rematerializing at various points around him.

Miranda tried to push up against the robot, but it pushed her down and gripped her neck tighter.

Fantastic Man solidified in front of Pinkney. Cape flapping in the breeze. Cocky grin in place. Majestic glow in effect. Wounds concealed.

"It's high time your malevolent machinations came to a close, you foul fiend."

Miranda tried to yell at him to cut the posturing and free Mr. Amazing, but she couldn't squeak out the words.

She struggled to pry the hand off. The effort progressed too slowly.

Pinkney shook his head and sneered. "I've seen you without your little tricks covering you up. I know who you are beneath this act."

"You don't know as much as you like to think, Pinkney." Fantastic Man said the name like it was an insult.

The robot squeezed Miranda's neck harder, overpowering her strength, restricting all air.

"You could have been so much more," Pinkney said. "Instead, you're a nonentity who's too ashamed to show his face. Anonymity is your only escape from failure."

The grin flattened. The glow faded. Cuts and bruises reappeared.

Fantastic Man socked him across the face.

Pinkney swayed in his spot, glazed eyes struggling to focus.

"As I suspected!" Fantastic Man said, with a too-boastful laugh as he discreetly massaged his punching hand. "A glass jaw!"

Pinkney's knees buckled. He collapsed onto his own arm, and his wrist controls crunched between the armor and the pavement, releasing sparks.

The robot released Miranda and she gasped. She rolled away the second it floated off her.

It hovered a few feet off the ground, its arms resting at its sides. As its eyes darkened, extinguishing the fiery scarlet power, Miranda took a cautious step toward the robot.

The eye slits flared up with tiny green flames, and she hopped back.

"I am Destructo." The robot's voice was staccato and electronic. "Original directive: Destroy all human life: Restored. Commencing operation."

It swiveled its head toward Pinkney, who was frantically hitting buttons on his damaged gauntlet. An emerald laser pounded his golden chest plate, slamming him against the tower's base.

Electricity crackled across the armor. Pinkney convulsed, screamed, and lost consciousness.

39

A robot was about to embark on a killing spree, and panic conquered Miranda's brain and obliterated all rational thought. She had no idea how to stop a killer robot made of unearthly metal, no idea how to protect everyone, no idea about anything except that people were counting on her to keep them safe.

"Get back!" she yelled to the police and anyone behind them. "Clear the area! It's not safe here!"

People reacted in slow motion. And the robot was turning toward them.

"Go!" she yelled louder, launching her strongest punch at Destructo's head, leaving only a minor dent.

Under the tower, Fantastic Man ripped off Mr. Amazing's headband. "Snap out of it, lad! We've got work to do! Help Ultra Woman—I'll tend to our enemy!"

Destructo clubbed Miranda with its thin steel arm, knocking her through the bushes.

"You dress like the creator," Destructo said. "But you are not she."

An explosion rattled her ears as Miranda ripped branches from her face. Screams followed.

The civilians finally started fleeing, and all it took

was the fiery destruction of a police car. The officers closest to the blast plunged to the ground, and a few of their colleagues rushed to their aid while several others advanced into the park and opened fire on the robot.

The bullets bounced off. The eye slits brightened again.

Instinct told Miranda to steer clear of gunfire, until she remembered she was bulletproof. So, with bullets whizzing by, she leapt onto Destructo's shoulders and clamped her arm under its chin. She grabbed the top of the head and pulled it back, just in time to send the laser firing upward through empty sky.

A cold hand snatched her ankle and slammed her onto the pavement. The head swiveled toward her.

And, untouched, the head swiveled another quarter-turn and lasers blasted the landscaping.

Mr. Amazing limped down the path, holding his hand toward Destructo as another emerald laser bore into the pavement. But the strain soon brought him to his knees, and the robot locked its aim on him.

Miranda swooped in, scooped him up, and carried Mr. Amazing onto the lawn, where she set him behind a fat tree.

"I want to help," he muttered, unable to pull himself back to his feet.

"Help by resting up." Miranda was about to dive back into the battle, but she paused, noticing his cuts, burns, and bruises. "I'm so sorry I wasn't here earlier."

She flew back across the park. The police were continuing their valiant but futile efforts to stop Destructo with conventional bullets. Ricochets abounded, though only Miranda was close enough to be hit. One bounced off her shoulder blade, convincing or perhaps deluding her that she was tough enough to prevail.

She punched Destructo's head as it fired again. The blow threw off the robot's aim and saved the cops from the next blast. Another vehicle exploded instead.

"Get out of here!" she shouted to the cops. "I'll handle—"

The robot swiped its fully extended arm at her, but she ducked, then grabbed it. Recalling how the scientists dismantled the robot at Hephaestus, she rotated the arm at the joint, just as they had—only several hundred times faster.

She yanked the arm out, then whacked Destructo with it. The metal head rolled with the hit, spinning a full revolution, but it did not retaliate. The detached arm, however, did fight back.

The arm bent, and the hand grabbed Miranda's neck, shoving her to the ground, where she and it wrestled. The police, meanwhile, resumed fire, no retreat in progress, still learning to take orders from amateur superheroes.

Miranda rolled back and forth, pulling at the arm, but the metallic appendage held tight, chilling her neck, restricting her air.

A green glow encroached on her peripheral vision. She angled to see—the robot was powering up and taking aim at an injured officer lying on the ground. Another cop was helping him to his feet, so slowly.

Fantastic Man appeared by their side to lend aid, which he could do only in his human form.

One or possibly all three were about to die, unless Miranda intervened.

With the mechanical arm still gripping her, she kicked herself off the ground and slid across the air, swerving to intercept as the beam discharged—at which point she remembered she was *not* laser-proof.

The metallic arm absorbed part of the hot force, but the majority cut past and pounded Miranda in the chest, slamming her into Fantastic Man and both against a police car.

Bright spots danced across her vision, and her muscles ached. The metallic arm flew back to Destructo and reattached itself.

"You okay?" she asked him as they both groaned.

"I'm ... fantastic," he said unconvincingly, one hand on the car as he pulled himself up.

The two officers hustled to a safer position, not that any safe positions existed here. Destructo blasted another vehicle.

"Help everyone get to safety," Miranda said. "I have

an idea."

"May I ask what?"

"No time!"

Miranda rushed up to Destructo and gave the time-out signal. Its eyes burned behind the slits.

"I met your creator!" she said quickly. "Your real creator. Dame Disaster."

The eyes' flames died out, and Destructo spoke. "Where is the creator?"

"She ... well, she's dead. You killed her, remember? In this park. Right over there." Miranda pointed to the site, and she marshaled her full confidence into an authoritative tone. "I've got some of her in me now, so that means you listen to me. And I say stop this. Right now. Just shut yourself down and enjoy a nice long rest."

"Acquisition of creator's genetic material is irrelevant," Destructo said. "Original programming stands. Destroy all human life."

The robot blasted a laser down at Miranda. She almost evaded. The shot nailed her arm, and she tripped into the bushes. The robot marched forward.

"Wait!" she yelled.

It kept marching, charging up another blast.

"You haven't destroyed me yet." Miranda stumbled back onto the path, ignoring her throbbing arm. "You can't 'destroy all human life' if you're willing to move on and leave me here, all un-destroyed."

Destructo paused, staring silently.

"I'm human life, aren't I?" she continued. "To fulfill your programming, you have to destroy me. Can't move on until I'm dead."

Its eyes lit up. "Logic ... validated."

The bushes burned upon receiving the next laser, but Miranda saved herself by going airborne. She hovered above the smoldering debris, and for the benefit of anyone who might have been watching, she flashed her most convincing Ultra Woman smile.

"Okay," she said. "But you'll have to catch me first."

Miranda took to the sky, and indeed, the robot pursued.

She knew the perfect battleground.

40

I'm going to die, Miranda thought as she soared over the water. *But if I die, everyone dies. That is not fair for everyone, and really not for me either.*

She kept swerving back and forth to avoid the laser fire. The latest blast missed her by inches; the heat reminded her to focus.

The uninhabited island wasn't much farther. No boats were nearby; no helicopters were parked on its beach. Just as she was hoping.

Miranda flew above the island's wooded center and landed in a dense forest. It was a peaceful environment, with a faint soundtrack of chirping birds and buzzing insects, free of human-made intrusions. Until Destructo arrived.

The robot blasted before landing. The emerald beam tore up dirt as Miranda retreated behind a sizable tree, and Destructo touched down, crunching twigs beneath its iron heels.

Miranda rushed out, pounded the back of its head, and withdrew behind a different tree. As anticipated, a laser sliced into that same tree, so Miranda bounded up and kicked the bark, sending the wood crashing onto the robot.

Destructo blasted through the falling lumber, which proved to be more of a nuisance than a genuine threat. As intended.

Speeding straight down, bolstered by superhuman momentum, Miranda stomped onto Destructo's shoulders, leaving deep imprints. She leapt off and flew behind cover.

No counterattack came. Peeking around the bark, she saw the damaged robot standing motionless.

Was that the end of the fight? She doubted it and quietly sank to the ground, preparing to launch her next attack. She was thinking the legs would make a good target—damage its mode of flying, strand it on the island…

Destructo's head started spinning—several revolutions per second—and it fired a continuous beam at varying angles.

Trees toppled, burying Miranda beneath smoldering wood, knocking her face-down.

The air was thick with sawdust and smoke. She spat out dirt, only to choke on the pollution.

The hum of lasers persisted. Eventually, she knew, they would find their way to her.

She reminded herself: *I die, everyone dies.*

The lumber, however many trees comprised it, wasn't as heavy as she would've thought. The wood yielded as she pushed up—though the bark, as if to protest, kept scraping her face.

When she reached the top of the pile, Destructo was waiting for her, its eye slits fiery with green power. Miranda froze, her tired muscles offering little support.

Before Destructo could shoot, a column of brilliant, shimmering light engulfed the robot, as if someone were firing a giant laser straight down onto the island.

It looked like an impressive display of force, but it turned out to be Fantastic Man.

His physical form replaced the light, and he stood before the enemy, staring at Destructo as it stared at him. He seemed so frail in front of that dense metal shell, and his frailty rendered his costume all the more ridiculous. A slight shudder escaped his defenses.

"I'm going to have to ask you to step away from the superhero," he said, his confidence prevailing.

"You pose no threat," Destructo said.

"Is that so?" Fantastic Man smirked at the robot, then tossed a glance back at Miranda. "I'll be in my photonic form."

Fantastic Man vanished, as did half the forest, exposing the subsoil a few feet below. Only Destructo remained visible, standing on seemingly nothing.

Miranda couldn't see her own hands, but she could feel them—and the strength they contained. She pitched herself at Destructo and smashed her fists against its shell, then repositioned herself for each successive punch. She directed the bulk of her attacks at its feet, hoping to disable its propulsion system.

Destructo gazed vacantly ahead as dents proliferated across its body. "Adjusting visual sensors to alternative wavelength."

Cold metal clamped Miranda's wrist in mid-strike. She was about to punch its eyes to stave off the inevitable laser blast, but she reconsidered—the robot would expect that.

"Need visibility!" she shouted.

Fantastic Man complied. Everything reappeared at once.

Ignoring her injuries, Miranda launched herself—and Destructo—above the trees. The robot clung tight to her arm, its electric humming growing louder. After a sharp turn, they dove into the ocean at full speed.

Once submerged, Destructo released and propelled itself toward the surface, but Miranda grabbed its leg and rammed her fist into its heel, crumpling the jets within. She likewise smashed its other heel.

She let go, and the robot sank. It fired up a parting blast, which she evaded, and Destructo shrank away into the depths.

Miranda leapt high out of the water. She intended to land on the beach, but the result was more like a slow crash.

Brushing off muddy sand, she looked up and found police tape stretched around four posts, marking the spot where the robot had murdered Officer Hoskins.

It won't harm anyone else, she told herself, breathing heavily. *It won't.*

Miranda watched the water. The fact that she saw only normal waves did nothing to calm her heart rate.

She jumped when Fantastic Man materialized. He appeared somewhat battered, but in much better condition than she was.

"Top-notch work, Ultra Woman!" He offered a helping hand, which she took.

As she rose, she kept checking the water. "Yeah, thanks for distracting it."

Fantastic Man's forehead wrinkled as he examined Miranda's new costume, which remained spotless. Not so much as a grass stain on it, and it had already dried off.

"Your uniform ... it's most impressive. Seems you've been busy. Walk me through all of it—minus personal details, of course. Start at the beginning."

Miranda, having grown accustomed to withholding information, took a second to gather her thoughts, then decided it was time to tell him everything she had experienced. If he happened to glean hints about her secret identity, so be it, but she considered that unlikely.

The water remained peaceful. It could so easily have lulled her to sleep, but she forced herself to stay alert. She looked at it rather than Fantastic Man as she spoke.

"Okay. Right." The beginning, she remembered. "So ...

the woman who was murdered? The one Officer Hoskins saw? I was there when she died—I was the last person to speak to her. That's when I got my powers. I—"

"Wait," Fantastic Man said, raising a finger. "You never mentioned *you* met her."

"It didn't seem relevant."

"It might have been! That was inexcusably poor judgment."

She sniffed at his anger. "Excuse me? You haven't exactly cultivated an environment of sharing, 'Fantastic Man.'"

"*Personal details* are what we don't share. You met an empowered being from another reality. That's not personal. If you knew the exact spot she died, I could have ..." He groped for the rest of that sentence but couldn't find it.

"What? What could have you done with that information?"

His hands tensed in front of him, trying to grab something that didn't exist. "I don't know!" The statement burst from his lips.

Miranda tilted her head as she studied him. "You don't really know much of anything, do you?"

He looked away and took a deep breath. His face sank, and the creases around his chin deepened. But he said nothing.

So Miranda blurted out, "What does Natalie think

of all this?"

His wide-open eyes snapped to her, but still he refrained from saying anything.

"I overheard you talking to Cadee," Miranda said. "So, look—maybe it's time we both opened up to each other, at least a little."

A hand hung over Fantastic Man's mouth. He lowered it. "You're wrong, and I suppose I'll have to take drastic measures to prove it."

Then he paused and it was infuriating.

Was he planning to fight her? Miranda assumed that was his definition of "drastic," and she pictured a tedious battle between photons and super-strength that would inevitably end in a stalemate. She did not want to exert any effort to such tedium. After Destructo, she felt decidedly lacking in the ability to exert anything.

The water remained calm. Her heart rate, she noticed, still wasn't.

"I was almost a founder of Hephaestus Enterprises," Fantastic Man said, his voice low and devoid of theatrics, every word carefully measured. "Cadee Luna, Warner Pinkney, and I dreamt it up in our undergrad days. But through a youthful … indiscretion … I got a young woman pregnant. So I tried to do the right thing."

He briefly rubbed his temple before continuing.

"We got married, and I deemed Hephaestus an impractical venture. Instead, I pursued a safer track, a career that pays well and will always be in need—I will not say what," he added quickly, raising a finger to preempt any question Miranda might have asked.

She shook her head to confirm she wasn't about to interrupt.

"I juggled postgraduate studies, full-time work, and life as a newlywed and new father. I provided." He hesitated. "And all those years, to my shame, I quietly resented the very family I was doing it for. My wife asked me to move out nearly six months ago."

His mouth hung open, as he seemed to wrestle with the question of whether to share further.

"My daughter and I have never had a warm relationship. But now I finally have an opportunity to be someone she can look up to. As Fantastic Man, I can be the person she's always deserved."

Miranda had no idea how to respond. She thought about her various ex-boyfriends and couldn't see any of them doing any better in that situation.

His tone turned harsher. "Now do you see why my secret identity is so important, especially in this day and age? Do you see why the man under this mask is not suited to be the world's first superhero? I can't have the public and media prying into all that."

Miranda pictured reporters hounding everyone she ever knew, dredging up her every past mistake, salivating at the prospect of showing the world how unfit she was.

"No, I guess that would be awful for your family," she said. "But ..."

"What?" Anticipatory exhaustion set in across his face.

"Honestly, it's a relief knowing you're human, too."

Fantastic Man's face fell into his palm. "You're so young," he muttered. "Consider it from the perspective of the average person. Think about what you're capable of. When you can lift a car with your bare hands, people don't want to see that you're just like them. They want you to be better."

"But that's a lie! I'm not! You're not! How—"

Waves thrashed behind her, and Miranda tensed, fatigue and anxiety paralyzing her.

No, she thought. *I won. I beat it.*

Fantastic Man, his eyes wide in alarm, attempted to shove Miranda aside but lacked the strength to budge her.

Then everything was green, and pain.

A laser blasted Miranda across the beach, hurling her back into the decimated woods. She crashed onto a fallen tree, her head swimming.

She forced herself to her feet. It was only pain, after all.

Destructo floated toward her, its jet boots operational and dents smoothed out.

"Repairs concluded. Resuming mission: Destroy this one, then everyone else," the robot said as it blasted her again.

"Okay, you're not destroyed," she said as Destructo

grew fuzzy in her eyes. "I'm ... not destroyed. We have so much in common, don't we?"

As it fired off another blast, Miranda lifted a fallen tree as a shield. The lumber absorbed most of the attack as she stumbled backward.

"No! Not destroyed." She clambered back up, out of breath. "Didn't you know ... I'm pretty much ... invulnerable?"

"You are lying," the robot said. "Enhanced resiliency does not equate to invulnerability."

"Says you."

She charged at Destructo and landed an embarrassing punch on its chest. Didn't even scruff the metal.

The robot swung its arm, swatting her away. She crashed onto her back, convinced she had turned into jelly.

"Commencing destruction of this one."

Destructo fired a continuous laser straight down at Miranda. The beam pushed into her abdomen with unbearable force, attempting to drill through her.

She screamed and felt her consciousness slipping away. *Should've beaten it. Failed everyone.*

So hot, and the force felt like a giant was stepping on her, grinding her into the dirt, eroding her will to resist, imploring her to surrender to the darkness. It would be easy, far easier than enduring this.

No failing. Can't fail ... everyone ...

She blacked out.

For how long, though, she had no idea. At some point, the beam relented, and Destructo stood over her, assessing its work.

"You are not destroyed," it said.

Miranda could barely move. Her blurry vision faded in and out, but she determined she was in a small crater and embedded in the hard dirt.

"Got that right, buddy," she mumbled, almost drifting out of consciousness. She willed herself awake. "Not destroyed!" She attempted a boastful laugh, but a cough surfaced instead.

"Rate of destruction inefficient," the robot said. "Calculating alternative methods of destruction."

"Take your time."

"Problem: Physical resiliency. Alternative: Gauge level of psychological resiliency."

"Huh?"

Destructo turned its head toward the city.

"Scanning for familial relations."

Miranda tried to pull herself up, but her back vetoed that action.

"No—can't … can't hurt me that way," she said. "I won't care. I'm too selfish. So self-centered, self-involved, all about me. Me, me, me. Hit me again."

"Statement incongruent with previous actions. Scanning … No familial relations detected within scanning radius."

Altered sci-fi DNA for the win, she thought.

"Compensating for genetic enhancements," Destructo said, again staring off into the distance for an intermi-nable minute. "Partial match detected on island city. Will destroy familial relation, then bring corpse here to commence psychological destruction."

The robot lifted off and flew toward Olympus, and Miranda feared she was too weak to save Bianca.

41

Standing up was a challenge, but Miranda managed it. Perhaps flying would be easier.

She leapt out of the crater and over the remaining trees, and crashed onto the beach. Sand trickled back to its source as she pushed herself up, and she worried this misfire already cost her too much time.

A body lay ahead, and Miranda's brain, lungs, and heart all stopped.

Fantastic Man. The side of his costume was frayed and blackened.

He stirred and groaned, and Miranda breathed.

"I'll be fine." He was clutching his side, and each word sounded painful. "You took the brunt."

Miranda started rambling at full speed. "It's going after my sister. It's all my fault. You were right. I should never have—"

"Go. Stop it."

She wasn't sure she could. Looking across the water, Miranda could still see the robot jetting toward Olympus City. She saw it alternately double and triple, but definitely still outside the city limits.

Miranda took a deep breath, gathered her strength,

and launched herself from the sand.

It wasn't her best flying, if it could even be called flying. She was hurtling above the water, relying primarily on the momentum of her leap, having no idea if she had enough momentum to cover the distance. She willed herself to remain airborne, calling on whatever reserves of flight power resided within.

Halfway toward the Olympus shore, the rushing wind was already calming down.

But she thought about the robot shooting a laser through Bianca, and her speed returned—allowing her to crash into the municipal landfill that much faster. Garbage exploded in all directions from her impact.

Gagging from the stench, she pulled herself out of the debris. No sign of the robot overhead. She was shaking from exhaustion, but too bad.

Another leap. She vaulted over the suburban outskirts and landed on a department store's roof, from which she immediately bounded toward a taller rooftop deeper into the city.

There.

Several streets remained between her and the robot, but she had it in her sights again. It was approaching, to her, the most familiar part of the city. She kept leaping from roof to roof, the constant rise and fall nauseating her, the whole world oscillating.

Until she tripped.

Miranda would have tumbled straight off a roof had she not grabbed the ledge in time. Her cape proceeded to flip over her head and shroud her face as she dangled twenty stories above the sidewalk, across the street from her apartment building.

One hand on the ledge, Miranda brushed the cape away from her eyes and found Destructo hovering a few stories lower. It faced her apartment building, its fiery green eyes targeting the roof.

Someone was on that roof, gazing through binoculars in the wrong direction, seconds away from likely death.

"Bianca!" Miranda shouted, her voice still hoarse, her muscles spent.

The wind blew the cape back in her face.

The cape. Fully intact. Not so much as a tear on it.

Miranda kicked off the building and mounted the robot. With her legs wrapped around its midsection, she pulled the head back as it was beginning to fire. The lasers shot harmlessly into the sky, missing everything, not even coming close to Bianca.

Bianca heard the commotion and turned to find her masked sister wrestling an airborne robot. "Miranda?"

"Go! It's after you!"

Miranda unlatched her cape. She threw it over Destructo's head while mechanical arms pried her legs off the metal. But she didn't fall—she clutched the cape and tied a hasty knot, right before the robot flung her onto the roof.

She rolled several times, side over side, stopping face-up. Bianca, lacking the sense to flee, rushed toward her.

"Are you okay?" Bianca asked frantically. "What the hell is going on?"

"Why are you still here?"

Destructo landed on the roof, its head still covered. Miranda hopped to her feet, positioned herself in front of Bianca, and immediately realized she was too small to fully shield her.

"Go!"

"Will it follow me inside and attack people there?" Bianca asked quickly. "Will it?"

The cape sprouted a bubble, then deflated, like someone breathing into a paper bag. Electric humming accompanied each exhalation, but the beams failed to penetrate the fabric.

Her fists quaking, Miranda took a wobbly step toward her opponent, but stopped when Bianca grabbed her shoulder.

"You're in no shape for that," Bianca said, hurriedly guiding her behind a utility shed.

Miranda supported herself by leaning on the brick. "Get inside."

"You need to rest."

"I'll rest when you're safe inside."

Bianca's fear spilled out: "Why is it trying to kill us?"

Destructo clomped blindly around the roof. Poking her head out, Miranda saw its arms groping for the cape. Its semi-articulate fingers lacked the dexterity to untangle knots, but Miranda's sloppy cape-tying effort improved its odds.

Miranda stared at that shrouded head, and she squinted slightly, an idea forming.

Bianca started, "Miranda, don't—"

"Time to be Ultra Woman right now."

Miranda charged at Destructo, leapt onto its shoulders, and planted her hands on both sides of its covered head. She swiveled the head, spinning it as fast as she could, endeavoring to unscrew it from its casing. Destructo's hands were feeling around its back, searching for her, and they climbed steadily toward the shoulders.

The head was loosening, and a metal hand brushed against her boot. Hoping she had loosened it enough, she yanked up on the head. It detached from the body, and she wrapped the excess cape around the bottom of the neck hole.

Then Destructo found her ankle and slammed her against the roof.

Spots blurring her vision, aches muddying her thoughts, Miranda concentrated on securing that cape—it must not spill open, no matter how much the head tried to blast its way free.

Although she succeeded in containing the head, she sure as hell wasn't getting up just yet, even with the headless Destructo about to thrash her. It was lowering itself onto one knee, positioning itself to achieve maximum damage with a single strike.

The easiest course of action, Miranda realized, would be to do nothing. Just let the pain come.

Bianca wrapped her arms around her, dragging her away. She couldn't do it fast enough, though, and she knew it—she implored Miranda to move.

Destructo thrust its arm down.

Jolting herself into action, Miranda sprang up to arrest the limb's descent. The attacking arm slipped into her grasp and came almost to a stop, no damage achieved. Her muscles ached and palm burned as Destructo continued pushing its arm toward its target.

"You really shouldn't be here," Miranda said, slowly falling to her knees as cracks spread beneath her feet. "Go."

"But—it's hurting you!"

"It'll kill you! Can't hold it off forever. Go! Just go!"

Miranda heard fast, retreating footsteps and no further protests. Once the footsteps faded out of earshot, Miranda collapsed, and the robotic arm plunged freely, aiming to impale her through the stomach.

But the arm stopped, seemingly on its own, its hand inches above her. It jerked slightly, nothing more.

Mr. Amazing landed beside the robot, his voice strained as he held his quaking hands at the threat. "I can keep it still ... more or less. Hit it with everything you've got."

She lost track of the head for a moment—it nearly slipped free of the cape. A laser fired straight up, and she quickly covered it again. The cape's constant bubbling and shifting challenged her grip, so she held it tighter.

Miranda twirled the bagged head like nunchakus, and she whacked Destructo with it, square in the chest. It clanged and left a dent. And the robot couldn't strike back.

The corner of her mouth curled up, just for a second, and she whacked it again and again, harder and faster each time.

"Destroy? You want to destroy?" she shouted, still hitting. "No! No destroying! No more destroying!"

Destructo was soon riddled with dents, but the damage was merely cosmetic. The body, struggling to move against Mr. Amazing's telekinetic grip, began to lurch. Miranda needed more, and as her cape swelled, she remembered she already had more.

"You might want to take a few steps back," she told him.

Miranda twirled the head again, ensuring it didn't know which way was which. As soon as she stopped, she removed the cape and pointed the eye slits at the body.

Lasers blasted the metal—so brightly that she had to look away.

Destructo exploded. No piece of it flew off the roof, thanks to Mr. Amazing's assistance, and that left only the head to contend with. Miranda rewrapped it within her cape, and she pushed her hands together, grunting as the metal skull gradually crumpled under the pressure.

Mr. Amazing said, "I can help with that."

"I've got this."

The cape's package condensed further and further, the metal screeching and groaning. Its internal power demanded release, however. The head burst apart, a small explosion. It didn't harm the cape, but it knocked Miranda off balance.

Mr. Amazing tried to help as she tottered backward, but he was hardly steadier. A chimney caught their fall; they slumped against it, into sitting positions, neither eager to rise anytime soon.

Panting, Mr. Amazing pointed a limp finger at her attire. "Nice costume."

"Oh. Thanks."

"Sorry I didn't catch you just now."

"All good. Totally fine with not standing."

Bianca cautiously approached them. She eyed the metal debris littering the roof, and her voice quavered as she asked, "Is everyone okay? Is it over?"

The shattered remains didn't move, and the stench of

burnt plastic lingered.

"Think so," Miranda said. She pointed to her teammate. "Meet Mr. Amazing. He helped."

Mr. Amazing managed a brief wave, and his arm collapsed to his side again.

"Um, hi." Bianca nodded weakly, lost in a haze. She hardly blinked as she wagged a finger on autopilot. "I'm going to find you both some water and a first aid kit. Just … stay put."

She went inside, leaving the superheroes slouching against the chimney.

"Robot was flashy," Miranda said. "Police or FBI or someone's probably on their way here. We might want to start thinking about getting up. At some point."

Mr. Amazing nodded at the debris. "We should also figure out how to dispose of all that."

"I'll fly it into space, throw it away in different directions."

"You can fly in space? How'd you figure that out?"

"Day took a turn."

Bianca's safe. Everyone's safe, Miranda assured herself, her head sinking toward her knees. Still, she couldn't help but ruminate on how close they came to a totally different outcome. If she were a second slower getting here, if Mr. Amazing hadn't arrived when he did, if she hadn't realized her cape was indestructible, if, if, if …

Almost disaster.

"I screwed up so bad," Miranda said.

"You stopped the robot."

"I should've been here much sooner."

"I'm sure you had a good reason. We can only be at one place at a time."

"Yeah, and I chose the wrong place, for the wrong reasons. And that robot, it almost—"

"It didn't kill anyone."

"It could have. My mistake ... almost turned into tragedy."

They sat in silence. Mr. Amazing turned toward her, then turned away, and he repeated the cycle, only more awkwardly.

Finally, he looked straight ahead and drew out a long sigh.

"I'm tired of this," he said, reaching for his mask.

Miranda watched as he was about to peel the mask off his face, but right before she could see any skin, she grabbed his wrist.

"Don't," she said. "We have to be more than we are."

Hesitantly, Mr. Amazing lowered his hand. And Miranda realized her sister had returned to the roof, water and first aid kit in hand.

Bianca stared at them, no doubt judging Miranda but abstaining from saying so. Tiny waves formed in both glasses. Miranda wanted to hug her, saw how much Bianca needed it.

Miranda hopped to her feet and forced a smile as she accepted the water. "Thank you, kind citizen."

She downed the glass in a few seconds. Mr. Amazing turned away, and Miranda averted her eyes as he lifted the lower half of his mask to drink.

"You're welcome." Bianca frowned, and strength gradually returned to her voice. "Let me look at your injuries. Since you clearly don't know, I'm a medical student."

"I'm already starting to feel better," Miranda said. "But please take a look at Mr. Amazing."

Mr. Amazing leaned away. "It's ... not necessary. Thank you, but I'll be—"

Bright light flashed from nothing. Bianca almost rushed away, but Miranda set a gentle hand on her shoulder.

"It's okay," she said.

Fantastic Man materialized. "I heard reports of an explosion in this neighborhood. Is it true? Have we vanquished that metallic menace?"

Miranda gestured to the debris, and she manufactured a cheesy smile, synchronizing it with Fantastic Man's. "Yes, it's experienced some ... technical difficulties."

Fantastic Man clasped both teammates' shoulders. "I had full faith the Terrific Trio would prevail."

Bianca's face contorted—she was cringing, questioning, and condemning all at once. Miranda, however, ignored her and studied Fantastic Man's mannerisms.

His poise was perfect, his confidence on point. He displayed not a trace of the inner man she had seen on the island. His costume still bore obvious signs of battle damage, and he seemed stiffer than usual, slower. Otherwise, he succeeded in hiding any pain his injuries may have caused him.

Noticing Bianca, his tone warmed up while remaining aloof, achieving a sort of impersonal compassion. "Are you all right, miss? Were you injured during the altercation?"

All she could say was "Um."

"It's all right, miss." Fantastic Man imbued himself with a soft, calming glow. "I'm Fantastic Man, and we're the Terrific Trio. You're safe now. Everyone is safe."

Bianca's wide eyes darted from the glowing man to her sister, who declined to reciprocate the eye contact.

Instead, Miranda said, "I believe this innocent bystander was hoping to be on her way. She's been through quite an ordeal, so let's not hold her up."

"Yes, of course," Fantastic Man said. "Young lady, if we can be of no further assistance, please don't let us keep you."

"Um, okay," Bianca said, turning again to Miranda.

Miranda simply nodded. "Ma'am."

Bianca's eyes narrowed slightly. " 'Ultra Woman.' "

The debris still needed tending to, so Miranda turned her attention to it. "I'll make sure this refuse is disposed of."

Her super-speed had recharged, not fully, but enough to expedite the chore. She swiftly gathered the parts and bundled them in her cape, then slung the sack over her shoulder.

"So that's the end of it?" Mr. Amazing asked.

He was far less skilled at hiding his weariness than Fantastic Man. Miranda recalled the false date Tuck arranged for him. Had he figured out it was a sham, or did disappointment still lay ahead? She concealed her anger as she decided the answer to Mr. Amazing's question was no—this was not the end of it.

"Almost," Fantastic Man said. "I'll tie up any loose ends with Pinkney. According to the hospital, his condition has stabilized, though he remains in a coma. Still, there's the question of how he escaped jail in the first place. He must have had some means of activating the armor remotely."

Miranda tightened her grip on the cape. "Let me handle that. I ... have a lead to follow."

"But—"

"Just trust me," she said. "It's something I need to do on my own. After that, we're a team."

Fantastic Man clutched his wounded side and mostly stifled a wince.

"Okay," he said after a long pause. "Go finish this."

Mr. Amazing asked, "Are you sure?"

"Yes," she said, ascending.

On the way up, Miranda sucked in deep breaths, saturating her lungs as she approached the upper atmosphere.

The frigid void greeted her on the other side, and she continued past a satellite. Once beyond its orbit, she unfurled her cape and sent some of the debris flying toward the sun, and the rest flying toward the outer planets.

She watched the scraps drift away, growing ever more distant from each other, never to reconnect.

Turning around, Miranda admired the Earth, the changed planet. And it would never change back. Right that second, it could have been generating any number of new threats that she would have to face someday.

Her responsibility, whether she liked it or not, whether she was good enough or not. But she'd have to be good enough, somehow.

She put her cape back on, and she flew back into the world.

It was time to have some words with Tuck Lewis.

42

Tuck was lounging by his pool, his expression blank as he browsed Miranda's phone. Her purse sat on the small table beside him.

"Put my phone down," Miranda said, hovering above the water, arms crossed, cape flapping behind her. Her tired, leaden muscles threatened to sink her, but she remained aloft—and remained what she hoped was a safe distance from Tuck's power.

Tuck didn't look at her. "You really should set up a PIN for this."

She scowled. Irritation swelled into loathing. How much easier her day would have been if not for this guy. He didn't intend for things to escalate as they did. Miranda understood that. Didn't matter. Her rage was rising from primal depths. The very sight of him repulsed her. She fantasized about snatching him up and tossing him around, far above the earth, savoring his terror.

She could also dunk him in his pool. She doubted he could summon the concentration to control her while he neared the point of drowning. Or she could throw rocks at him—and deliberately miss, of course, but scare the hell out of him as super-accelerated pebbles shot through his property.

Miranda knew she shouldn't do any of that. She clenched her teeth and struggled to steady her breathing. Her skin itched, but it wasn't Tuck's doing this time. He wasn't controlling her; she was remembering how he had.

"Who's Peyton?" Tuck asked.

The phone disappeared from Tuck's palm, and following abrupt turbulence, he was hanging upside-down over a mile of empty air. Miranda held him by his ankle, her reclaimed phone in her other hand, as the wind buffeted them. His startled yelp wasn't satisfying enough.

"Do you even know what happened today?" Miranda shouted. "Do you know what you caused?"

Shock gave way to an icy calm, and Tuck shook his head.

"Yes. I know." He yelled to be heard over the wind, but was otherwise sedate, almost in a trance. It infuriated Miranda all the more.

She rattled his ankle, just a little. She had to remind herself she could no longer smack a man without consequence.

"Was it worth it?" she asked.

"No. Not at all."

Forgetting herself, Miranda almost crushed her phone. She stopped her hand from squeezing, and she tapped the screen on to see what Tuck had been reading.

Peyton had sent a flurry of texts that afternoon, both

to make sure Miranda was okay and to gush about the latest superheroic activity. In one of the more recent texts, she raved about Ultra Woman finally wearing a proper costume. In another, Peyton identified her future ambition as wanting to *be* Ultra Woman. However, a message from earlier in the day captured Miranda's full attention.

Why isn't Ultra Woman there? Peyton had asked, punctuating the message with a frowning face.

Tuck hung in Miranda's grasp; he was limp, pathetic, waiting for her to decide his punishment. She wanted to punish him, for several valid reasons but also for a selfish one—he failed to live up to her expectations.

She couldn't punish him. She didn't have the right.

Miranda flew them back down to the poolside.

"You're going to turn yourself in to the police," she said, hovering above him. "You're going to confess to helping a fugitive, and you will accept whatever consequences the courts decide."

Tuck gazed down at nothing as he considered her words.

"I have a better idea." He immediately raised his empty hands. "Relax. I'm not going to hurt you or anyone. I promise."

Miranda was skeptical, but curious. She backed up, just in case.

"I'm going to reach into my pocket," Tuck explained. "I've got a device that will summon the ship. I will not ask you to board it. I will not use my powers on you."

Slowly, he did what he said. Miranda watched for any deviation—there was none. Tuck pulled out a tiny remote control and hit a button. Dame Disaster's vessel, surrounded by a mist, appeared beside him. A shimmering force field replaced the window Miranda had smashed.

"I have a lot to learn," Tuck said.

His humility sounded sincere, but Miranda maintained her skepticism.

"Miranda, you've shown me how much better I need to be. So I'm going to work on that. I'm going to board this vessel and have it take me to that other world. Just me. I'll observe the pure heroes there. Maybe I'll join one of their teams, even if it means being the worst among them. But I have to start somewhere."

He took a single step toward the vessel.

"You can stop me if you want," he said. "I won't resist you. But I hope you'll let me have this chance. I don't want to be the villain."

Part of Miranda insisted it was too late, demanded she haul him in and let the public see him for what he really was. But she wasn't sure what that would accomplish, and she was so tired.

Tuck waited for Miranda's response. She simply sank to the ground and turned to the side, keeping him in the corner of her eye.

"I better not see or hear about you anytime soon," she said.

"Thank you," he said.

He climbed aboard. The engine hummed, and the vessel soon vanished from the Earth, leaving silence in its wake.

Miranda gazed at the vast property around her, the sort of home she dreamed of having for so long. It now seemed barren. The pool water was too still, without anyone to enjoy it. The house, too many empty rooms. The fleet of collectible cars, beyond the enjoyment of any passengers.

Did she still want this?

The home itself had nothing to do with acting. This was neither the art of filmmaking nor the craft of performance. When Miranda succeeded, she would do things differently.

She looked at her phone and scrolled down to Peyton's latest text, which asked, *You're ok, right?*

Miranda typed her response: *Yeah, all good here. Saw Terrific Trio stop the robot in my neighborhood. Don't tell Mom & Dad. Talk later.*

She appended a smiley face to the text, and started wearing one herself.

43

Arriving at her apartment building and lacking any civilian clothing, Miranda needed to speed inside as a blur. She abruptly opened and slammed her door, unleashing a gust through the tight space and startling Bianca in mid-sip.

Wine spilled onto the carpet, barely missing Bianca's suitcase, which sat beside her on the couch. Bianca immediately set the glass on the side table and apologized for the mess. Her arms were shaking; one hand was clasped tight to her chest. She went to the kitchen nook for paper towels.

Miranda lightly touched her arm. "Are you okay?"

"I ... yeah, but ..." Bianca stared at Miranda. "Your eyes. They're different. It's weird."

"They are?" Miranda zipped over to the bathroom mirror, and she flinched at her narrower, now-green eyes. "Wow, you're right. Totally different."

The costume also colored her hair a deep red, but once she removed the mask, her entire face returned to normal. She could figure out how it worked later. For now, she threw baggy, normal clothes over the tights.

Bianca was already cleaning up the spill, so Miranda

grabbed a towel and got on the floor beside her.

"I feel awful you got thrown into the middle of this," Miranda said, rubbing the towel over a damp, red spot.

"You're doing that wrong."

"Probably." She hugged Bianca. "Today should never have happened. You should not have been that close to danger. I won't let it happen again."

"You can't promise that." Bianca sighed, pulled away, and stood up. "Is this how everything is now? Killer robots and mad scientists in suits of armor?"

Miranda also rose, forgetting about the developing stain. She never expected to see the security deposit again anyway.

"I think it's only the start," she said.

Bianca rubbed the bridge of her nose. "Then I guess we'll be needing Ultra Woman. But—"

"I can't tell anyone else."

"This is such a huge part of your life now."

"I can't and I won't."

"But you need—"

Miranda's hands found their way to her hips as she cast a serious look up at her sister. "I need to keep everyone safe."

"So you're just bottling up half your life? Not healthy, Miri."

"I can handle it."

"Do you think *I* can?"

Miranda's arms went limp at her sides. "What? What do you mean?"

"We almost died today, both of us, and I'm supposed to never talk about it, not with anyone?"

"You can always talk to me."

"Even when you're Ultra Woman and you pretend you don't know me?"

Miranda waited for the right words, perfectly composed, to emerge from her mouth and put Bianca's mind at ease. They never came. She saw the luggage and could think of nothing else.

"Are you leaving?"

"Yeah." Bianca stared at her suitcase, then turned to Miranda, not even trying to conceal her suspicions. "Were you able to make it to your audition before ... everything?"

"Um ..." Guilt swelled up within Miranda. This morning's selfishness pained her. "Yeah, but it was a total bust."

"Okay." Bianca raised an eyebrow, obviously aware that Miranda was omitting significant details. But she didn't press it. Instead, she grabbed her luggage and started for the door. "It's time for me to go home. I won't tell anyone."

"Please don't hate me for this."

"I could never hate you."

Miranda advanced toward the door. "I'll ride with you to the airport. I really do appreciate you coming ..."

She trailed off as Bianca gently raised a hand to stop her.

"No," Bianca said, sounding increasingly fatigued. "I—look, I need some time to think and process everything. By myself."

Miranda frowned. "Okay. If that's what you want."

"Just ... be safe. As safe as you can be with all this. Do a lot of good out there."

Bianca left, and the apartment walls felt even tighter than usual.

Surrendering to her exhaustion, Miranda crashed onto her couch and stared out the window, at the city that was still standing.

I did that, she thought, the corner of her mouth curling up.

A few hours remained before her show that evening. Miranda preferred to sleep for a full day, so she set an alarm on her phone before closing her eyes.

The play had seven more performances, and she still had no idea what she'd do after that. Her heart started beating faster, and she didn't fall asleep. She thought about Bianca riding to the airport alone—Bianca would always feel alone from now on, and it was Miranda's fault.

Miranda considered checking in with Ken, at least as a friend, but wasn't sure if it would be too awkward now. She picked up the phone and stared at the blank screen, plotting out what she might say, hypothetically.

A notification popped up. A new text from Alyssa.

Saw your city in the news again, Alyssa's message said.

Are you OK? Are you sure you want to live in that craziness? BTW thanks for stopping by the other day. Hope the rest of the trip went smooth.

The text relieved Miranda, left her feeling silly for having worried about their friendship. Except ... she wasn't entirely wrong. Right there in the text was a reminder that Miranda had lied to her. They were, in fact, drifting. As their youth receded into the past, they would share less and less in common. But it would never quite get to zero. Their history could never be erased.

Miranda responded, *It WAS crazy, but all good now!* And she couldn't resist adding, *You know you want to move here after school. No place like it!*

She set the phone down and realized she was especially looking forward to tonight's performance, couldn't wait to envelope herself in laughter and applause. On the stage, she could feel like herself.

The sky looked gorgeous. Miranda had hardly noticed the perfection the weather had achieved that afternoon. Perhaps a leisurely flight would wake her up, and along the way, she might even come across people Ultra Woman could help.

Miranda put on her mask, and she leapt into the sky.

EPILOGUE

The Olympus City skyline changed over the next several weeks as crews dismantled the central tower from the top down. The city council devised a different plan for a replacement structure.

The majority of the property would remain a public park, but in the center now stood Terrific Hall. Imposing marble columns lined the top of the steps, emphasizing the Ancient Greek architectural style, but the front entrance was mostly intended for show. The building's only three users tended to prefer the roof entrance fifty feet above the park grounds.

The one-room interior was mostly hollow in Terrific Hall's earliest days of operation, the central feature being the oversized, triangular conference table with a high-back chair on each side. A gigantic computer dominated the rear wall. Otherwise, the vast room was empty.

It was a place the Terrific Trio could meet privately while remaining close to the people they protected. Park visitors frequently looked up, hoping to glimpse arriving or departing superheroes.

Her scarlet cape billowing behind her, Ultra Woman slowed down, smiled, and waved to her fans as she descended toward the roof, and the public always greeted her with applause—genuine, enthusiastic applause. She had earned plenty of goodwill over the previous few months.

Entering through the open skylight, she found Fantastic Man and Mr. Amazing already seated at the table, in a comfortable silence. Mr. Amazing had upgraded his costume in response to hers, ditching the tweed jacket and opting for more traditional tights and a cape. He still wasn't colorful. With the exception of a large red "A" on his chest, he was otherwise gray from head to toe, and he maintained the full-face, featureless mask. But he looked more like a superhero now.

Ultra Woman floated directly into her designated chair.

"Sorry I'm late," she said in a calm, professional tone. "I got tied up stopping a bank robbery."

"No worries, Ultra Woman," Fantastic Man said. "That is the job, after all. But let's delay no further!"

He picked up a remote control and turned on the computer screen. An image of Warner Pinkney's mugshot appeared.

"I'm sure we all remember our 'friend' Dr. Pinkney," Fantastic Man said. "He's escaped custody. I had been keeping tabs on his condition. He recently awoke from his coma, and according to the prison warden, his behavior has taken an odd turn. He seems to have sustained permanent psychological damage from his robot-in-

334 • DANIEL SHERRIER

flicted injuries, but as we've just learned, he retains his blatant disregard for human life. There have been several deaths."

"Who has he killed?" Mr. Amazing asked, leaning forward.

"I believe you mean '*Whom* has he killed?' " Fantastic Man said, wagging a finger. "We are not above the laws of grammar."

"Of course. My apologies."

His expression solemn, Fantastic Man continued, "Pinkney murdered several prison guards in the course of his escape—and that was without the aid of his full armor, which is being kept in a secure location. We'll have to ensure it remains there."

Ultra Woman leaned forward. "How did he do it?"

"While in custody, despite the careful scrutiny of the guards, Pinkney somehow constructed a makeshift gauntlet, in which he installed a miniature laser pistol. He shot the guards on sight, then blasted his way to freedom."

Mr. Amazing said, "But last time he was just targeting people with powers. Killing the guards doesn't fit with that."

"He's changed, in ways we may not be able to predict, but certainly not for the better," Fantastic Man said. "It appears no one is safe from his misguided notions. He's now calling himself Doctor Hades."

Fantastic Man noticed Ultra Woman's contemplative gaze.

"Ultra Woman? Do you have something to add?"

Miranda thought about the possibility of Pinkney reclaiming the armor, maybe building another Destructo or something worse. She had no idea how dangerous he would be as this Doctor Hades. Whatever he had become, they'd have to confront it, and prevail.

Fear bubbled up, as well as shame about the fear, but she buried those feelings beneath a stoic front. Time to be perfect. Time to not be Miranda.

"Yes," Ultra Woman said. "Doctor Hades won't harm anyone else, not on our watch. Let's go stop the supervillain."

ACKNOWLEDGMENTS

This book has been years in the making, with multiple rewrites and previous incarnations as unpublished comic book scripts and plays. I owe thanks to many people.

Thanks to my editor, Matthew Limpede of Limpede Ink, for his guidance and insightful feedback throughout the process of writing this final version; to my second editor, Todd Barselow, for cleaning up my mistakes; to cover designer Justin Burks for making the book look good; to my uncle Joe Sergi for letting me tag along at various book festivals and conventions and generally showing me the ropes of being an author; to Abby Adams for volunteering her expertise to critique an earlier draft; to Taliesin Nexus for accepting me into their first Calliope Writers Workshop, where publishing professionals and fellow attendees provided constructive criticism of an early version of the story; to the members and staff of the Comics Experience online workshop for the critiques of my scripts when I was envisioning this as a comic book series; to my college playwriting professor, Laurie Wolf, and my friends and classmates for their feedback and support of the original version of this story, the play *Super!*, especially Christopher Boyd, Austin Elmore, Sara Strehle, Katie Nebel, David Gray, and John Moss; to the numerous comic book writers, artists, and editors who have provided me creative fuel since I was a child; and, of course, thanks to my family, without whom none of this would have been possible.